BIONICLE®

ENCYCLOPEDIA

BIONICLE®

FIND THE POWER,
LIVE THE LEGEND

The legend comes alive in these
exciting **BIONICLE®** books:

BIONICLE®

ENCYCLOPEDIA

by Greg Farshtey

SCHOLASTIC INC.

New York Toronto London Auckland Sydney

Mexico City New Delhi Hong Kong Buenos Aires

Dedicated with respect and gratitude
to Crystal Matrix, Peter Dolan, and
BIONICLE fans everywhere

ISBN 0-439-74561-6

12 11 10 9 8 7 6 5 4 3 2 1   5 6 7 8 9 10/0

Cover Design by Henry Ng
Interior Design by Henry Ng and Bethany Dixon
Printed in the U.S.A.
First printing, October 2005

ACID SHIELD:

Tool carried by the LEHVAK. This shield secreted a special acid that could eat through any substance on MATA NUI (2) in a matter of seconds.

AHKMOU (OCK-moo):

MATORAN carver originally from PO-METRU. His rivalry with ONEWA led him into a deal with the DARK HUNTER NIDHIKI to obtain the six GREAT DISKS. Frustrated in this and captured by Onewa, he reluctantly joined the TOA METRU in their efforts to find the disks and defeat the MORBUZAKH plant. He was briefly a part of the merged being MATORAN NUI, but split off to pursue his own destiny.

Ahkmou was one of six Matoran initially rescued from the COLISEUM by the Toa Metru. During the voyage to MATA NUI (2), Ahkmou's sphere was lost. It lay on the bottom of an underground river until found by MAKUTA. By that time, evidence had been discovered by the Toa Metru that Ahkmou may have been destined to become a Toa of Stone.

Ahkmou would later reappear on Mata Nui as a trader, selling KOLHII BALLS infected with Makuta's darkness.

AHKMOU

AIR KATANA:

LEWA NUVA's tools, which allowed him to glide on air currents.

AIRSHIP:

Matoran flying vehicles used to transport cargo in METRU NUI. Airships were operated using a complicated system of KANOKA DISKS with the *levitation* and *increase weight* powers. When pulleys caused the *levitation* disks to strike the framework, the craft rose. When another set of pulleys brought the *increase weight* disks into contact with the frame, the craft would lose altitude. Forward thrust was provided by a portion of CHUTE capped at both ends, with only a small amount of liquid PROTODERMIS under high pressure allowed to jet from the back. Airships were built, maintained, and piloted by LE-MATORAN.

The VISORAK destroyed all of the airships in the MOTO-HUB when they invaded the city. Later, the TOA HORDIKA constructed six vessels to carry the sleeping MATORAN to the island of MATA NUI (2).

AKAKU (ah-KAH-koo):

The Mask of X-Ray Vision, which allowed the wearer to see through solid objects. Many Akaku were fitted with special lenses that allowed for telescopic vision as well.

AKAKU

AKAKU NUVA (ah-KAH-koo NOO-vah):

The more powerful Mask of X-Ray Vision worn by KOPAKA NUVA. He used this mask to spot the damage done to KO-KORO by the RAHKSHI. Like all KANOHI NUVA masks, its power could be shared by the user with those in close proximity. See KANOHI NUVA.

AKAMAI (OCK-kah-MY):

A TOA KAITA, the result of the merging of Toa TAHU, Toa POHATU, and Toa ONUA. Akamai fought the MANAS, MAKUTA's monstrous crablike guardians. Akamai wore the KANOHI AKI.

AKAMAI NUVA (OCK-kah-MY NOO-vah):

A TOA KAITA NUVA that could have been formed by TAHU NUVA, ONUA NUVA, and POHATU NUVA. There is no record that this being was ever brought into existence.

AKI (OCK-kee):
The Gold Mask of Valor, possessed of the powers of Shielding, Speed, and Night Vision.

AKILINI (AH-kih-LEE-nee):
The major sport of METRU NUI. Akilini was said to have been created by a MATORAN named KODAN, with the original version featuring a ball (see KODAN BALL). Later, it evolved into a popular sport in which players launched KANOKA DISKS through hoops. Akilini was played on small fields throughout Metru Nui and in the COLISEUM. The disks used by the winning team in a tournament would be sent to TA-METRU to be turned into KANOHI masks.
At its most basic, akilini was played on a round field surrounded by posts upon which hoops were mounted. The field was not free of obstacles — in fact, the prevailing wisdom was: the more, the better. Matoran would surf on Kanoka disks up and down structures, through chutes, and even through tunnels in the ARCHIVES, popping up only long enough to make a shot. "Street akilini" became so popular, and such a menace to pedestrians, that the VAHKI eventually had to crack down on it.

AMAJA CIRCLE (ah-MAH-yah):
A circular sandpit at KINI-NUI used by the TURAGA to tell stories using stones.

RULES OF AKILINI

1. Akilini matches are played between more than one, but not more than four, teams.
2. An akilini team consists of at least two, but not more than six, players.
3. At least one player on each team must serve as a defender. A defender is forbidden to take shots and may only launch disks to deflect the shots of opponents. A maximum of two players may serve as defenders.
4. At least one player on each team must be a launcher. If the team has more than two players, a maximum of four players may serve as launchers.
5. One point is scored for every disk that passes cleanly through an opposing team's hoop. Disks that strike the hoop are not considered goals.
6. Akilini tournament play ends when one team reaches 21 goals.
7. Disks in play may be retrieved by any launcher or defender from the launching team but may not be recovered by opposing players.
8. Disks that leave the playing field are considered to be open to all and may be retrieved by players from any team.
9. Players must keep at least one foot on their transport disk at all times. Transport disks may not be launched. Launching disks may not be used for transport.
10. Players who go more than one bio outside of the field of play on any side will be considered out of bounds. However, players may go as far above or below the field of play as they wish and still be considered in bounds.
11. Players may not make physical contact with a defender at any time.
12. Players may make physical contact with launchers, but only after their disk has been launched. Striking, tackling, or otherwise making physical contact with a launcher in the process of making a shot is considered "roughing the launcher" and will cost the offending team one launching disk.

AMANA VOLO SPHERE (ah-MAH-nah VOH-loh):
A powerful globe of dark energy discharged from certain RAHI upon the removal of an infected mask. These free-floating balls of energy could be absorbed by other beings and could restore health.

AQUA AXES:

GALI NUVA's tools. In addition to their cutting edge, they doubled as fins for swimming at great speed.

ARCHIVES:

The living museum of ONU-METRU, which extended far below the surface and below many other metru as well. Here could be found virtually every tool, artifact, and creature of METRU NUI's past. Staffed by a large number of ONU-MATORAN, it was once the workplace of WHENUA before his transformation into a TOA METRU.

RAHI kept in the Archives were held in stasis for safety purposes. Each Rahi was placed inside an inner stasis tube which was surrounded by a clear casing. While in the stasis tube, their life processes were slowed to an extreme degree. They were alive, but not aware, and could remain in that state for thousands of years. Damage to the outer case would not affect the Rahi, but damage to the inner case would cause it to awaken.

The Archives were known to contain levels, sublevels, and maintenance tunnels. Some sublevels featured creatures considered too dangerous to exhibit publicly. The museum could be accessed through a number of entrances, all of which were guarded. The locking mechanism was a series of hidden switches that had to be hit in a certain order.

Creatures known to have been in the Archives included RAHKSHI, the TWO-HEADED TARAKAVA, the USSAL hybrid, a NUI-RAMA, a MUAKA, and the ARCHIVES BEAST. KRAHKA and other creatures lived in the maintenance tunnels beneath the Archives.

The RAHAGA used the Archives as a base for years prior to the coming of the VISORAK and hid the AVOHKII there. A massive earthquake later shattered the Archives, releasing all of its exhibits into the city.

ARCHIVES MOLE

ARCHIVES BEAST:

A strange creature housed in the ONU-METRU ARCHIVES and believed to have some connection to the *reconstitutes at random* KANOKA DISK power. When encountered by TOA NUJU and Toa WHENUA, it had taken on the appearance of an empty room. Its attempts to trap the Toa were frustrated by a blizzard created by Nuju.

ARCHIVES MOLES:

Small, harmless creatures who migrated from PO-METRU to the ARCHIVES. They fed on insects and microscopic protodites and were known for their ability to cooperate with each other. These RAHI later made their way to LE-WAHI on MATA NUI (2).

ARTAKHA [arr-TOCK-ah]:

A place of peace and contentment for all MATORAN. Its location has never been discovered, and many Matoran now believe it to be a myth. The first mention of Artakha is in an ancient legend which speaks of a trouble-free site to which skilled Matoran workers were allowed to migrate.

ARTAKHA BULL [arr-TOCK-ah]:

A swift, strong, plant-eating RAHI who relied on its sharp horns for defense. The Artakha bull was considered to be one of the earliest RAHI known to MATORAN and was rumored to be extremely intelligent. The species lived in LE-METRU on METRU NUI, but none were ever seen on MATA NUI (2).

ARTAKHA BULL

ASH BEAR:

A large ursine creature known for its powerful teeth and claws. The TOA METRU encountered a wounded member of this species in the ARCHIVES and combined their powers to heal the she-creature. Hundreds of years later, this same ash bear would briefly menace JALLER and TAKUA in LE-WAHI, before being subdued and calmed by LEWA NUVA.

ASSEMBLER'S VILLAGE:

Small settlements scattered throughout PO-METRU on METRU NUI, home to the crafters who assemble Matoran goods. Parts were shipped to these villages via CHUTE, boat, AIRSHIP, and USSAL cart, and these were then painstakingly assembled by skilled PO-MATORAN. Due to the relative isolation of these villages, they were extremely vulnerable to RAHI attack. In the past, assembler's villages had been menaced by STONE RATS, KINLOKA, ROCK RAPTORS, and scores of other beasts. The TOA METRU fought NIDHIKI and KREKKA here, in a village later destroyed by a KIKANALO stampede.

AVOHKII (ah-VOH-kee):

KANOHI Mask of Light worn by TOA TAKANUVA.

The origins of the Mask of Light remain a mystery, but what is known is that at some point in the past, the BROTHERHOOD OF MAKUTA stole the mask from its creators and hid it in one of their fortresses. Later, after discovering the Brotherhood's treachery, the TOA HAGAH raided the fortress and stole the mask themselves. Even after being turned into RAHAGA, they were able to successfully spirit the mask away.

The Rahaga hid the mask in the ARCHIVES in METRU NUI. The compartment in which it was concealed could only be opened using six MAKOKI STONES, which the Rahaga hid around the city to keep them from the VISORAK. The TOA HORDIKA retrieved all six stones and found the Avohkii, which gave off a bright glow. Fearing that the glow would attract the attention of the Visorak, Toa Hordika ONEWA used his RHOTUKA SPINNER to conceal the mask in a block of stone.

The TOA METRU later transported that stone to the island of MATA NUI (2) and hid it in a lava cave. Legend stated that the HERALD of the Toa of Light would have to find the mask, it could not be given to him, and so the location of it was kept secret. A MATORAN named TAKUA would eventually stumble upon the Mask of Light while exploring the cavern.

Takua and JALLER were charged by the TURAGA with the duty of finding the Toa of Light. Their adventure took them to many places on the island and exposed them to danger from RAHI and RAHKSHI. Takua later donned the mask and transformed into Takanuva, the Toa of Light. (How the mask was able to trigger such a transformation when normal Great Masks do not has not yet been revealed. It is rumored that the mask may have been infused with Toa power during its creation, and so acted like a TOA STONE.)

The Avohkii can project powerful beams of light energy and banish the darkness. It also brings understanding, turning anger into peace and enemies into allies.

AXE:

TOA tool carried by LEWA, used to focus his air power.

BAHRAG (BAH-rag):
CAHDOK and GAHDOK, the twin queens of the BOHROK swarms. The Bahrag directed the rampages of the Bohrok, unaware that there were MATORAN living on the surface of MATA NUI (2). They possessed the elemental powers of the six Bohrok, plus the ability to create lifelike illusions. They created and were in contact with the KRANA that inhabited each Bohrok. The Bahrag were defeated by the TOA NUVA and imprisoned in a cage of solid PROTODERMIS. The Bahrag were later the subject of a failed rescue attempt by the BOHROK-KAL.

BIO (BY-oh):
A unit of Matoran measurement. A bio is equal to roughly 4.5 feet or 1.37 meters in Earth measurement. A TOA averages 1.6 bio in height (7.2 feet/2.19 meters). There are 1,000 bio in a KIO.

BLADE BURROWER:
A creature of the ONU-METRU ARCHIVES. It used its powerful claws to carve tunnels that looked MATORAN-made, and then used the tunnels to lure archivists to their doom. Blade burrowers hunted mainly by smell, having poor eyesight, and rarely ventured to the higher levels of the Archives.

BLADE BURROWER

BOGGARAK (BOE-ger-rack):
One of the six breeds of VISORAK who invaded METRU NUI. Although not strong swimmers, Boggarak were capable of "skating" atop the water, speedily darting to and fro toward their prey. Their RHOTUKA SPINNERS had two powers. When used underwater, they caused the target to swell up and float helplessly to the surface. When used on land, they completely dehydrated the target, reducing it to a pile of dust. Boggarak were also capable of emitting a sonic hum that could transmute solid matter. ROODAKA's personal guard was made up of Boggarak. These Visorak also decimated a squad of VAHKI.

BOG SNAKE:
Nasty, venomous serpents that lived in the muddy shallows off ONU-METRU and fed on small amphibians. ONU-MATORAN walking along the shoreline learned to be extremely careful so that they did not disturb a bog snake nest.

BOHROK

BOHROK (BOH-rock):
Insectlike mechanoids who menaced the island of MATA NUI (2) shortly after the TOA arrived there. Each Bohrok contained a KRANA that provided additional power as well as direction to the machine. The krana, in turn, were in mental contact with the BAHRAG, who were the ultimate authority over the Bohrok swarms. Bohrok nests extended from below the surface of Mata Nui to below the city of METRU NUI. Each nest was home to hundreds of Bohrok and BOHROK-VA. There were six known breeds of Bohrok: GAHLOK, KOHRAK, LEHVAK, NUHVOK, PAHRAK, and TAHNOK (see individual entries).

HISTORY

The first recorded encounter between MATORAN and Bohrok occurred in Metru Nui, when ONU-MATORAN miners stumbled upon a nest filled with sleeping Bohrok. Not certain what the creatures were or why they could not be awakened, the miners turned the Bohrok over to the ARCHIVES. They were put on display and at the same time studied by Matoran researchers. (The name "Bohrok" came from a word carved in the wall of the nest.)

Their first discovery was that the Bohrok themselves were completely inorganic and not "alive" in the sense that Matoran understand life. They also learned that the dormant krana inside them were completely organic and living creatures, although the connection between krana and Bohrok was not yet known. Interestingly, an examination of the Bohrok revealed no traces of any assembly. An Onu-Matoran archivist, MAVRAH, theorized that perhaps the Bohrok were not built but were in fact originally biomechanical creatures that had somehow evolved to the point where all organic matter was lost. It would have meant their transformation from possibly a living, thinking state to a form of artificial life incapable of independent thought. Archivists were split on his theory, and since there was no way to prove it one way or the other, it was forgotten over time.

No active Bohrok presence ever existed on Metru Nui. In fact, the Bohrok and krana remained asleep for another 1000 years after the fall of the city. The only other thing to be learned about them during this time was the result of VAKAMA's visions of the Bohrok attacking and destroying the island of Mata Nui.

Following his defeat by the Toa of Mata Nui, MAKUTA sent a signal that awakened the swarms. They immediately made for the surface of Mata Nui and went on a rampage, destroying mountains, forests, waterways, and every other obstacle that got in their way. It seemed as if their sole purpose was to eradicate everything on the surface of the island. The Toa and Matoran mobilized to stop them, fighting battles across the entire island. Interestingly, the Bohrok showed no interest in harming Toa, TURAGA, or Matoran unless those beings prevented the swarm from carrying out its task.

The most devastating blow dealt by the Bohrok was the capture of almost the entire population of LE-KORO, including Turaga MATAU and Toa LEWA. These prisoners were fitted with krana in place of their masks and thus became slaves of the swarm. They were eventually freed, thanks to the efforts of Toa ONUA and four Matoran: KONGU, TAKUA, TAMARU, and NUPARU.

The Toa eventually tracked down the Bahrag and brought the fight to them. The defeat and imprisonment of the Bohrok queens caused the swarms to become disorganized and no longer any threat. The Matoran removed the krana from most of the Bohrok and put the machines to work rebuilding the villages.

Later, the Bohrok were summoned back to their nests by the BOHROK-KAL to await the call to invade Mata Nui again. The intervention of the TOA NUVA prevented the Bohrok-Kal from freeing the Bahrag, and so the signal was never sent. The Bohrok remain asleep as of this writing.

POWERS

The six breeds of Bohrok had elemental powers similar to the Toa for the most part, controlling fire, water, earth, stone, and ice. The Lehvak, however, were not connected to the air element but instead were identified with swamp terrain. The Bohrok were also capable of snapping their heads forward, delivering a powerful blow, as well as launching the krana they carried at a foe. If a krana affixed to the face of a target, that being would become mentally enthralled by the swarm.

PERSONALITY

Although different breeds of Bohrok had preferred tactics in battle, they could not be said to have actual personalities.

EQUIPMENT

Each breed of Bohrok carried two shields through which elemental power could be focused. These were the ACID SHIELD, EARTH SHIELD, FIRE SHIELD, ICE SHIELD, STONE SHIELD, and WATER SHIELD.

BOHROK-KAL [BOH-rock KAHL]:

Six mutated BOHROK who challenged the TOA NUVA in an effort to free the BAHRAG, and so unleash the swarms against the island of MATA NUI (2) a second time. Each Bohrok-Kal contained a KRANA-KAL, which provided additional power and controlled the mechanoid. There were six Bohrok-Kal: GAHLOK-KAL, KOHRAK-KAL, LEHVAK-KAL, NUHVOK-KAL, PAHRAK-KAL, and TAHNOK-KAL (see individual entries). They were defeated by the Toa Nuva.

BOHROK-KAL

HISTORY

The six Bohrok-Kal appeared on Mata Nui following the defeat of the Bahrag. Their stated mission was to free the Bohrok queens so that the swarms could be active again. It later became clear that the Kal had been created by the Bahrag for just this purpose.

How the Bohrok-Kal were created has never been determined, though it is believed by some that the Bahrag discovered a means of distilling energy from a mutagenic substance, possibly Visorak venom or some variation of that. The energy was then used to bathe both the Bohrok and their KRANA, resulting in a number of mutations.

The Bohrok-Kal rapidly proved to be quite different from the Bohrok. They had different powers. Their krana-kal were capable of communication with other species and were not mentally linked to the Bahrag as the Bohrok krana were.

Knowing the Toa Nuva would attempt to prevent their rescue of the Bahrag, the Bohrok-Kal infiltrated the Matoran villages and stole the NUVA SYMBOLS. By doing so, they robbed the Toa Nuva of their elemental powers, severely weakening them. The Kal then began searching the island for the location of the Bahrag.

The Toa Nuva tried desperately to stop the Kal, doing everything from gathering KANOHI NUVA to forming WAIRUHA NUVA. Meanwhile, the Bohrok-Kal had discovered where the Bahrag were imprisoned. The prison was guarded by EXO-TOA running on automatic, but these were easily defeated by the Bohrok-Kal.

Faced with no choice, TAHU NUVA called upon the most powerful mask in his possession, the VAHI, or Mask of Time. He used its power to slow down time around the Kal and prevent them from freeing the Bahrag.

The Nuva symbols proved to be the Kal's undoing. Through force of will, the Toa Nuva were able to trigger the power stored in the symbols and cause it to flow into the Kal. This resulted in an overload as the Kal absorbed more power than they could control. They were defeated and have not been a threat since that time.

POWERS

The Bohrok-Kal's powers included control of magnetism, gravity, plasma, electricity, sound, and vacuum.

EQUIPMENT

Each breed of Bohrok-Kal carried two shields through which its power could be focused. These were the ELECTRIC SHIELD, GRAVITY SHIELD, MAGNETIC SHIELD, PLASMA SHIELD, SONIC SHIELD, and VACUUM SHIELD.

PERSONALITY

The Bohrok-Kal tended to be arrogant and cruel. Whereas the Bohrok did not go out of their way to harm living beings, the Bohrok-Kal were not only willing to attack Toa and Matoran but even members of the swarms.

BOHROK-KAL KAITA JA (BOH-rock KAHL KIGH-ee-TAH JAH): A merged being formed by the combination of KOHRAK-KAL, LEHVAK-KAL, and GAHLOK-KAL. It was dominated by the KRANA JA-KAL and controlled the powers of magnetism, vacuum, and sound. It defeated WAIRUHA NUVA in battle.

BOHROK-KAL KAITA ZA (BOH-rock KAHL KIGH-ee-TAH ZAH): A merged being formed by the combination of TAHNOK-KAL, PAHRAK-KAL, and NUHVOK-KAL. It was dominated by the KRANA ZA-KAL, and controlled the powers of gravity, plasma, and electricity. It was never sighted on MATA NUI (2).

BOHROK VA (BOH-rock VAH): Miniature mechanized assistants and couriers for the BOHROK swarms. The Bohrok Va traveled back and forth from the BAHRAG nest to the Bohrok in the field, carrying KRANA to those Bohrok who had lost theirs. The Va were also capable of hurling krana at opponents — if the krana affixed to the target's face, that being would become a servant of the swarm. Bohrok Va were present throughout MATA NUI (2) during the Bohrok invasion and frequently clashed with MATORAN, but rarely with the TOA.
When the Toa defeated the Bahrag, and thus the Bohrok swarms, the Matoran believed the Bohrok Va had been rendered harmless. They allowed both the Bohrok and Bohrok Va into the villages to repair some of the damage done by the swarms. But the Matoran had made a potentially fatal mistake. Since the Bohrok Va were not guided by krana like the Bohrok, the defeat of the Bahrag did not lessen their threat. They immediately began rendering aid to the BOHROK-KAL, assisting them in infiltrating the villages to steal the NUVA SYMBOLS.
When the Bohrok were summoned back to their nests in preparation for the freeing of the Bahrag, the Bohrok Va went with them. The TOA NUVA's defeat of the Bohrok-Kal prevented the Bahrag from being unleashed again. The Bohrok Va remain in the nests, awaiting the signal that will call them to action once more.
There were six breeds of Bohrok Va: GAHLOK VA, KOHRAK VA, LEHVAK VA, NUHVOK VA, PAHRAK VA, and TAHNOK VA.

BOMONGA (bo-MAHN-gah):

Former TOA HAGAH of Earth, later mutated by ROODAKA into a RAHAGA. Bomonga had been part of an elite TOA team charged with being MAKUTA's personal guard. When the Toa discovered Makuta was oppressing and enslaving MATORAN, they turned on him and attacked a fortress of the BROTHERHOOD OF MAKUTA. Bomonga was struck by one of Roodaka's RHOTUKA SPINNERS and mutated into a shrunken creature with the head of a RAHKSHI. He was later rescued by Toa IRUINI and Toa NORIK, who also ended up being mutated.
What masks and tools Bomonga carried as a Toa has not yet been revealed.
As a Rahaga, Bomonga specialized in capturing RAHI hiders, such as FIREFLYERS and BLADE BURROWERS. He carried a Rhotuka Spinner that could fly in absolute silence and then adhere to and paralyze a target. Bomonga was known for his patience and his ability to remain motionless for long periods of time while waiting for a target to pass nearby.

BORDAKH (bore-DOCK):

VAHKI model assigned to GA-METRU on METRU NUI. These mechanoids were cunning and enjoyed to chase for the sake of chasing. Their staffs of loyalty made a target so enthused about maintaining order, he would turn in his friends to the Vahki if necessary. NOKAMA and MATAU clashed with Bordakh while trying to recover the Ga-Metru GREAT DISK.

BOXOR (BOX-oar):

A defense vehicle designed by NUPARU, an ONU-MATORAN inventor. It was used by the MATORAN on MATU NUI (2) to defend themselves against the BOHROK swarms. A Matoran could ride inside the vehicle and manipulate its two arms to fight the invaders. Boxors were later disassembled for transport to METRU NUI. See NUPARU.

BRAKAS (BRAH-kahs):

Mishievous monkeylike creatures who once roamed freely throughout LE-METRU and GA-METRU. They were such pests that the MATORAN petitioned Turaga DUME to have them banned. VAHKI later rounded up all specimens and put them in the ARCHIVES, from which they escaped. They later appeared on MATA NUI (2), where they continued to be an annoyance, often stealing fruit from KORO storehouses. Brakas are known for their distinctive "kau kau" cry.

BROTHERHOOD OF MAKUTA (mah-KOO-tah):

A secretive, powerful, and dangerous group of renegades who have turned against the GREAT SPIRIT MATA NUI (1). According to legend, they were originally the beings closest to the heart of the Great Spirit, charged with creating whatever was needed to do the will of Mata Nui and safeguard the MATORAN. At some point, for reasons of greed, ambition, or a darker emotion, MAKUTA, who would later become a foe of the TOA, began oppressing and enslaving Matoran. The Brotherhood did nothing to stop him, even aiding him as he turned his knowledge and power against those he had sworn to protect.
Over the centuries, the Brotherhood continued to grow in power while remaining relatively small in number. They were allied with the DARK HUNTERS and turned benevolent technology like the EXO-TOA into tools of conflict. Later, the Brotherhood would clash with the Dark Hunters over the apparent death of NIDHIKI and KREKKA. The Brotherhood experimented with mutating RAHI as well as creating specialized beings like VOPORAK. It is known that

survived well into the era of the TOA NUVA. A clash between protectors of the Matoran and the Brotherhood would seem to be inevitable.

BULA (BOO-lah):

A berry that grew on MATA NUI (2) and was famous for its ability to restore energy. MATORAN could absorb energy from direct physical contact with the berries, something that was particularly helpful when on long journeys.

CABLE CRAWLER:

A LE-METRU RAHI who made a home in the cables that overhung the district. Nocturnal hunters, cable crawlers fed on small birds and were extremely difficult to capture. They had the added ability of being able to unleash an energy blast that disrupted a foe's sense of balance.

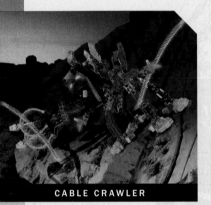

CABLE CRAWLER

CAHDOK (KAH-dahk):

This monstrous blue creature was one of the two BAHRAG twins.

CANYON OF UNENDING WHISPERS:

Geographic feature in PO-METRU on METRU NUI, located near the PRISON OF THE DARK HUNTERS. The canyon got its name because of the abundance of echoes. VAKAMA, NOKAMA, MATAU, and the KIKANALO battled VAHKI here while attempting to save the other TOA METRU.

CATAPULT SCORPION:

A dangerous PO-METRU RAHI. The catapult scorpion had the ability to materialize a ball of molten magma at the end of its tail, which rapidly cooled to solid rock. The scorpion could then hurl it at enemies. Catapult scorpions fed on raw PROTODERMIS and were considered to be extremely hostile. None were ever reported on MATA NUI (2).

CATAPULT SCORPION

CAVE FISH:

A GA-METRU creature that defended itself by absorbing liquid PROTODERMIS through its skin. It used the fluid to "inflate" itself and give the appearance of being a larger creature. GA-MATORAN later used dead cave fish to absorb leaks in the protodermis purification vats. Cave fish were often seen in the waters around MATA NUI (2).

CHARRED JUNGLE:

A forest of burnt trees in TA-WAHI on MATA NUI (2). TAKUA trailed TAHU through the jungle and discovered TA-KORO.

CHIEF ARCHIVIST:

Administrator in charge of the ARCHIVES in METRU NUI. Only the Chief Archivist had keys to certain sublevels of the structure. TURAGA DUME instructed the Chief Archivist to put an end to MAVRAH's researches.

CHRONICLER:

A MATORAN designated to record important events on the WALL OF HISTORY. The best-known Chronicler in METRU NUI was a PO-MATORAN named KODAN. His first experience was recording the defeat of the KANOHI DRAGON by TOA LHIKAN and 10 other Toa. He later traveled with some of Lhikan's fellow Toa on one of their missions, but neither he nor they ever returned. TURAGA DUME chose not to appoint a new Chronicler. No one knew at the time that the true Dume had been replaced by MAKUTA in disguise.

After the Matoran traveled to MATA NUI (2), the six TURAGA appointed TAKUA to serve as Chronicler. His position would lead to his being present at many of the most important events in Mata Nui history.

When Takua became TAKANUVA, Toa of Light, a GA-MATORAN named HAHLI stowed away on the USSANUI on its journey to Makuta's lair. Once there, she volunteered to serve as Chronicler in Takua's stead. It is a position she still holds as the Matoran prepare to journey back to Metru Nui.

CHRONICLER'S STAFF:

The tool carried by the MATORAN charged with the task of recording events on the WALL OF HISTORY. In addition to being decorative, the staff can be used to scratch letters into the wall. The original Chronicler's staff was lost when KODAN disappeared. TURAGA NOKAMA carved another one for TAKUA to carry during his time of service. It has now been passed on to HAHLI.

CHUTE LURKER

CHUTE LURKER:

A dangerous RAHI known for its habit of hiding in chutes and ambushing travelers. The Rahi were both omnivorous and amphibious, though they seemed to prefer avoiding breathing air as much as possible.

CHUTE SPEAK:

Name given to the slang used by residents of LE-METRU in METRU NUI.

CHUTE STATION 445:

The busiest transport hub in PO-METRU. TOA ONEWA caught up to AHKMOU here.

CHUTES:

Primary transport system for the city of METRU NUI. Chutes were long cylindrical tubes made of liquid PROTODERMIS held in place by a sheath of magnetic energy. The protodermis flowed through the chutes at a high rate of speed, carrying cargo and MATORAN from place to place. Passengers were required to hold their breath while riding in a chute.

Most chutes ran aboveground, often supported by solid protodermis braces. Some chutes ran underground or underwater, but most of these were in poor repair and largely abandoned by the Matoran. These chutes were used by both RAHI and VISORAK to reach the city.

Chutes ran in a preset direction. Attempting to change that direction could cause severe damage to the system. KONGU was forced by NIDHIKI and KREKKA to reverse the flow of a chute in an effort to capture the TOA METRU.

Chutes could be boarded at a chute station or by "chute jumping," leaping onto a chute during the brief moments when the magnetic energy wavered and the outer layer could be penetrated. This was both dangerous and illegal.

Chutes faced a number of potential problems. A weakened magnetic energy sheath would cause liquid protodermis to leak out. Poorly constructed braces could break and cause the chute to collapse. It was also possible for a portion of the magnetic energy to break off and form a FORCE SPHERE.

CITY OF LEGENDS:

Nickname given to the city of METRU NUI. The name was actually coined as a dark joke by the SHADOWED ONE during the conflict between the TOA and the DARK HUNTERS. He claimed that Metru Nui would be "well and truly a city of legends since, as is well known, most legends are about the dead."

CLAW CLUBS:

TOA HORDIKA ONEWA's tools, these could be used for climbing, hurling stones, or charging up Onewa's RHOTUKA SPINNER.

CLIMBING CLAWS:

POHATU NUVA's Toa tools. These claws could be hurled at opponents or combined to form a sphere called a KODAN BALL.

COLISEUM:

COLISEUM

The sporting arena, power station, and seat of government for METRU NUI. The largest building in the city, it sat at the meeting point of the six metru boundaries. It was home to TURAGA DUME. The central arena of the Coliseum was used for citywide AKILINI tournaments as well as VAHKI training exercises. Below that were storage areas. Farther down, there was a power station that relied on the flow of liquid PROTODERMIS to generate energy for the city.

The TOA METRU made their first major public appearance at the Coliseum, where they were challenged by MAKUTA (posing as Turaga Dume) to prove themselves to be TOA. The Coliseum floor was activated, causing the surface to move like ocean waves and huge pillars of protodermis to rise up in an irregular pattern. When the Toa failed to keep their footing, they were branded as impostors and their capture was ordered. NUJU, ONEWA, and WHENUA were captured in a whirlpool and VAKAMA, MATAU, and NOKAMA were forced to flee.

The Toa Metru later returned here to confront Makuta and attempt to save the MATORAN. The city's population had been placed in spheres and rendered comatose, and those spheres were then loaded into the storage area. The Toa managed to recover six of the spheres even as Makuta drained the energy from the city's power plant. They were forced to leave the remainder of the spheres behind as they made their escape from the city.

Later, the Toa Metru returned to Metru Nui in an effort to save the rest of the Matoran. They discovered that the Coliseum had been taken over by the VISORAK horde and its leaders, SIDORAK and ROODAKA.

COLONY DRONE:

Harmless creatures whose RHOTUKA SPINNER energies were a food source for the VISORAK. The hordes brought large groups of colony drones with them whenever they went to a new land, keeping them penned up and under guard.

COMET:

A popular type of KOLHII BALL. AHKMOU sold comet balls infected with MAKUTA's darkness to unsuspecting MATORAN. His scheme was uncovered by TAKUA, and the tainted spheres were destroyed by Takua and POHATU.

COPPER MASK OF VICTORY:

Ceremonial masks awarded to the winners of Matoran village games. These were originally forged on METRU NUI and worn by the champions of AKILINI tournaments.

CRYSTAL CLIMBER

CRYSTAL CLIMBER:

RAHI originally from KO-METRU, these creatures lived among the KNOWLEDGE TOWERS, feeding on ICE BATS. They were considered pests due to their habit of infesting tower chambers and refusing to leave. They later migrated to the frosty wastes of MOUNT IHU on MATA NUI (2).

CYCLONE SPEAR:

Tool carried by TOA IRUINI. The cyclone spear could create massive windstorms strong enough to sweep away hundreds of foes at a time. Use of the spear weakened Iruini, making it necessary for him to be careful how often he used it.

DAIKAU (DIGH-cow):

A carnivorous plant that grew wild in the jungles of LE-WAHI on MATA NUI (2). It fed primarily on insects and small birds but was not above snatching a passing MATORAN if one wandered too close. Its apparent ability to think led the Matoran to classify it as a RAHI.

DARK HUNTERS:

A shadowy band of mercenaries and bounty hunters whose existence has been rumored for centuries. They are said to be as powerful as TOA but far less moral, willing to take on any job if the reward is great enough. In the past, Dark Hunters have been paid with everything from skillfully crafted tools to secrets to political power.

Rumors put the numbers of Dark Hunters as anywhere between a dozen and a few hundred. They are allegedly led by a charismatic and powerful individual known only as the SHADOWED ONE, a being said to be respected even by MAKUTA. When a request for Dark Hunter assistance comes in, the Shadowed One decides how many Dark Hunters he will dispatch and who they will be. Often, he pairs up agents who on the surface seem like poor teams, such as NIDHIKI and KREKKA. In the end, they are inevitably successful, for all Dark Hunters know the price of failure.

The Dark Hunters have a history of conflict with Toa and METRU NUI. Early in the reign of DUME, the Shadowed One wished to establish a base in the city, but Dume refused. This resulted in a huge struggle between the Toa, led by LHIKAN, and the Dark Hunters. During this conflict, Toa Nidhiki attempted to betray the city and eventually defected to the enemy. The Toa eventually won the fight, leaving the Shadowed One embittered and determined to grind Metru Nui to dust beneath his heel.

As an organization, the Dark Hunters were at one time allied with the BROTHERHOOD OF MAKUTA. In addition, both ROODAKA and SIDORAK were frequent employers of Dark Hunters, using them to spy on each other. Later, Makuta himself, in the guise of Turaga Dume, would call for Dark Hunters to be sent to Metru Nui to capture Toa Lhikan. It is possible, though unproven, that he may have also used Dark Hunters to capture or eliminate some of Lhikan's fellow Toa. The Dark Hunters later clashed with the Brotherhood when Makuta caused the deaths of Nidhiki and Krekka.

The Dark Hunters jealously hide their secrets and enforce their own rules. Summoning a Dark Hunter for no reason or refusing to pay them can result in truly hideous consequences. The worst offense of all is causing the death of a Dark Hunter, either directly or indirectly, a crime that risks attracting the direct attention of the Shadowed One.

DERMIS TURTLE:
Amphibious creatures who lived in GA-METRU and later migrated to GA-KORO. They were credited by MATORAN with being able to predict the weather — they retreated into their shells when storms were coming.

DERMIS TURTLE

DIGGER:
A unique tool used by ONU-MATORAN miners on MATA NUI (2), the digger consisted of a short wooden staff with a pointed metal spiral at the end. It could be planted and twisted to loosen rock, much like a drill.

DIKAPI (DIGH-kah-PEY):
A flightless desert bird known for its ability to run great distances without tiring. Although present on MATA NUI (2), these creatures were never seen on METRU NUI. It's believed they may have arrived on the island from some other underground region.

DISK OF TIME:
A KANOKA DISK made by combining all six of the GREAT DISKS. This disk had the power to speed up or slow down time around a target. VAKAMA later carved the disk into the VAHI, the Mask of Time.

DISKS:
See KANOKA DISKS.

DOOM VIPER:
Multi-headed serpent whose toxic breath was capable of killing any living thing it touched. Doom vipers came to GA-METRU via a trading boat from another land and proved extremely hard to capture. None seem to have made it to MATA NUI (2).

DOOM VIPER

DRAGON LIZARD:
See HIKAKI.

DRIFTS:
The icy snowfields of MOUNT IHU. POHATU NUVA followed KOPAKA NUVA through this treacherous area during the search for the KANOHI NUVA masks. TAKUA and JALLER later traveled this way as well on their quest for the Seventh TOA, encountering vicious RAHKSHI during the journey.

DRILL STAFF:
TURAGA WHENUA's tool and badge of office, also known as the drill of ONUA. The drill staff is an altered version of the EARTHSHOCK DRILLS that Whenua carried as a TOA; it transformed when Whenua became a TURAGA.

DUME (doo-MAH):
Former Toa of Fire and TURAGA of METRU NUI. Dume's history as a TOA has not yet been revealed, although it is believed that he had some hand in LHIKAN's becoming a Toa. After becoming a Turaga, Dume led Metru Nui for thousands of years, helping it to become a thriving metropolis.

Under Dume's rule, the MATORAN constructed the KRALHI and the VAHKI. Dume also authorized MAVRAH's researches into ancient sea RAHI, then later ordered the experiments stopped when they threatened the city. It was also Dume who first summoned Lhikan and ten other Toa to battle the KANOHI DRAGON that menaced Metru Nui.

Perhaps Dume's bravest act was opposing the DARK HUNTERS when they wished to establish a base in Metru Nui. Despite threats from the SHADOWED ONE, Dume refused to allow the mercenaries anywhere within the boundaries of the city. This set off a major conflict between the Dark Hunters and a small band of Toa in the city, led by Lhikan. The Toa were eventually victorious, despite the defection of Toa NIDHIKI and his attempts to betray the city into Dark Hunter hands (see NIDHIKI).

Centuries later, Dume was captured by MAKUTA and placed inside a sphere that rendered him comatose. Makuta then impersonated Dume as part of his plan to capture all of the Matoran in the city. Although the TOA METRU uncovered the ruse, they were unable to rescue Dume prior to their escape from the city. Later, as TOA HORDIKA, they were successful in rescuing him. Dume chose to remain in the city after the Toa and Matoran left.

DWELLER IN THE DEEP:
A massive underwater beast that lived in the sea beneath the GREAT TEMPLE. TOA NOKAMA encountered it during her search for the GA-METRU GREAT DISK, which turned out to be wedged between two of the creature's sharp teeth. The dweller's preferred prey was GREAT TEMPLE SQUID.

EARTH SHIELD:

Tool carried by NUHVOK. These shields could weaken a structure from below, causing it to tumble down. The Nuhvok used their earth shields in their successful invasion of LE-KORO.

EHRYE

EHRYE (AIR-yay):

A KO-MATORAN. Ehrye worked as a messenger in KO-METRU but dreamed of obtaining employment in a KNOWLEDGE TOWER. He blamed NUJU for preventing him from getting a better job and resolved to use his knowledge of the location of the Ko-Metru GREAT DISK to get what he wanted. NIDHIKI and KREKKA trapped Ehrye on a rooftop in their efforts to get the Great Disks, and he had to be saved by Toa Nuju. Later, Ehrye merged with VHISOLA, ORKAHM, NUHRII, TEHUTTI, and AHKMOU to form the MATORAN NUI and help the TOA METRU defeat the MORBUZAKH. Shortly after that, Ehrye was captured by the VAHKI and put into a sphere that rendered him comatose. Evidence was later discovered that Ehrye may have been destined to become a Toa of Ice.
Ehrye was eventually rescued by the Toa Metru and brought to MATA NUI (2).

ELECTRIC SHIELD:

Tool carried by TAHNOK-KAL capable of releasing hundreds of thousands of volts at once.

ENERGIZED PROTODERMIS:

The rarest form of PROTODERMIS, capable of inducing permanent mutations or causing instant destruction. Energized protodermis was silver in color and appeared to be charged with an unknown form of energy, but the origin of the substance was not known by the MATORAN. ONU-MATORAN miners occasionally stumbled across small samples of it beneath METRU NUI, and GA-MATORAN scholars attempted to analyze it, but to no avail. In some strange way, energized protodermis appeared to be linked to the destiny of those beings exposed to it. A being destined to be transformed by energized protodermis would be; a being who was not so destined would be dissolved by the liquid. Energized protodermis apparently worked on inanimate objects as well, having been seen to transform KANOHI masks and give a semblance of life to solid stone. It is believed the rock creature called VATUKA may have been created using this substance.
MAKUTA worked with the ENERGIZED PROTODERMIS ENTITY to use the substance to mutate RAHI, for reasons still unknown. Later, the TOA METRU discovered an energized protodermis pool in one of Makuta's lairs outside of the city, guarded by the energized protodermis entity. During the ensuing battle, the entity used its substance to mutate Rahi to fight the Toa. Later, the KARZAHNI (2) was destroyed after exposing itself to this fluid in an effort to gain greater power. Centuries after the Matoran left Metru Nui for MATA NUI (2), TAHU and his team of TOA were immersed in tubes of energized protodermis following a battle with the BAHRAG. Rather than being destroyed by it, the Toa were transformed into TOA NUVA. The chamber in which this occurred was later buried under tons of rubble.

ENERGIZED PROTODERMIS ENTITY:

A sapient being that consisted exclusively of ENERGIZED PROTODERMIS in a humanoid form. It was encountered by the TOA METRU in one of MAKUTA's lairs. It revealed that it had been allied with Makuta in experiments to mutate RAHI, as well as being a vital part of the creation of KARZAHNI (2) and the MORBUZAKH. The Toa Metru asked for a small portion of its substance to trade for a cure for NOKAMA's wounds, but the entity refused and engaged them in battle. The entity fought primarily through surrogates, Rahi creatures mutated by its substance. In the end, the Toa Metru defeated the Rahi and threatened to bring the chamber down on the protodermis pool if the entity did not comply. The entity allowed them to take a vial full of its substance but then attempted to slay the Toa Metru as they departed. Toa ONEWA brought down the last pillar supporting the ceiling and buried the entity under tons of rock.

It is highly unlikely the energized protodermis entity was killed in this incident. Since it was capable of appearing wherever any of its substance might be, it probably disappeared before the impact and reappeared at another pool somewhere else. It is no doubt planning revenge for its defeat.

ENSIGN:

A badge worn by members of the TA-KORO GUARD, bearing the volcanic emblem of that force.

EXO-TOA [EX-oh TOE-ah]:

Armored suits capable of enhancing the powers of the beings that wore them. The Exo-Toa were constructed under the orders of the BROTHERHOOD OF MAKUTA, both as a failsafe against a possible rampage by the BOHROK and as automated guardians of the Brotherhood's many fortresses. A number of Exo-Toa were destroyed by the TOA HAGAH during their attack on a Brotherhood base.

Centuries later, the Exo-Toa were stumbled upon by TAHU and his team of TOA while attempting to stop the BAHRAG. They donned the armor and used its advanced equipment, including electro-rockets, to challenge the Bohrok queens. However, the armor inhibited the Toa's elemental powers, making them as much a hindrance as a help.

Later, the six Exo-Toa suits, again running on automatic, challenged the BOHROK-KAL as they tried to free the Bahrag. The Kal destroyed the Exo-Toa. Unknown to anyone, NUPARU salvaged some of the armor and is hoping to study it on the journey back to METRU NUI.

FADER BULL:

Plant-eating PO-METRU RAHI capable of limited teleportation to escape enemies.

FAU SWAMP [FOW]:

The marshy ground of LE-WAHI. Too soft and muddy to build homes upon, the presence of the Fau Swamp forced the LE-MATORAN to make their homes in trees. MATAU became lost in the swamp on his first visit to MATA NUI (2) and often complained about the terrain afterward. The swamp was later home to a large number of RAHI.

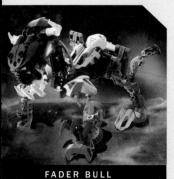

FADER BULL

FIELDS OF CONSTRUCTION:

A large, open area in PO-METRU where assorted pieces were assembled to make goods for use throughout METRU NUI.

FIKOU (fee-KOO):

Tree spiders that nested in LE-METRU cables, ONU-METRU tunnels, and, later, LE-WAHI vines. The Fikou were known for spinning incredibly intricate webs and for jumping out suddenly at passing prey.

"FIKOU WEB" (fee-KOO):

Nickname given by ONU-MATORAN to a complex series of maintenance tunnels beneath the ONU-METRU ARCHIVES. The TOA METRU encountered RAHKSHI and KRAHKA here while attempting to repair a leak that threatened the Archives.

FIRE ENTITY:

A creature made completely of flame encountered and defeated by TOA VAKAMA during the TOA METRU's journey back to METRU NUI. Its exact nature was never discovered, but Vakama saw it as a reflection of himself if he were ever to let his power run out of control. He defeated the fire entity by using his Toa power to draw every last bit of heat from the chamber, causing the entity to freeze. It evidently survived, for it was gone when the other Toa arrived to find Vakama, unconscious from his effort.

FIRE GREATSWORDS:

Twin Toa tools carried by LHIKAN, through which he could focus his flame power. They could also be fitted together to form a shield and a flying board.

FIRE PITS:

Flame geysers in the center of TA-METRU, believed by the MATORAN to have been the source of all fire in the district. They were surrounded by a fence and guarded by VAHKI patrols. Due to the danger of the pits, Matoran had to receive special permission from TURAGA DUME to access them. TOA VAKAMA and NUHRII broke into the fire pit area to retrieve the Ta-Metru GREAT DISK, and fought a MORBUZAKH vine inside one of the pits.

FIRE SHIELD:

Tool carried by the TAHNOK. It was capable of melting any substance on the island of MATA NUI (2). Tahnok used fire shields in attacks on TA-KORO, PO-KORO, and elsewhere.

FIREFLYERS:

Flying insects with a fiery sting. Swarms of fireflyers were known to nest in furnaces and maintenance tunnels beneath TA-METRU.

FIRESTAFF:

TURAGA VAKAMA's tool and badge of office. His firestaff is in fact his mask-making tool that he used while living on METRU NUI as a MATORAN. This same tool was used by Vakama to create the KANOHI VAHI, the Mask of Time.

FORCE SPHERE:

A particularly dangerous phenomenon observed in CHUTES in the city of METRU NUI. When part of a chute was damaged, a portion of the magnetic force holding the liquid PROTODERMIS in place could fold in on itself and break off. It could then travel through the chute, absorbing everything that it passed and growing larger. At a certain size, it would wreck the chute and then implode, destroying everything contained within it. The LE-METRU GREAT DISK was freed from a force sphere by TOA MATAU.

FOUNTAINS OF WISDOM:

Decorative structures in GA-METRU from which jets of liquid PROTODERMIS emerged.

FROST BEETLES:

Insectoid KO-METRU RAHI rumored to have Matoran-level intelligence as a result of having consumed MEMORY CRYSTALS. These creatures were never spotted on MATA NUI (2).

FROST BEETLE

FROSTELUS (frost-TELL-lus):

Icebergs floated in the far northern waters around METRU NUI, having appeared suddenly following the earthquake that struck the city. No one realized that these were not natural forms — they were, in fact, homes and "armor" for the beings called Frostelus. Somewhere on the borderline between RAHI and TOA-TURAGA-MATORAN, Frostelus may have been former victims of the VISORAK or some previously undiscovered species. How they came to be so near Metru Nui, and what their intentions were, remains unknown.

FURNACE SALAMANDER:

Lizardlike RAHI that lived inside the foundries and furnaces of TA-METRU. Excellent climbers and jumpers, they were also capable of gliding short distances.

FURNACE SALAMANDER

FUSA (FOO-sah):

A kangaroo-like RAHI and a natural enemy of the MUAKA. Fusa defended themselves using their powerful hind legs and could be extremely dangerous when cornered or in captivity.

G

GA (GAH):

A Matoran prefix meaning "water."

GA-KINI (GAH-kin-NEE):

A temple dedicated to GALI located in GA-WAHI on MATA NUI (2).

GA-KORO (GAH-koar-OH):

Village on MATA NUI (2) and home to the GA-MATORAN. Ga-Koro was led by TURAGA NOKAMA and protected by TOA GALI. The village floated atop the waters off the northeastern coast of the island. Whirlpools and strong currents combined to make the village a dangerous place for outsiders to visit. TAKUA aided the village when it was invaded by RAHI, shortly after the arrival of Gali. Ga-Koro was menaced by PAHRAK during the BOHROK invasion.

GA-MATORAN (GAH-mat-OR-an):
A resident of GA-KORO or GA-METRU. Ga-Matoran had blue armor and often wore blue masks. All Ga-Matoran were female. On METRU NUI, most Ga-Matoran were students or teachers. On MATA NUI (2), their labors tended to involve boating, fishing, and other aquatic pursuits.

GA-METRU

GA-METRU (GAH-MET-troo):
Spiritual and educational center of METRU NUI and home to the GREAT TEMPLE and the FOUNTAINS OF WISDOM. Ga-Metru was the site of numerous PROTODERMIS canals, as well as temples and schools. According to legend, Ga-Metru was the second region of the city built and was the one most favored by MATA NUI (1). Protodermis was pumped from the sea into Ga-Metru, and the purification process took place here. This metru was protected by TOA NOKAMA, who discovered a GREAT DISK in the waters beneath the Great Temple.

GA-SUVA (GAH-soo-VAH):
A shrine to GALI NUVA in GA-KORO. KANOHI masks and Gali Nuva's symbol were kept here.

GA-WAHI (GAH-wah-HEE):
Region in northeastern MATA NUI (2), site of GA-KORO. Ga-Wahi was dominated by the waters of NAHO BAY and was home to numerous aquatic RAHI, including RUKI, MAKUTA FISH, TARAKAVA, and TAKEA. Seaweed and lily pads in the bay provided a foundation for the village to float upon.

GAAKI (gah-KEE):
Former TOA HAGAH of Water later mutated by ROODAKA into a RAHAGA. Gaaki had been part of an elite Toa team assigned to be MAKUTA's personal guard. When they discovered Makuta was oppressing and enslaving MATORAN, they turned on him and attacked a fortress of the BROTHERHOOD OF MAKUTA. Gaaki was struck by one of Roodaka's RHOTUKA SPINNERS and mutated into a shrunken creature with the head of a RAHKSHI. She was later rescued by Toa IRUINI and Toa NORIK, who also ended up being mutated.
What masks and tools Gaaki carried as a Toa has not yet been revealed.
As a Rahaga, Gaaki specialized in capturing RAHI swimmers, such as TAKEA and MAKUTA FISH. She carried a Rhotuka Spinner with the *floater* power, which attached to its target and carried the Rahi to the surface of the water. She also carried a staff that she used to bait Rahi by striking the water with it.

GAHDOK (GAH-dahk):
This red creature was one of the two BAHRAG twins. See BAHRAG.

GAHLOK-KAL

GAHLOK [GAH-lahk]:

One of the six breeds of BOHROK, insectlike mechanoids controlled by KRANA who menaced the island of MATA NUI (2). The Gahlok were tied to the element of water, and their WATER SHIELDS could draw moisture from any source and redirect it at an opponent. The Gahlok were known for being sly and tricky, rarely reacting the same way twice to a given situation. Although most often seen in GA-WAHI, their most successful strike was the flooding of ONU-KORO. The Gahlok returned to their nests after the coming of the BOHROK-KAL and remain there still.

GAHLOK-KAL [GAH-lahk-KAHL]:

One of the six mutant BOHROK who made up the BOHROK-KAL. Its tool was a MAGNETIC SHIELD, which could be used for defense or offense. After being fed TOA power via the TOA NUVA SYMBOLS (see BOHROK-KAL), Gahlok-Kal's power went wild and drew every metallic object in the room toward it. Its robotic body was crushed in the ensuing collision.

GAHLOK VA [GAH-lahk VAH]:

One of the six BOHROK VA, Gahlok Va was connected to the water element. Their primary tools were twin hooks which could be used to climb slippery surfaces or defend themselves in combat. Although not fleet swimmers, they had incredible endurance, enabling them to travel long distances without stopping.

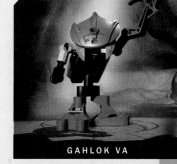

GAHLOK VA

GALI/GALI NUVA [GAH-lee/GAH-lee NOO-vah]:

TOA of Water and protector of GA-KORO.

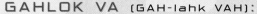

HISTORY

All that is known about Gali and her past prior to her first appearance on MATA NUI (2) comes from MATORAN legend. She was one of six Toa who had been floating in the ocean around the

GALI

island for 1000 years. They were inside unique canisters and each was partially disassembled. A signal unwittingly sent by TAKUA called the canisters to shore. Gali emerged on the shores of GA-WAHI and almost immediately had to act to save Ga-Koro from the rampage of a TARAKAVA.

Gali soon made contact with the other five Toa — KOPAKA, LEWA, ONUA, POHATU, and TAHU. Together and separately, they searched for KANOHI masks and battled the RAHI servants of MAKUTA. From the start, she had to spend a lot of time keeping Kopaka and Tahu from arguing. During a fight with the Rahi, Gali hit her head and had a vision in which the two TOA KAITA appeared and told her that it would be the destiny of the Toa to form those two powerful beings. Later, she would indeed briefly merge with Lewa and Kopaka to form Toa Kaita WAIRUHA and fight the MANAS.

During the BOHROK invasion, Gali teamed with Pohatu, Onua, and Kopaka to trap a swarm of TAHNOK in TIRO CANYON.

Following the defeat of the twin Bohrok queens, the BAHRAG, the six Toa were transformed by ENERGIZED PROTODERMIS into TOA NUVA. When Kopaka and Tahu decided to break up the team, Gali objected strongly. But no one, not even Onua, supported her. It would be some time before she forgave her friends. Later, after the BOHROK-KAL had stolen the Toa Nuva's powers, Gali teamed with TURAGA NOKAMA to search for KANOHI NUVA masks and was almost killed by a GREAT TEMPLE SQUID.

Gali was the first to see the coming of the RAHKSHI, and she sped to TA-KORO to warn the village. But despite the best efforts of herself and Tahu, they were unable to prevent the village of fire from being destroyed or the Toa of Fire from being poisoned. Later, she led the other Toa in a healing ritual to save Tahu's life.

Gali Nuva and other Toa Nuva are now journeying back to METRU NUI with the Turaga and Matoran.

POWERS

Gali controls the power of water. She can start or stop tidal waves and floods, draw moisture from the air and hurl it in a devastating water blast, or lash an opponent with fierce rainstorms. She is a strong swimmer and can survive prolonged periods of time at great depths.

PERSONALITY

On a Toa team filled with strong personalities, it normally falls to Gali to be the peacemaker. More than once, she has had to get between Tahu and Kopaka to keep them focused rather than fighting. Of all the Toa, she and Pohatu are probably closest to their respective Matoran, taking time to help them and guide them in between adventures.

GALI NUVA

EQUIPMENT

Gali carried HOOKS that allowed her to scale slippery surfaces. As Gali Nuva, she carried twin AQUA AXES that could be attached to her feet to serve as scuba fins. Gali most often wore the Kanohi KAUKAU or KAUKAU NUVA, the Great Mask of Water Breathing.

GATE GUARDIAN:

A deceptive creature that created a false image of itself to fool enemies. The Gate Guardian seen by others was small, perhaps 1.5 feet high. In reality, the creature was much bigger, but virtually impossible to see. An attacker targeting the small image would find itself beaten back by the larger, invisible Gate Guardian. The image mimicked the movements of the true creature. The only way to defeat a Gate Guardian was to first find some way to reveal its true form. NOKAMA was able to use her water power to do this on METRU NUI. It is believed that Gate Guardians were allied with the VISORAK.

GATE GUARDIAN

GHEKULA [GECK-you-LAH]:

Amphibious creatures most often found in swampy waters. It was considered bad luck to harm one. Prior to selling infected KOLHII BALLS in PO-KORO, AHKMOU attempted to make a living selling "lucky Ghekula" to superstitious MATORAN, until TURAGA ONEWA put a stop to it.

GNOMON:

The centerpiece of a sundial. Gnomon were in use on both the sundial on MATA NUI (2) and the massive sundial kept by MAKUTA in the COLISEUM.

GRAVITY SHIELD:

Tool carried by NUHVOK-KAL. This shield could completely eliminate gravity in a large area or increase it by up to 1,000 times. Nuhvok-Kal used this shield to erase gravity around a swarm of TAHNOK and send them flying into space.

GREAT BEINGS:

Immensely powerful entities who, according to MATORAN legend, dispatched the GREAT SPIRIT MATA NUI (1) from paradise to care for all living things. It is believed that the Great Beings came into existence long before Mata Nui — and dwarf even him in sheer power. How many Great Beings there are and where they reside is unknown.

GREAT DISKS:

Six KANOKA DISKS of great power. According to legend, one was hidden in each of the six districts of METRU NUI. Their powers were *reconstitutes at random, freeze, weaken, enlarge, regenerate,* and *teleport.* Each Great Disk had a power level of 9.
Shortly after becoming a TOA METRU, VAKAMA had a vision that hinted the Great Disks were needed to save the city. He and the other Toa Metru went on a dangerous quest and succeeded in finding all six disks, despite efforts by NIDHIKI, KREKKA, and AHKMOU to stop them. They later used the disks to defeat the MORBUZAKH.
The heroes believed the recovery of the disks would prove them worthy to be TOA in the eyes of the MATORAN, but such did not prove to be the case. However, Vakama was successful in merging the disks into a DISK OF TIME and later carving the VAHI from it.

GREAT FURNACE:

Once the second highest structure in METRU NUI (after the COLISEUM), the Great Furnace was a massive foundry in TA-METRU used for the creation of VAHKI parts and other essential items. The heat from the furnace was so intense that even MATORAN could stand it for only a few minutes at a time before they had to retreat to a slightly cooler outer ring in the structure. The Great Furnace operated day and night, producing the largest amount of material of any forge or factory in the metru. Shortly before the coming of the TOA METRU, mysterious vines began attacking workers in the Great Furnace. The workers eventually fled the structure, leaving it abandoned but still functioning. The Great Furnace became the home of the king root of the MORBUZAKH plant, from which it launched its attacks on the rest of the city. It was also the site of the final battle between the Toa Metru and the Morbuzakh, which resulted in the destruction of both the plant creature and the building. The Great Furnace was never rebuilt.

GREAT MASKS:
See KANOHI.

GREAT SPIRIT:
Designation given to MATA NUI (1) by the MATORAN. A Great Spirit is considered to be extremely powerful, though not at the level of a GREAT BEING. The GREAT TEMPLE in GA-METRU and KINI-NUI were both dedicated to the Great Spirit Mata Nui.

GREAT TEMPLE:
Arguably the most important building in METRU NUI, the Great Temple was the spiritual center of the city. It was built on a spit of land apart from the rest of GA-METRU and revered by MATORAN from all districts. It was heavily patrolled by VAHKI BORDAKH to protect it from RAHI attack.
The Great Temple was the home of the TOA SUVA, a round stone structure said to be the source of TOA power. The suva boasted six slots into which TOA STONES could be

GREAT TEMPLE

placed. Toa LHIKAN stole six Toa stones from this site and gave them to six Matoran — MATAU, NOKAMA, NUJU, ONEWA, VAKAMA, and WHENUA. These six were later transformed from Matoran into TOA METRU. KANOHI Masks of Power were also stored in the Great Temple.
Amazingly, the structure survived, relatively intact, the earthquake that struck Metru Nui. TOA HORDIKA Nokama and RAHAGA GAAKI encountered a GATE GUARDIAN here while searching for GREAT MASKS. The RAHAGA and Toa Hordika also journeyed here in search of clues to the location of KEETONGU.

GREAT TEMPLE SQUID:
Multi-tentacled beasts that lurked in the waters beneath the GREAT TEMPLE in GA-METRU. Long a menace to divers, the Great Temple squid feared only their natural enemy, the DWELLER IN THE DEEP. Each squid had twelve tentacles, each ending in a snapping beak, as well as a larger beak that acted as a mouth. Their sheer strength rivaled that of a TOA.
GALI NUVA was once trapped in the tentacles of a Great Temple squid that had made its way into an underwater tunnel between METRU NUI and MATA NUI (2).

GREAT USSAL RACE (uss-SUL):
The major sporting event of ONU-KORO on MATA NUI (2). This competition pitted riders on USSAL crabs against each other in a test of speed and skill. ONEPU won the race five times.

GUKKO (GUCK-koh):
These large, four-winged birds originally made their nests in the cables above LE-METRU. After the MATORAN fled METRU NUI to MATA NUI (2), the Gukko followed and found a home in the jungles of LE-WAHI. The LE-MATORAN eventually learned to tame the Gukko birds. Gukko riders became the main defense force of LE-KORO. RAHAGA KUALUS insisted that Gukko was not the correct name for the species and that the term might have even been an insult in the language of these RAHI. Kualus and TOA HORDIKA NUJU are believed to have been the first to ride Gukko birds.

GUKKO BIRD FORCE:

A defense squad made up of LE-MATORAN mounted on GUKKO. Their most memorable feats were coming to the aid of the CHRONICLER's Company and their attack on a NUI-RAMA nest. The Gukko Bird Force was led by KONGU.

GUURAHK (GER-rahk):

One of the six RAHKSHI sent by MAKUTA to stop the HERALD and recover the KANOHI AVOHKII. Guurahk's staff emitted a powerful cone of energy capable of disintegrating anything it struck. This Rahkshi's special talent was the ability to divine the weakest point in any object or foe and target it. Along with LERAHK and PANRAHK, Guurahk destroyed the village of TA-KORO. These three Rahkshi were later trapped in a prison of glass, thanks to the combined powers of LEWA NUVA and TAHU NUVA.

HAFU (HAH-foo):

Extremely skilled PO-MATORAN carver. Hafu was widely considered the best of all the artisans in PO-KORO, as well as a great storyteller. Unfortunately, Hafu had a very high opinion of himself and tended to talk mostly about himself and his achievements. Hafu was part of the CHRONICLER's Company assembled by TAKUA to defend KINI-NUI against RAHI attack. Hafu's greatest moment occurred when he sacrificed some of his most beautiful statues to block the entryway to Po-Koro against the invading TAHNOK. Hafu later served on the Po-Koro KOLHII team with HEWKII, narrowly losing to the GA-KORO team.

HAHLI (HAH-lee):

A GA-MATORAN and current CHRONICLER of the TOA NUVA's adventures. Prior to the coming of the TOA, Hahli spent most of her time fishing and mending nets, too shy to voice her ideas or opinions. But she was thrust into danger during the BOHROK invasion and worked with MACKU to prevent the PAHRAK from entering GA-KORO. Following the defeat of the BOHROK-KAL, Hahli was unexpectedly tapped by TURAGA NOKAMA to play on the Ga-Koro KOLHII team. Hahli led her team to victory against PO-KORO and TA-KORO squads. She had formed a close friendship with JALLER, captain of the TA-KORO GUARD, at this time, though the relationship had not progressed beyond that.

After TAKUA became TAKANUVA, the Seventh Toa, Hahli stowed away onboard his USSANUI vehicle to MAKUTA's lair. There she revealed herself to him and offered to be his Chronicler. He sent her back to the surface to gather the other Toa, the Turaga, and the MATORAN and bring them down with her. This she did, returning in time to see Takanuva and Makuta merge into TAKUTANUVA.

Hahli was one of the Matoran who passed through the gateway leading to the shores of the silver sea around Metru Nui. She carried the late Jaller's mask with her. Takutanuva stopped her and used part of his life force to bring Jaller back to life.

Since that time, Hahli has served as Chronicler, present for almost all of Turaga VAKAMA's tales of METRU NUI.

HAPAKA (hah-PAH-kah):

Large hounds briefly employed by GA-MATORAN to drive away KAVINIKA, with mixed success. Although the Hapaka were certainly fierce enough for the job, they were also easily distracted by the chance to chase other RAHI.

HAU (HOW):

The Mask of Shielding. This mask created a force field around the user, protecting him from physical attack. Its sole limitation was that it could protect only against attacks that are expected, and so was ineffective against ambushes. TOA TAHU was wearing a Hau when he first appeared on MATA NUI (2), and it was Toa LHIKAN's mask of choice as well on METRU NUI. After his transformation into a TURAGA and subsequent death, Lhikan's Noble Hau was given to JALLER, a TA-MATORAN. In addition, the Hau is the symbol of the GREAT SPIRIT MATA NUI (1).

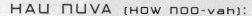

HAU

HAU NUVA (HOW noo-vah):

The more powerful version of the HAU worn by TAHU NUVA. This mask was able to project a stronger force field than the Hau, and the effect could be maintained for a longer duration. Like all Nuva masks, its power could be shared by the user with those in close proximity.

HEATSTONE:

A small, yellowish rock which gave off natural heat. It could be used to warm a chamber when open flame was not advisable. Heatstones are believed to be related to LIGHTSTONES, but most likely derive their power from a different source.

HAU NUVA

HERALD:

According to MATORAN legend, the Herald was the being charged with bringing the KANOHI AVOHKII, the Mask of Light, to the TOA of Light. This would bring about the dawn of a new age in which darkness would be defeated and peace would reign. TAKUA was the chosen Herald, but he attemped to pass the responsibility on to JALLER. After Jaller's death, it was discovered that Takua was not only the Herald but was, in fact, destined to become TAKANUVA, the Toa of Light.

HEWKII (HOO-kee):

PO-MATORAN carver and diskmaker. During the time that he lived on METRU NUI, Hewkii was famous throughout the city for the quality of his KANOKA DISKS. So excellent was his workmanship that TURAGA DUME was forced to make a rule that players from other metru could not use PO-METRU disks in AKILINI tournament play.

On MATA NUI (2), Hewkii was a KOLHII champion and a trusted aide to Turaga ONEWA. He was one of the only Po-Matoran strong enough to crush rocks with both his feet and his head. Athletic and powerful, he led the PO-KORO team to numerous kolhii championships and won the COPPER MASK OF VICTORY multiple times. Hewkii was credited with inventing the most popular current form of kolhii when he used his staff to save MACKU from a flying rock during

HEWKII

the BOHROK invasion. Paired with HAFU, Hewkii challenged TA-KORO and GA-KORO squads in a kolhii match, but narrowly lost to Ga-Koro.

HIKAKI (hih-KAH-kee):
A small lizardlike creature that thrived on molten PROTODERMIS and often shared territory with the FURNACE SALAMANDER. It was found most often in the vicinity of the MANGAI volcano on MATA NUI (2). Also known as the Dragon Lizard.

HIVE:
Bases for the VAHKI order enforcers in METRU NUI. Each hive contained an energy cradle through which Vahki could be recharged. When the METRU NUI power plant was destroyed, the resulting energy surge wrecked the hives as well.

HOOKS:
Tools carried by TOA GALI that allowed her to climb on slippery surfaces.

HORDIKA (hoar-DEE-kah):
A Matoran word meaning "half beast." It was applied to the venom of the VISORAK, which could transform TOA into half-hero, half-RAHI forms.

HORDIKA

HOTO (HOH-toh):
Fire bugs known for tunneling through solid stone using the searing heat given off by their bodies to melt the way. On both METRU NUI and MATA NUI (2), they were considered a pest, often causing buildings and tunnels to collapse.

HUAI SNOWBALL SLING (HOOH-eye):
A popular sport in KO-KORO. Winners of the competition would receive a COPPER MASK OF VICTORY.

HUFA-MAFA RIVER (HOOH-fah MAH-fah):
A river that ran southwest from NAHO BAY on MATA NUI (2). MACKU thoroughly explored this waterway in the early years of her time on the island. She was almost killed here by a TAKEA shark that had wandered into the river and become lost.

HUNA

HUNA (HOO-nah):
KANOHI Mask of Concealment. TOA VAKAMA wore the Great Mask of Concealment, which could make him invisible, although he would still cast a shadow. As a TURAGA, Vakama wore the Noble version of this mask, which had the same effects but a shorter duration.

HUSI (HOO-see):
Ostrichlike birds that once roamed free on the rocky crags of PO-METRU before being hunted almost to extinction by MUAKA and other predators. They were later placed in the ARCHIVES for their own protection. Some Husi escaped after the quake shattered the facility and later made their way to MATA NUI (2).

ICE BAT:
Winged creatures of KO-METRU, known for their destructive flights through KNOWLEDGE TOWERS. Their presence accounted for the reluctance of AIRSHIP pilots to fly over Ko-Metru.

ICE BLADE:
KOPAKA NUVA's twin Toa tools, through which he focused his ice power. The ice blade could be split in two and be used as power ice skates for rapid travel.

ICE PICK OF NUJU (noo-joo):
TURAGA NUJU's tool and badge of office.

ICE SHIELD:
[1] Tool carried by the KOHRAK. These shields were capable of freezing anything, including molten rock or open flames. Kohrak used their ice shields in an early attack on TA-KORO. [2] Defensive tool carried by KOPAKA.

ICE SWORD:
Toa tool carried by KOPAKA through which he channeled his elemental power.

ICE VERMIN:
Small RAHI who became serious threats to METRU NUI after the earthquake. In some strange way, their RHOTUKA SPINNERS absorbed the seismic energy of the quake. They were then able to use them to cause earth tremors or make enemies actually shake apart.

ICE VERMIN

IGNALU (igg-NAH-loo):
Lava surfing competition popular in TA-KORO. Participants used LAVABOARDS to travel rapidly across the flows. Winners of this competition received a COPPER MASK OF VICTORY.

IHU (EEE-hoo):
KO-MATORAN who acted as mentor to NUJU at the start of his career in the KNOWLEDGE TOWERS. Ihu taught Nuju that the most important thing in life was what you learned while living and how you used that knowledge. Ihu was killed when NUI-RAMA attacked the CHUTE in which he was riding. Later, TOA Nuju would name a mountain on MATA NUI (2) in his honor (see MOUNT IHU).

INFECTED MASKS:
Term used for KANOHI masks which have been tainted by the darkness of MAKUTA. Infected masks are created when a KRAATA makes physical contact with a mask. They can also be infected at long range by a SHADOW KRAATA. An infected mask takes on a rusted, pitted appearance. Anyone wearing such a mask becomes subservient to the will of Makuta. TOA LEWA was once forced to wear an infected mask and temporarily served Makuta.

INFERNAVIKA (in-FURN-nah-VEE-kah):

A small bird that made its home near the molten PROTODERMIS waste pipes on the coast of TA-METRU. Its love of ultra-hot places kept it safe, as few other creatures ventured near. These creatures would later migrate to MATA NUI (2) and make a home amid the lava near TA-KORO.

IRUINI (EYE-roo-NEE):

Former TOA HAGAH of Air, later mutated by ROODAKA into a RAHAGA. Iruini had been part of an elite TOA team charged with being MAKUTA's personal guard. When they discovered Makuta was oppressing and enslaving MATORAN, they turned on him and attacked a fortress of the BROTHERHOOD OF MAKUTA. Iruini and NORIK got separated from the other Toa but managed to defeat the EXO-TOA and the DARK HUNTERS and drive Makuta off. They then went to rescue their friends, only to discover they had been turned into shrunken, twisted creatures with the faces of RAHKSHI by Roodaka. Although they saved their fellow Toa, they too were turned into Rahaga.

As a Toa, Iruini carried a CYCLONE SPEAR and a RHOTUKA SPINNER with the ability to heal. He wore the KANOHI KUALSI, the Great Mask of Quick Travel.

As a Rahaga, Iruini specialized in capturing Rahi climbers, such as BRAKAS and CABLE CRAWLERS. He carried a Rhotuka spinner with the *snag* power, which attached to its target and tangled up limbs like a net. He also carried a staff, the movements of which could hypnotize RAHI.

JALLER (JAH-luh):

Heroic TA-MATORAN. Jaller was employed as a tool maker in METRU NUI and was close friends with TAKUA, another worker. He often covered for Takua with the VAHKI, keeping his friend out of trouble. During transport to MATA NUI (2), Jaller's KANOHI mask was badly damaged. TURAGA VAKAMA replaced the mask with the late Turaga LHIKAN's Noble HAU. (Being a MATORAN, Jaller could not access the powers of the mask.)

Jaller rapidly became an important figure during the construction of TAK-KORO, helping to defend the site from RAHI attacks. Vakama appointed him captain of the TA-KORO GUARD, a position he has held for over 1000 years. He showed great heroism during the BOHROK invasion, aiding the village of GA-KORO against a PAHRAK attack. He was rewarded with a name change during NAMING DAY ceremonies. He continued his friendship with Takua, and the two of them made up Ta-Koro's KOLHII BALL team, with Jaller serving as goalie. He also struck up a budding romance with HAHLI, a GA-MATORAN.

Prior to an important kolhii match, Jaller went in search of the missing Takua only to find him in a forbidden lava cavern. He was there when Takua stumbled upon the legendary Mask of Light. Unwilling to accept responsibility for being HERALD of the Toa of Light, Takua tricked the Turaga into believing it was Jaller's destiny to fulfill that role. Jaller got even by insisting Takua accompany him on his search for the Seventh Toa. The two braved many dangers on their quest, including encounters with an ASH BEAR, RAHKSHI, and MAKUTA himself.

JALLER

During the final battle between the TOA NUVA and the Rahkshi, Jaller sacrificed his life to save Takua. Later, TAKUTANUVA, a merged entity made up of TAKANUVA and Makuta, gave up part of its life force to restore life to Jaller. Since that time, the valiant Ta-Matoran has helped to oversee the construction of transport craft for the return to Metru Nui.

KAHGARAK [KAH-gah-rack]:

A powerful species related to the VISORAK used as guards by the hordes. Kahgarak ranged in height from 6 feet to 12 feet, and in width from 9 feet to 18 feet. Their coloring also varied. The Kahgarak's RHOTUKA SPINNERS had the power to envelop a foe in a zone of shadow. Their target would be unable to see or communicate with the world outside and would remain trapped unless another Kahgarak opened a gap in the zone. This power also meant that Kahgarak were the only creatures who could release the dreaded ZIVON from its domain of darkness, not to mention send it back there. A Kahgarak was responsible for the Zivon, TAHTORAK, and the KRAHKA all being transported to the realm of shadow, from which they have not yet returned. Kahgarak have, in the past, also been fitted with projectile launchers for use in sieges.

KAHGARAK

KAKAMA [kah-KAHM-mah]:

The Mask of Speed. This mask allowed the user to run great distances in an instant. POHATU wore the KANOHI Kakama when he first appeared on MATA NUI (2), and often put its power to good use. In one of his earliest adventures, he ran around the base of an erupting volcano at super speed, creating a trench into which molten lava could safely flow.

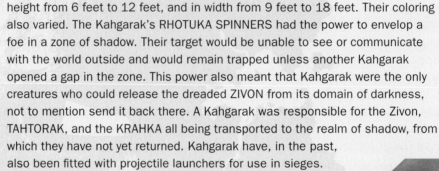

KAKAMA

KAKAMA NUVA

KAKAMA NUVA [kah-KAHM-mah NOO-vah]:

The more powerful version of the KAKAMA worn by POHATU NUVA. This mask not only allowed super speed travel, but also gave the user complete control of the molecules of his body. This allowed someone wearing the Kakama to pass through solid objects without harm by simply vibrating at a different speed than the object. Like all Nuva masks, its power could be shared by the user with others in close proximity. The TOA used a combination of the Kakama Nuva and MIRU NUVA's powers to "fly" out of the BAHRAG chamber following their transformation into TOA NUVA.

KANAE BAY [kah-NIGH]:

A body of water on the southern shore of LE-WAHI. For a number of years, LE-MATORAN came here to attempt to overcome their dislike of water by swimming in the clear waters. The efforts proved to be a dismal failure and MATAU finally persuaded them that trees were far better than water, anyway.

KANE-RA [kah-NAY-rah]:

One of the largest plant-eating land RAHI, the Kane-Ra bull would prove to be a menace on MATA NUI (2). Several specimens made it from METRU NUI to the island, only to be fitted with INFECTED MASKS and put under the influence of MAKUTA. Later, the TOA removed these masks and the Kane-Ra retreated to the valleys, no longer a threat.

KANE-RA

KANOHI (kah-no-hee):

Matoran word meaning "mask." The Kanohi Masks of Power were vital to the survival of the MATORAN and the power of the TURAGA and TOA. Kanohi masks were created using KANOKA DISKS and were made in TA-METRU in METRU NUI.

There are three known types of Kanohi mask:

Matoran Masks: Worn by Matoran villagers, these masks do not have any extra powers. Wearing them is essential for Matoran, however, as having a mask off for too long can lead to a condition resembling a coma. Matoran masks are fashioned to look like Great Masks and Noble Masks. They are made from Kanoka disks with a power level of 6 and under.

Noble Masks: Less powerful than Great Masks, these are commonly worn by Turaga, but also used by Toa. Noble Masks are made from Kanoka disks with a power level of 7. Noble Masks were stored in the GREAT TEMPLE of Metru Nui. Noble Masks were brought from Metru Nui to MATA NUI (2) by the TOA METRU. They were later stolen from the Matoran villages by RAHI under MAKUTA's command, and remained missing until found by TAHU and the other Toa a thousand years later.

Great Masks: These masks can be used effectively only by Toa, and are made from Kanoka disks with a power level of 8. Great Masks were stored in the Great Temple in Metru Nui. An assortment of these masks was brought to Mata Nui by the TOA METRU and hidden in various spots on the island. They were later found by Tahu and his team of Toa.

Use of a mask power requires a high level of mental discipline and willpower. For this reason, Turaga are no longer able to use Great Masks despite having once been Toa, and Matoran cannot use mask powers at all.

Whether extremely powerful masks like the VAHI, KRAAHKAN, and AVOHKII can be considered Great Masks or are something more is unclear.

Known Kanohi include the AKAKU, AKAKU NUVA, HAU, HAU NUVA, HUNA, KAKAMA, KAKAMA NUVA, KAUKAU, KAUKAU NUVA, KOMAU, KUALSI, MAHIKI, MATATU, MIRU, MIRU NUVA, PAKARI, PAKARI NUVA, PEHKUI, RAU, and RURU.

See also KANOHI NUVA and INFECTED MASKS.

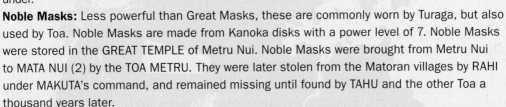

KANOHI DRAGON

KANOHI DRAGON (kah-no-hee):

A mysterious beast said to have vanished from METRU NUI more than a thousand years before the coming of the TOA METRU. According to legend, TOA LHIKAN and ten of his comrades fought a great battle and defeated the monster. A creature of fire, the Kanohi dragon could fly and relied on its flame breath, smoldering tail blades, and claws in combat. Its name came from the Kanohi masks that seemed to line its body. Some MATORAN claimed they were real masks, while others said they were decoys designed to lure Toa in close.

KANOHI NUVA (kah-no-hee noo-vah):

Masks exposed to ENERGIZED PROTODERMIS and transformed. Kanohi Nuva were more powerful than standard masks, and granted the user the ability to share the mask's power with anyone in close proximity. Kanohi Nuva included the AKAKU NUVA, HAU NUVA, KAKAMA NUVA, KAUKAU NUVA, MIRU NUVA, and PAKARI NUVA. They were worn by the TOA NUVA.

KANOKA DISK [kah-NO-kah]:

Round disks of PROTODERMIS used for both sport and defense in the city of METRU NUI. Kanoka disks were made using liquid protodermis that had been purified in GA-METRU. Disks were made in every metru in the city and each had a special power. Each disk was stamped with a three-digit code, with the first digit representing the metru in which the disk was made, the second its power, and the third its level of power.

There were eight basic Kanoka powers: *enlarge, freeze, reconstitutes at random, regenerate, remove poison, shrink, teleport,* and *weaken.* These eight powers could also be combined in various ways to create new powers. A Kanoka's power and level of power were determined by the properties and purity of the protodermis used and the skill of the MATORAN making the disk. The metru in which it was made also determined the special flight properties of the disk.

Kanoka disks were used in various Matoran sports, including AKILINI, and for defense against RAHI. Disks were also made into KANOHI masks. Those disks with a power level of 6 or less became Matoran masks and had no power. Disks with a power level of 7 became Noble Masks, with a significant amount of power. Disks with a power level of 8 became Great Masks, with an enormous amount of power. Only six disks were ever known to have a power level of 9, the GREAT DISKS, which were used by VAKAMA to create the Kanohi VAHI. In addition to being launched and thrown, Kanoka disks were also used in other ways in Metru Nui. *Levitation* and *increase weight* disks were incorporated into the design of airships, and *regeneration* disks built into buildings.

KANOKA LAUNCHER [kah-NO-kah]:

A tool carried by MATORAN and used for hurling KANOKA DISKS. Launchers had to be manually loaded and activated. These were used both for defense and in the sport of AKILINI.

KANOKA DISK—MASK OF POWER CHART

Listed below are the various Masks of Power that have appeared in BIONICLE and, where known, the Kanoka disks used to create them.

Kanohi Hau, Mask of Shielding — Growth + Regeneration disks

Kanohi Miru, Mask of Levitation — Teleport + Weaken disks

Kanohi Kakama, Mask of Speed — Teleport + Reconstitutes at Random disks

Kanohi Pakari, Mask of Strength — Regeneration + Enlarge + Removes Poison disks

Kanohi Kaukau, Mask of Water Breathing — Regeneration + Shrink + Removes Poison disks

Kanohi Akaku, Mask of X-Ray Vision — Regeneration + Teleport disks

Kanohi Mahiki, Mask of Illusion — Reconstitutes at Random + Weaken disks

Kanohi Huna, Mask of Concealment — Enlarge + Shrink + Freeze disks

Kanohi Komau, Mask of Mind Control — Freeze + Weaken + Removes Poison disks

Kanohi Rau, Mask of Translation — Removes Poison + Enlarge disks

Kanohi Ruru, Mask of Night Vision — Enlarge + Teleport disks

Kanohi Matatu, Mask of Telekinesis — Teleport + Shrink disks

Kanohi Kiril, Mask of Regeneration — Regeneration disk

Kanohi Kualsi, Mask of Quick Travel — Teleport disk

Kanohi Pehkui, Mask of Diminishment — Shrink disk

Kanohi Kraahkan, Mask of Shadows — Unknown

Kanohi Avohkii, Mask of Light — Unknown

Kanohi Vahi, Mask of Time — Disk of Time, made by combining all six Great Disks

KAPURA (KUH-purr-UH):

A TA-MATORAN. On METRU NUI, Kapura worked as a vat controller. During the time when the MORBUZAKH threatened the city, Kapura was dispatched to scout abandoned areas of the metru and retrieve any valuable items he might find.

On MATA NUI (2), Turaga VAKAMA worked with Kapura to teach him the secret art of traveling long distances very quickly by moving very slowly. Although some considered Kapura to be not very bright, Vakama saw great potential in him and made him a trusted aide. Kapura served as part of the CHRONICLER's Company, a small group assembled by TAKUA to defend KINI-NUI against RAHI attack.

KARZAHNI (KARR-zah-NEE):

[1] Legendary ruler of a domain much feared by MATORAN in the dim past. According to ancient tales, in the time before the GREAT SPIRIT, Matoran labored in darkness. Those Matoran who excelled at their work were sent to ARTAKHA and allowed to work in the light. Those who worked poorly were sent to another place, one ruled by Karzahni, from which they never returned. The name "Karzahni" eventually became a term Matoran used to scare each other, with each new tale about him becoming more and more exaggerated and frightening. [2] An intelligent plant creature created by MAKUTA with the help of the ENERGIZED PROTODERMIS ENTITY. Makuta named his creation Karzahni after the legendary ruler of a dread domain in ancient Matoran history. From the first, Karzahni proved to be too willful and ambitious to suit Makuta's needs, so eventually the master of shadows exiled his creation into the tunnels that linked METRU NUI to MATA NUI (2). There Karzahni brooded and planned its revenge on its creator. When the TOA METRU defeated Makuta, Karzahni shifted its hatred to them. After NOKAMA was mortally wounded by the RAHI NUI, Karzahni struck a bargain with the Toa Metru: if they would retrieve for it a sample of ENERGIZED PROTODERMIS from Makuta's lair, it would cure Nokama. Karzahni wanted the energized protodermis because it believed that the liquid would transform it into a far more powerful being.

The Toa Metru completed the quest and returned to Karzahni. Once there, NUJU revealed that he had deduced the plant creature was dying, the result of a fatal flaw Makuta bred into all of his creations. Forced to keep his bargain by Vakama, Karzahni cured Nokama and took the

KANOKA RESEARCH AND INFORMATION

Keep track of your KANOKA disk collection! Each time you get a KANOKA disk, check out the first two digits of its code – the METRU of origin and the power. Then write the code in the appropriate box below. And don't forget to enter the codes on BIONICLE.com to earn valuable KANOKA points!

Disc Effects on Targets	TA-METRU Stronger, can knock obstacles out of the way.*	GA-METRU Can change direction in mid-air, guided by the thrower's thoughts.*	PO-METRU Deflects other discs from their course.*
	143	226	337

CODES • CODES • CODES • CODES • CODES • CODES • CODES • CODES

	TA-METRU	GA-METRU	PO-METRU
(1) reconstitutes at random			
(2) freezes			
(3) weakens			
(4) removes poison			
(5) enlarges			
(6) shrinks			
(7) regenerates			
(8) teleports			

Disc Effects on Targets	KO-METRU Dodges obstacles to get to target.*	LE-METRU Flies further.*	ONU-METRU Always returns to thrower if diverted from course.*
	473	574	685

CODES • CODES • CODES • CODES • CODES • CODES • CODES • CODES

	KO-METRU	LE-METRU	ONU-METRU
(1) reconstitutes at random			
(2) freezes			
(3) weakens			
(4) removes poison			
(5) enlarges			
(6) shrinks			
(7) regenerates			
(8) teleports			

*Flight characteristics refer to story only, and do not reflect actual product performance.

vial of energized protodermis from the Toa. But when it poured the contents onto itself, the liquid burned the plant from within. In a matter of moments, Karzahni was dead.

When the Toa reached the shore of the silver sea around Metru Nui, they realized that they needed a ship to cross it. A VAHKI TRANSPORT was found, but there was nothing to keep it afloat. Toa ONEWA and Toa MATAU chopped up the dead plant's trunk and strapped the wood onto the bottom of the craft, making it seaworthy. None of the Toa noticed a small, green shoot growing from one of the logs. Whether it is a sign Karzahni will return someday remains to be seen.

KAU KAU STAFF [KOW KOW]:
TURAGA MATAU's tool and badge of office. Interestingly, its name is not related to the KANOHI KAUKAU mask. The name was a joke suggested by ONEWA based upon the noise made by BRAKAS in the trees. The nickname stuck and it has been called a kau kau staff ever since.

KAUKAU [KOW-KOW]:
The Mask of Water Breathing. Wearing this mask enabled the user to breathe underwater for an extended period of time. TOA GALI wore this mask when she first appeared on MATA NUI (2).

KAUKAU

KAUKAU NUVA [KOW-KOW NOO-vah]:
The more powerful version of the KAUKAU worn by GALI NUVA. In addition to allowing underwater respiration, this mask made it possible for the wearer to stay under longer and to breathe at greater depths. Like all Nuva masks, its power could be shared by the user with those in close proximity.

KAUKAU NUVA

KAVINIKA [KAH-vih-NEE-kah]:
Wolflike creatures originally used as guards at some MATORAN facilities in METRU NUI. Their violent natures made them too dangerous and they were banned by TURAGA DUME, but efforts to drive them out of the city met with failure. Strangely, their population actually seemed to increase after the earthquake in Metru Nui. The RAHAGA believed that something in one of the GA-METRU labs caused the RAHI to duplicate. Kavinika did make their way to MATA NUI (2), surviving in the depths of the LE-WAHI jungle.

KAVINIKA

KEELERAK [KEY-le-rack]:
One of the six breeds of VISORAK that invaded METRU NUI. The ends of a Keelerak's legs are razor sharp, and they have been known to leap high in the air and whirl at high speed, becoming Visorak "buzzsaws." Keelerak RHOTUKA SPINNERS have an acid venom that can melt any substance.

KEERAKH [key-RAHK]:
The VAHKI model assigned to KO-METRU in METRU NUI. These mechanoids were known for their uncanny ability to predict where a target would run, allowing them to get there first. They were rarely seen by KO-MATORAN except for those who had broken the law and been apprehended. Keerakh carried STAFFS OF CONFUSION, which could scramble a target's sense of time and place and leave

KEERAKH

him disoriented. NUJU and WHENUA battled KEERAKH on top of a KNOWLEDGE TOWER during their search for the GREAT DISKS.

KEETONGU [KEE-tahn-GOO]:

KEETONGU

A powerful RAHI previously unknown on METRU NUI and believed to be a myth by the populations of other lands. After the TOA METRU were mutated into HORDIKA, RAHAGA NORIK told them Keetongu was their only hope for a cure. Legend states that Keetongu's single "eye" can see the good or evil in any being, and that he will grant his cure only to those who are noble of spirit. His rotating shield array can absorb any power used against him and his blade claw can cleanse a being of VISORAK venom. Keetongu's true power is said to come from his armor and his spinners. The armor channels the power absorbed by the shield array, and the spinner can then send that energy back at his attacker. In this way, Keetongu can counteract any attack made upon him. The Toa Hordika and Rahaga launched a search for him in Metru Nui, in hopes that he would cure the Toa of their affliction.

KERAS [KEE-rahs]:

Large coral crabs found in the ocean off GA-METRU. At one time, MATORAN hoped that keras could be as useful to them as USSAL crabs were, but the hostile nature of the keras made that impossible.

KIKANALO

KIKANALO [KEE-kah-nah-LOW]:

Herd beasts that roamed the canyons of PO-METRU before coming to MATA NUI (2). These creatures used their horns to dig up little bits of PROTODERMIS left behind by PO-MATORAN carvers. In addition to their great strength, Kikanalo are capable of letting loose a roar that can blow away enemies like dust in a windstorm. A Kikanalo herd aided the TOA METRU against the VAHKI in Po-Metru. During that adventure, Toa NOKAMA was able to use her Mask of Translation to communicate with the beasts, discovering that they were in fact quite intelligent.

KINI-NUI [kih-NEE NOO-ee]:

The GREAT TEMPLE on the island of MATA NUI (2), constructed in part by the TURAGA and MATORAN shortly after their arrival on the island. TAKUA and the CHRONICLER's Company fought to defend this site from RAHI attack. Later, the Toa brought their KANOHI masks here and received GOLDEN MASKS that contained a full range of six powers. They entered Kini-Nui using the MAKOKI STONES and fought the MANAS, the SHADOW TOA, and MAKUTA. Later, Kini-Nui would be the site of the first appearance of the RAHKSHI on Mata Nui.

KINLOKA [kin-LOW-kah]:

A large, nasty species of rodent, Kinloka were the result of an experiment by the BROTHERHOOD OF MAKUTA to produce a RAHI with a more efficient digestive system. The result was a creature that was constantly hungry and ate anything. Although native to LE-METRU, they were seen all over METRU NUI. No reports of sightings were ever made on MATA NUI (2).

KINLOKA

KIO [KY-oh]:

A unit of MATORAN measurement equal to 1,000 BIO. A kio measures 4,500 feet or 1,371 meters in Earth measurement. A kio is also equal to .85 miles or 1.37 kilometers. METRU NUI is 47.6 kio long and 24 kio wide. By contrast, MATA NUI (2) is 357 kio in length and 178 kio in width. There are 1,000 kio in a MIO.

KIRIKORI NUI [kih-rih-KOAR-EE noo-ee]:

Locustlike insects known for their appearance in the skies over METRU NUI every ten years or so. They would alight in PO-METRU and GA-METRU, consume all the vegetation in sight, and then disappear. Their point of origin was unknown. Much to the dismay of the TURAGA, they later appeared on MATA NUI (2). MATORO was credited with discovering that they were afraid of NUI-KOPEN. Fake RAHI wasps were later constructed to try to scare the Kirikori Nui away.

KNOWLEDGE TOWERS:

Large crystalline structures in KO-METRU which were the workplaces of KO-MATORAN scholars. Knowledge Towers were not built but grown. Special knowledge crystals were thrown into cradles throughout the district, from which the towers grew at a rapid pace. Each Knowledge Tower boasted extensive library space, living quarters for scholars, observatories to monitor the stars, and special areas designed to hold ancient tablets and other valuable items. Many Ko-Matoran both lived and worked in the towers, never venturing out of doors. Before becoming a Toa, NUJU was employed in a Knowledge Tower. The Knowledge Towers were badly damaged in the earthquake that rocked METRU NUI.

KNOWLEDGE TOWERS

KO [KOE]:

A Matoran prefix meaning "ice."

KO-KINI [KOE-kih-NEE]:

A temple dedicated to KOPAKA located in KO-WAHI on MATA NUI (2).

KO-KORO [KOE-koar-OH]:

Village on MATA NUI (2) and home to the KO-MATORAN. Ko-Koro was hidden beneath a massive ice block that separates two glaciers, and surrounded by huge crevasses that could swallow the unwary. KO-KORO was led by TURAGA NUJU and protected by TOA KOPAKA. The village was severely damaged by the RAHKSHI.

KO-MATORAN [KOE-mat-OR-an]:

A resident of KO-KORO or KO-METRU. Ko-Matoran had white armor and commonly wore white or light-blue masks. Ko-Matoran in METRU NUI were primarily scholars. On the island of MATA NUI (2), they were master trackers and trap builders. They tended to be quiet and not very social in both locations.

KO-METRU [KOH-MET-troo]:

Home of the thinkers in METRU NUI. Dubbed the "quiet metru" by MATORAN from other districts, Ko-Metru was the site of the KNOWLEDGE TOWERS and TOWERS OF THOUGHT. The entire area was dedicated to learning and the

KO-METRU

interpretation of prophecies. Just as living creatures and artifacts were stored in the ARCHIVES, so were all written records of Matoran past, present, and future stored here. Ko-Metru was protected by TOA NUJU. One of the six GREAT DISKS was found here, hidden in ice at the top of a Knowledge Tower.

KO-SUVA [KOH-soo-VAH]:
A shrine in the village of KO-KORO to honor KOPAKA NUVA. The NUVA SYMBOL was originally stolen from here by the BOHROK-KAL. Kopaka's Masks of Power were also kept on the suva.

KO-WAHI [KOH-wah-HEE]:
Icy region on MATA NUI (2) that encompassed MOUNT IHU and the DRIFTS. The village of KO-KORO was located here. Snowfall and avalanches are common here. TAKUA and JALLER traveled through Ko-Wahi on their quest to find TAKANUVA. A temporarily powerless KOPAKA NUVA and POHATU NUVA were menaced by a MUAKA in Ko-Wahi.

KODAN [KOH-dann]:
A PO-MATORAN in METRU NUI and the CHRONICLER for TOA LHIKAN's team. Kodan began his career as Chronicler when Lhikan arrived in the city with ten other Toa to fight the KANOHI DRAGON. Kodan continued to fill this role for centuries. He vanished along with two Toa on a mission for TURAGA DUME (actually MAKUTA in disguise).

Kodan was also credited with the invention of the sport of AKILINI. Numerous legends have arisen about how he first came up with the idea or how he first set up a crude akilini field in a PO-METRU canyon. However, over the years other metru have insisted that the idea for the sport actually came from one of their MATORAN. In the resulting confusion, no one is really certain anymore who deserves the honor. After Kodan disappeared and was presumed dead, a monument was erected to him in Po-Metru giving him credit for the discovery.

KODAN BALL [KOH-dann]:
A sphere formed by POHATU NUVA's CLIMBING CLAWS. In shape and size, it resembles the sphere used in METRU NUI for the very earliest versions of the sport of AKILINI. It was that resemblance which led TURAGA ONEWA to suggest the name "Kodan ball" to Pohatu Nuva. KODAN was the PO-MATORAN said to have invented the sport of Akilini. (See KODAN.)

KOFO-JAGA [KOH-foh JAH-gah]:
Small, fiery scorpions known for attacking in swarms, these were most often found near abandoned forges in TA-METRU and near the MANGAI volcano in TA-WAHI. They were attracted to the smell of molten PROTODERMIS and preferred dark places.

TA-METRU MATORAN investigating empty factories knew to carry bright LIGHTSTONES to protect themselves (temporarily) from these creatures. A swarm of Kofo-Jaga once drove off much larger and more powerful MANAS crabs.

KOHRAK [KOH-rahk]:
One of the six breeds of BOHROK, insectlike mechanoids controlled by KRANA who menaced the island of MATA NUI (2). The Kohrak were tied to the element of ice, and their ICE SHIELDS could freeze anything, even open flames. The Kohrak's bodies gave off such intense cold that other Bohrok avoided their company. The Kohrak were part of the initial attack on TA-KORO which was repulsed by TAHU

KOHRAK

and his team of TOA. They spent much of their time on the lava plains and in the valleys of TA-WAHI. The Kohrak returned to their nests after the coming of the BOHROK-KAL and remain there still.

KOHRAK-KAL [KOH-rahk KAHL]:

KOHRAK-KAL

One of the six mutant BOHROK who made up the BOHROK-KAL. Kohrak-Kal's tool was a SONIC SHIELD capable of creating a sound barrier that could repel most forms of attack. It could also cause objects to vibrate until they shattered. After being fed TOA power via the TOA NUVA's symbols (see BOHROK-KAL), Kohrak-Kal was shaken apart by its own energies.

KOHRAK VA [KOH-rahk VAH]:

One of the six BOHROK VA, Kohrak Va were connected to the element of ice. They relied on stealth and camouflage, hiding in snowdrifts to keep an eye on the movements of the TOA and MATORAN. When cornered, they used their claws to defend themselves.

KOHRAK VA

KOLHII [KOAL-lee]:

The most popular sport on MATA NUI (2). Kolhii was created by TURAGA ONEWA during a dispute between the carvers of PO-KORO and the miners of ONU-KORO. Seeking a way to settle the matter without violence, Onewa conceived of a competition between the two koro, and Turaga WHENUA readily agreed.

In kolhii, two or more teams compete to get a KOLHII BALL into an opponent's goal. Variants of kolhii include a match where the ball can only be kicked, to the most popular version, in which KOLHII STAFFS are used to hurl the ball. Defending players carry KOLHII SHIELDS to deflect shots away from their goals.

PO-MATORAN have traditionally been the champions of the sport, to the point that POHATU is considered to be the patron TOA of kolhii. Prior to the coming of the Toa to Mata Nui, most matches were intramural within koro, due to the dangers of traveling to other villages. With the defeat of MAKUTA's RAHI, travel become much easier and inter-koro games were played once again. Kolhii became a centerpiece of Matoran life and matches an occasion of great celebration. Variants of the sport include an Onu-Koro version played on USSAL crabs and an aerial version played by LE-MATORAN flying on GUKKO birds.

Following the defeat of the BOHROK-KAL, the Toa and Matoran worked together to erect a great kolhii stadium. It was in the immediate aftermath of a match between TA-KORO, GA-KORO, and Po-Koro that it was discovered that TAKUA carried the Mask of Light.

KOLHII BALL [KOAL-lee]:

A sphere made of lightweight airstone bound in steel used in the sport of KOLHII. The most popular type of kolhii ball was the COMET, although it fell out of favor after AHKMOU sold several infected samples to MATORAN. These infected spheres brought the Matoran owners under the sway of MAKUTA.

KOLHII SHIELD [KOAL-lee]:

Tool carried by defenders in the sport of KOLHII, used to deflect shots.

KOLHII STAFF [KOAL-lee]:

A long staff with a macelike hammer on one end and a scooped hurler on the other, used in the sport of KOLHII. The hammer is used to deflect opponent's shots, while the hurler is used to toss the KOLHII BALL to a teammate or toward an opponent's goal.

KOMAU [koh-mow]:

KANOHI Mask of Mind Control. This mask allowed the wearer to make others do his bidding, although it could work only on targets that had a mind (and thus was ineffective against VAHKI and some forms of RAHI). ONEWA wore the Great Mask version of this as a TOA, and the Noble Mask version as a TURAGA.

RULES OF KOLHII

1. Teams must number more than one but no more than six.
2. Teams may include any number of players greater than one, but no team may have more players than any other.
3. Prior to the game, all teams must agree to the number of goals required for victory.
4. The first team to reach the number of goals agreed to is the winner.
5. All goals are good goals (counting for a score) as long as they are not own goals (goals scored by a player in his own net). Own goals are not goals.
6. Each player is allowed one defender who carries a kolhii shield. No other player may use that shield, except when rule #11 is invoked.
7. All players may carry one kolhii staff, and one only.
8. Any number of kolhii balls may be played, but balls in play must number less than either the number of teams or the number of players per team, whichever number is the smallest.
9. Any player who strikes another player did not play well. Shield and staff strikes occurring during play and deemed innocent in intent are not considered a violation of this rule.
10. Any player who does not play well brings dishonor to his or her koro.
11. In the event of an invasion of the playing field by RAHI or other forces, play is postponed until the problem is dealt with.

KONGU

KONGU [KAHN-goo]:

A LE-MATORAN hero. On METRU NUI, Kongu was simply another worker, assigned to oversee the chute controls in the MOTO-HUB. The only excitement in his life came when he was captured by the DARK HUNTERS NIDHIKI and KREKKA and forced to reverse the flow in the CHUTES in an effort to trap the TOA METRU.

On MATA NUI (2), Kongu developed an incredible skill at dealing with RAHI. He became the best bird wrangler in all of LE-KORO and captain of the GUKKO BIRD FORCE. Kongu aided TAKUA on a rescue mission to save other MATORAN from a NUI-RAMA nest. Later, he was part of a successful mission to save Toa LEWA, Turaga MATAU, and the other Le-Matoran from being controlled by the BOHROK swarm through the KRANA they had been forced to wear. Kongu worked with TAMARU, Takua, and NUPARU on this dangerous task, which was credited with saving the entire KORO.

KOPAKA/KOPAKA NUVA [koh-PAH-kah/koh-PAH-kah NOO-vah]:

TOA of Ice and protector of KO-KORO.

Nothing is known about Kopaka's history prior to his first appearance on the island of MATA NUI (2). He was one of six Toa who had been floating in the ocean around that land for 1000 years. They were inside unique canisters and each was partially disassembled. A signal unwittingly sent by TAKUA called the canisters to shore. Kopaka emerged on the shores of KO-WAHI and almost immediately encountered MATORO. This MATORAN brought Kopaka to TURAGA NUJU, who explained that the island was besieged by the forces of MAKUTA.

KOPAKA

Kopaka's first act of heroism was saving Matoro from a NUI-RAMA. Shortly after, he encountered POHATU when the Toa of Stone accidentally buried him in a rockslide. The two proceeded to find a Kanohi HAU atop MOUNT IHU. Then Kopaka spotted a gathering of other beings, who turned out to be ONUA, TAHU, LEWA, and GALI.

Despite some misgivings, Kopaka agreed to team up with the other Toa. Together and separately, they searched for KANOHI masks and battled the RAHI servants of MAKUTA. Early on, Kopaka and Tahu began to get on each other's nerves, a condition that would only grow worse with time. He briefly merged with Gali and Lewa to form TOA KAITA WAIRUHA and fight the MANAS.

During the battle against the BOHROK, it was Kopaka who discovered that the enemy was not alien to the island of Mata Nui, but in fact came from underground. He also prevented Tahu from charging into a Bohrok nest and possibly getting killed.

Following the defeat of the twin Bohrok queens, the BAHRAG, the six Toa were transformed by ENERGIZED PROTODERMIS into TOA NUVA. Tahu and Kopaka fought shortly after, an argument which led to the break-up of the team. This damaged Kopaka's friendship with Gali for some time. Later, after the BOHROK-KAL had stolen the Toa Nuva's powers, Kopaka teamed with Pohatu to search for KANOHI NUVA masks.

Kopaka encountered TAKUA and JALLER during their search for TAKANUVA, saving them from a RAHKSHI attack. Discovering that Ko-Koro had been badly damaged by the invaders, Kopaka bid the Matoran farewell as he went to aid his village.

Later, Kopaka teamed with Tahu Nuva, Onua Nuva, and Pohatu Nuva to imprison KURAHK and VORAHK in frozen magma.

Kopaka Nuva and other Toa Nuva are now journeying back to Metru Nui with the Turaga and Matoran.

Kopaka was the master of ice. He could stop or start blizzards; hurl ice darts; travel via ice slides; freeze an opponent solid in an instant; and, as a Toa Nuva, even freeze open flames. He also had a natural resistance to extreme cold.

Kopaka was the least social of all the Toa, preferring to spend time by himself. While he usually recognized the importance of being on a team, he was never comfortable with it. When not adventuring, he could be found alone on Mount Ihu. He had little patience for fools or reckless behavior. He and Tahu clashed repeatedly, almost coming to blows once. Of all the Toa, it was only Gali and (though he would never admit it) Pohatu whom he considered friends.

EQUIPMENT

Kopaka carried an ICE SWORD and ICE SHIELD (2). As Kopaka Nuva, he carried an ICE BLADE which could be split in two and used as ice skates. Kopaka most often wore the Kanohi AKAKU or AKAKU NUVA, the Great Mask of X-Ray Vision.

KOPEKE [KOH-peek]:

A highly respected KO-MATORAN carver, known for his ice bridges and sculptures in honor of TOA KOPAKA. On METRU NUI, Kopeke worked at a variety of jobs, including messenger and chute station attendant. But it was on MATA NUI (2) that his true artistic gifts began to show themselves.
In addition to being a fine sculptor, Kopeke was also an athlete. He excelled at both HUAI SNOWBALL SLING and KOLHII.
Kopeke served as part of the CHRONICLER's Company and helped to defend KINI-NUI against RAHI attack.

KORO [KOAR-oh]:

Matoran word meaning "village." There were six villages on MATA NUI (2): GA-KORO, KO-KORO, LE-KORO, ONU-KORO, PO-KORO, and TA-KORO.

KRAAHKAN [krah-KAN]:

The Great Mask of Shadows worn by MAKUTA. The Kraahkan was capable of creating darkness, anger, and fear. Its origin is unknown, although legends hint that it may have been created by mask makers enslaved by the BROTHERHOOD OF MAKUTA. The mask was capable of changing shape along with Makuta as needed. TAKANUVA defeated Makuta in part by removing this mask from his face.

KRAAHU [KRAH-hoo]:

A specialized version of a VAHKI designed by NUPARU for use against RAHI stampedes and in other emergencies. Unlike the standard Vahki model, the Kraahu's knowledge centers are scattered throughout its structure. This allows the Kraahu to actually split apart and have its various pieces act independently. Kraahu parts give off an electrical charge that is triggered on contact. When intact, the Kraahu can emit clouds of stun gas.

KRAATA [KRAH-tah]:

Wormlike, sentient portions of MAKUTA's substance, created by him as the basis for RAHKSHI. Although Makuta could in theory create an infinite number of kraata, bringing them into being seems to diminish his energy temporarily. Kraata move like snakes and are capable of spreading infection to any inanimate object they touch, most often KANOHI masks. A kraata exposed to ENERGIZED PROTODERMIS will evolve over time into Rahkshi armor. Another kraata must then occupy the armor to activate and control it.
Kraata come in a variety of colors, with the colors indicating the power of the individual kraata. The Rahkshi created from those kraata will have identical powers.

Kraata go through six stages of development, with the evolution the result of time and experience. A select few kraata evolve to a seventh stage (see SHADOW KRAATA).

Although there were Rahkshi on METRU NUI, kraata were not a major factor there. The sole exception was TOA NOKAMA's realization that the Rahkshi he had encountered had to be KRAHKA in disguise because the armor lacked a controlling kraata.

These creatures were, however, a significant problem on MATA NUI (2), sent forth by Makuta to infect masks and bring RAHI and MATORAN under his sway. Many of these kraata were trapped by the TURAGA and placed into stasis tubes hidden in a PO-WAHI cave. The Turaga chose not to kill the kraata they encountered, believing that their energy would simply revert to Makuta.

Kraata were in control of the six Rahkshi who attacked Mata Nui. TAKANUVA's vehicle, the USSANUI, was constructed from the parts of these Rahkshi and powered by kraata. Their presence enabled the craft to detect Makuta's location and bring the Toa of Light right to it.

Kraata Colors and Powers

A kraata's power can be identified by its mix of colors. These powers can be used by the Rahkshi formed from the individual kraata. See the Rahkshi chart on pages 90–91 for the colors of different Rahkshi breeds.

Kraata Color	Power
Reddish Gold/Bright Red	Fear
Lemon Metallic/Bright Yellowish Green	Poison
Dark Gray/Metallic Gray	Hunger
Sand Yellow Metallic/Brick Yellow	Shattering
Sand Blue Metallic/Medium Blue	Disintegration
Light Gray Metallic/White	Anger
Lemon Metallic/Dark Gray Metallic	Weather Control
Bright Yellow Green/Bright Yellow	Elasticity
Black/Bright Orange	Heat Vision
Dark Green/Bright Yellow	Illusion
Lemon Metallic/Bright Red	Teleport
Lemon Metallic/Sand Blue Metallic	Quick Healing
Lemon Metallic/Dark Green	Laser Vision
Dark Gray Metallic/Lemon Metallic	Gravity
Bright Blue/Bright Red	Electricity
Black/Bright Yellow	Sonics
Bright Yellow/Bright Yellow Green	Vacuum
Dark Gray/Sand Blue Metallic	Plasma
Bright Orange/Black	Magnetism
Black/Bright Red	Fire Resistance
Bright Yellow/Dark Green	Ice Resistance
Bright Red/Lemon Metallic	Mind Reading
Dark Gray/Bright Yellow Green	Shapeshifting
Reddish Gold/Bright Yellow	Darkness
Reddish Gold/Black	Plant Control
Sand Yellow Metallic/Reddish Gold	Molecular Disruption (inorganic)
Sand Blue Metallic/Lemon Metallic	Chain Lightning

Sand Blue Metallic/Light Gray Metallic	Cyclone
Dark Green/Lemon Metallic	Density Control
Sand Yellow Metallic/Bright Yellow	Chameleon
Bright Red/Bright Blue	Accuracy
Sand Yellow Metallic/Black	Rahi Control
Bright Yellow/Black	Insect Control
Sand Blue Metallic/Dark Gray	Stasis Field
Black/Sand Yellow Metallic	Limited Invulnerability
Bright Red/Black	Power Scream
Bright Yellow/Sand Yellow Metallic	Dodge
Bright Yellow Green/Dark Gray	Silence
Bright Yellow/Reddish Gold	Adaptation
Light Gray Metallic/Sand Blue Metallic	Slow
Black/Reddish Gold	Confusion
Reddish Gold/Sand Yellow Metallic	Sleep

KRAATA-CU [KRAH-tah-KOO]:
Controlling organism of the RAHKSHI KURAHK. Possessed the anger power. See KURAHK.

KRAATA-UL [KRAH-tah-UHL]:
Controlling organism of the RAHKSHI GUURAHK. Possessed the disintegration power. See GUURAHK.

KRAATA-VO [KRAH-tah-VOH]:
Controlling organism of the RAHKSHI VORAHK. Possessed the hunger power. See VORAHK.

KRAATA-XI [KRAH-tah-ZEE]:
Controlling organism of the RAHKSHI PANRAHK. Possessed the shattering or fragmenting power. See PANRAHK.

KRAATA-YE [KRAH-tah-YAY]:
Controlling organism of the RAHKSHI LERAHK. Possessed the poison power. See LERAHK.

KRAATA-ZA [KRAH-tah-ZAH]:
Controlling organism of a RAHKSHI TURAHK. Possessed the fear power. See TURAHK.

KRAAWA [KRAH-wah]:
A RAHI with the special ability to absorb any force directed against it and use that energy to grow. The Kraawa was kept in the most secure portion of the METRU NUI ARCHIVES. How many specimens exist is unknown. An attempt by a kraawa to escape was blamed for the shattering of a container holding microscopic PROTODITES, and the subsequent spread of those creatures throughout the Archives.

KRAAWA

KRAHKA [KRAH-kah]:

Intelligent, shapeshifting RAHI who lived in the area beneath the ARCHIVES maintenance tunnels in METRU NUI. Krahka was able to take on the form and powers of any living thing she had seen, as well as combine those forms and powers. She also gained knowledge with the transformation, enabling her to master the MATORAN (2) language among other things.

Krahka first encountered the TOA METRU when they went into the maintenance tunnels to stop a leak that threatened the Archives. After capturing WHENUA, she impersonated him to lead the others into a trap. Believing the Toa and MATORAN (1) a threat to her domain, she intended to lure the Matoran into the tunnels and trap them, then claim the city for herself. She was defeated after using her power to take on aspects of all six TOA, when the mental strain proved too much for her. Turning herself into a lava eel, she escaped, with Toa VAKAMA making no effort to stop her.

She resurfaced after the VISORAK took over Metru Nui, challenging ROODAKA to single combat. Roodaka won and used Krahka as part of a plan to undermine the confidence of the TOA HORDIKA. Krahka later turned on Roodaka and sided with the Toa and RAHAGA against the Visorak horde. Summoning the TAHTORAK, Krahka rode it into battle against the horde and the ZIVON. During the struggle between the Tahtorak and the Zivon, Krahka spotted a KAHGARAK about to unleash a spinner that would send the Tahtorak into the zone of darkness. Knowing she could not save him, Krahka slammed into the Zivon, forcing it into physical contact with its foe. When the spinner hit, all three — Tahtorak, Zivon, and Krahka — were transported into the zone. None of them have been seen since.

Krahka believed that she was the only member of her species, but Rahaga POUKS revealed that many more had once existed in another land. They were overrun by the Visorak and are presumed lost.

KRAHKA

KRALHI [KRAHL-hee]:

The initial attempt to create an order-enforcing machine in METRU NUI was the Kralhi, designed by NUPARU under orders from TURAGA DUME. The Kralhi was able to launch an energy bubble from its tail at a target. The bubble would then envelop the target and drain a percentage of his energy. Unfortunately, this system proved inefficient as it left the MATORAN lawbreakers too weak to work. Dume decided to have the Kralhi retired, but the machines refused to be shut off. Some hid in KO-METRU, some in the ARCHIVES, and others ended up in the tunnels connecting Metru Nui to MATA NUI (2). The latter group allied with MAVRAH against the TOA METRU and were destroyed as a consequence. The Kralhi were replaced in Metru Nui by the VAHKI.

KRANA [KRAH-nah]:

Living creatures that reside in and operate BOHROK mechanoids. There were eight types of krana: KRANA BO, KRANA CA, KRANA JA, KRANA SU, KRANA VU, KRANA XA, KRANA YO, and KRANA ZA (see individual entries). Each provided the Bohrok with a different power or ability. Krana were created by the BAHRAG by introducing an unknown form of energy into ENERGIZED PROTODERMIS. Krana came into being from a combination of the two.

Krana were unable to function independently, and relied on a telepathic link to the Bahrag. When that link was cut off by the Bahrag's defeat and imprisonment, the krana ceased to be a threat. If a krana was removed from a Bohrok, the mechanoid ceased to function properly. Bohrok were capable of ejecting their krana onto the face of an opponent. Once the krana was attached, the target's mind fell under the sway of the Bohrok swarm. TOA TAHU, Toa LEWA, TURAGA MATAU, and almost the entire population of LE-KORO experienced this harrowing ordeal.

During the battle with the Bohrok, the Toa collected the eight forms of krana from each species. Once they were fitted into niches in the floor of an underground chamber, six passages opened up revealing the way to the EXO-TOA armor. The Toa used that armor in their final battle with the Bahrag.

MATORAN also collected krana from Bohrok as a means to render the mechanoids helpless. Most of these krana wound up buried in a pit. Having survived thousands of years of dormancy, it is likely the krana simply willed themselves back into a suspended state to await rescue.

KRANA BO (KRAH-nah BOH):
One of the eight KRANA that served as controlling brains for the BOHROK. The krana bo gifted a Bohrok with the ability to see in the dark.

KRANA BO-KAL (KRAH-nah BOH-KAHL):
One of the eight KRANA-KAL that served as controlling brains for the BOHROK-KAL. The krana bo-kal granted the power of X-ray vision. A Bohrok-Kal with this creature could see in the dark and through most substances. Only the walls of caves and tunnels beneath MATA NUI (2) were impervious to this power.

KRANA CA (KRAH-nah KAH):
One of the eight KRANA that served as controlling brains for the BOHROK. The krana can give a Bohrok the power to shield itself and others from attack.

KRANA CA-KAL (KRAH-nah KAH-KAHL):
One of the eight KRANA-KAL that served as controlling brains for the BOHROK-KAL. A Bohrok-Kal with this creature could sense the minds of the BAHRAG and thus locate them no matter where they were.

KRANA CA-KAL

KRANA JA

KRANA JA (KRAH-nah JAH):
One of the eight KRANA that served as controlling brains for the BOHROK. The krana ja gave a Bohrok the power to detect distant obstacles in the swarm's path.

KRANA JA-KAL (KRAH-nah JAH-KAHL):
One of the eight KRANA-KAL that served as controlling brains for the BOHROK-KAL. This krana-kal granted its Bohrok-Kal a radar sense, enabling it to detect distant obstacles. It also magnified the senses of the Bohrok-Kal, particularly smell and hearing.

KRANA-KAL [KRAH-nah-KAHL]:

Living creatures that reside in and operate BOHROK-KAL mechanoids. As with the KRANA, there were eight types of krana-kal: KRANA BO-KAL, KRANA CA-KAL, KRANA JA-CAL, KRANA SU-CAL, KRANA VU-KAL, KRANA XA-KAL, KRANA YO-KAL, and KRANA ZA-KAL. Each provided the Bohrok-Kal with a different power or ability. Unlike the krana, the krana-kal could function independently of the BAHRAG's influence and communicate with members of other species. If a krana-kal was removed from a Bohrok-Kal, the mechanoid ceased to function properly. At least some of the krana-kal escaped the destruction of the Bohrok-Kal.

KRANA-KAL

KRANA SU [KRAH-nah SOO]:

One of the eight KRANA that served as controlling brains for the BOHROK. The krana su gave a Bohrok the power of enhanced strength.

KRANA SU-KAL [KRAH-nah SOO-KAHL]:

One of the eight KRANA-KAL that served as controlling brains for the BOHROK-KAL. This krana-kal gave a Bohrok-Kal enhanced strength and resistance to heat and cold.

KRANA VU [KRAH-nah VOO]:

One of the eight KRANA that served as controlling brains for the BOHROK. The krana vu gave a Bohrok the ability to fly short distances.

KRANA VU-KAL

KRANA VU-KAL [KRAH-nah VOO-KAHL]:

One of the eight KRANA-KAL that served as controlling brains for the BOHROK-KAL. A Bohrok-Kal with this creature could move across the ground or through the air at high speed.

KRANA XA [KRAH-nah ZAH]:

One of the eight KRANA that served as controlling brains for the BOHROK. This krana was used only by swarm commanders and gave them the ability to form complex strategic plans.

KRANA XA-KAL [KRAH-nah ZAH-KAHL]:

One of the eight KRANA-KAL that served as controlling brains for the BOHROK-KAL. This krana-kal was the most important of them all. It gave its Bohrok-Kal the power to free the BAHRAG from their prison, in conjunction with the activation of the NUVA CUBE.

KRANA YO [KRAH-nah YOH]:

One of the eight KRANA that served as controlling brains for the BOHROK. The krana yo gave a Bohrok the power to tunnel through any substance on the island of MATA NUI (2).

KRANA YO-KAL [KRAH-nah YO-KAHL]:

One of the eight KRANA-KAL that served as controlling brains for the BOHROK-KAL. This krana-kal gave its Bohrok-Kal the ability to sense stress points in the earth, making for more efficient tunneling. It could also sense underground movement.

KRANA ZA [KRAH-nah ZAH]:

One of the eight KRANA that served as controlling brains for the BOHROK. The krana za made it possible for a Bohrok to communicate telepathically with others in the swarm.

KRANA ZA-KAL [KRAH-nah ZAH-KAHL]:

One of the eight KRANA-KAL that served as controlling brains for the BOHROK-KAL. This krana-kal was capable of communicating telepathically with other krana-kal, as well as reading minds and sensing strong emotion in the area.

KRANUA [KRAH-noo-ah]:

A specialized version of a VAHKI designed in secret by NUPARU and built by a select team of PO-MATORAN engineers. Its intended purpose was crowd control, particularly mass RAHI breakouts from the ARCHIVES. The powerful and bulky Kranua was capable of transforming its body into animated grains of PROTODERMIS, allowing it to flow through narrow openings before re-forming. The TOA METRU encountered a Kranua on their initial journey back to METRU NUI. After a brief but furious battle, VAKAMA used his fire power to fuse the sandy grains of the Kranua into glass. MATAU later tipped the crystalline Kranua over, shattering it.

KREKKA [kreh-KAH]:

One of the two DARK HUNTERS sent to METRU NUI at the request of MAKUTA. Krekka's partner was NIDHIKI.

Krekka was originally part of a guardian/servant class on the same island from which SIDORAK came. Extremely strong and powerful but not very bright, Krekka earned a living by convincing intruders to go away, often in very painful ways. Unfortunately, he made the mistake of trying to do this to an emissary of the BROTHERHOOD OF MAKUTA. Exactly what happened next is not clear, but some believe the encounter was responsible both for Krekka deciding to leave home and for the loss of one of his eyes. For a number of years, Krekka journeyed from island to island, usually getting into trouble and brawling his way out of it. This attracted the attention of the Dark Hunters, and Krekka was recruited into their organization. By order of the SHADOWED ONE, he was partnered with Nidhiki. It was an uneasy partnership at best, with Nidhiki being much smarter and more cunning than his bestial companion. But the Shadowed One had good reason for the decision he made. Nidhiki had betrayed the TOA in the past, and no one truly trusts a traitor. Krekka, on the other hand, would stick to a mission no matter what and make sure that Nidhiki did not stray too far from their objectives. For insurance, it was made extremely clear to Nidhiki that if anything happened to Krekka, the Dark Hunters would hold him responsible. Nidhiki and Krekka were sent to Metru Nui to aid Makuta in his plan to seize the GREAT DISKS and capture all the MATORAN in the city (see MAKUTA). Among their deeds were the capture of Toa LHIKAN and the recruitment of AHKMOU to help them get the Great Disks. They clashed repeatedly with the TOA METRU during and after this time (see NIDHIKI). Both Dark Hunters were drawn into Makuta's substance and became part of his new body. Neither has been seen since, and they are presumed dead.

KREKKA

In addition to his enormous strength, Krekka carried a KANOKA DISK launcher and was capable of launching energy webs at his foes. He could also shift into an aerodynamic mode for flight. He was able to survive falls from great heights. Unlike Nidhiki, Krekka was not a Toa in the past.

KUALUS [KOO-ahl-luss]:

Former TOA HAGAH of Ice later mutated by ROODAKA into a RAHAGA. Kualus had been part of an elite Toa team charged with being MAKUTA's personal guard. When they discovered Makuta was oppressing and enslaving MATORAN, they turned on him and attacked a fortress of the BROTHERHOOD OF MAKUTA. Kualus was struck by one of Roodaka's RHOTUKA SPINNERS and mutated into a shrunken creature with the head of a RAHKSHI. He was later rescued by Toa IRUINI and Toa NORIK, who also ended up being mutated.

What masks and tools Kualus carried as a Toa has not yet been revealed.

As a Rahaga, Kualus specialized in capturing flying RAHI, such as ICE BATS and GUKKO. He carried a Rhotuka spinner with the *boomerang* power, which would adhere to a flying target and then bring it right to him. His staff could be used to send a high-pitched signal to Rahi, summoning them or warning them of danger.

Kualus was capable of speaking a strange language that was evidently understood by some Rahi, and of understanding some of their language. He later taught this skill to Toa NUJU, who eventually abandoned speaking Matoran altogether in favor of this Rahi dialect.

KUALSI [KOO-ahl-see]:

Mask of Quick Travel, worn by TOA IRUINI. This mask allows the wearer to travel by teleportation, although only to a spot that is in his or her sight line.

KUMA-NUI [KOO-mah-NOO-ee]:

A giant rat creature found in the maintenance tunnels beneath the ARCHIVES, particularly in the TA-METRU and KO-METRU areas. A small number of these later migrated to MATA NUI (2). KORO defense forces were routinely dispatched to keep them away from the villages.

KUMU ISLETS [KOO-moo]:

A group of small islands at the southern tip of MATA NUI (2). Efforts to colonize them met with failure owing to the large number of extremely dangerous RAHI who made their home there.

KURAHK [KER-rahk]:

One of the six RAHKSHI sent by MAKUTA to stop the HERALD and recover the KANOHI AVOHKII. Kurahk's power, directed through its staff, caused his targets to grow enraged and often turn on each other. Along with TURAHK and VORAHK, Kurahk was responsible for the destruction of the village of ONU-KORO. Kurahk was trapped in an ice prison due to the efforts of ONUA NUVA, POHATU NUVA, TAHU NUVA, and KOPAKA NUVA.

KURAHK

LAKE OF FIRE:

A molten body of liquid PROTODERMIS on MATA NUI (2), site of the village of TA-KORO. The superheated lava was spanned by a bridge that could be lowered into the lake when danger threatened. Ta-Koro was later destroyed by the RAHKSHI and sank into the lake.

LAKE PALA (PAH-lah):

A small body of water in southeastern MATA NUI (2).

LAVA:

Molten PROTODERMIS. Streams of this substance flowed from the MANGAI volcano on MATA NUI (2). It was farmed by TA-MATORAN, and IGNALU, or lava surfing, was a popular sport in the village.

LAVABOARD:

A flat, narrow piece of hardened PROTODERMIS used by TA-MATORAN in TA-WAHI to surf on lava. MATORAN use tree trunks from the CHARRED FOREST to make their boards, for they do not melt in molten magma.

LAVA EEL:

A serpentlike creature of TA-METRU. When agitated, the surface temperature of a lava eel's skin increased to the point where it could melt through metal. Small lava eels were often kept as pets by TA-MATORAN, until they grew larger and more destructive, at which point they were normally abandoned.

LAVA FARM:

Areas worked by the TA-MATORAN in TA-WAHI. When the MATORAN lived on METRU NUI, objects could be crafted in TA-METRU from piped-in molten PROTODERMIS, then easily shipped to other districts for assembly and use. On the island of MATA NUI (2), things were not so simple owing to the number of RAHI serving MAKUTA who made the manufacture and transport of items more difficult. Ta-Matoran began harvesting lava from the MANGAI volcano and cooling it, then using tools to shape it into items that might be needed (these were rough carvings, nowhere near the level of what PO-MATORAN could do). These would then be shipped via underground tunnel to other villages. The BOHROK's initial attack on Ta-Wahi damaged some of the lava farms.

LAVA RAT:

A small rodent commonly found in TA-WAHI on MATA NUI (2). The lava rat was immune to fire and known for its tendency to burst into flames without warning. An old Matoran legend tells of an uneasy trip across water by a TAKEA shark carrying a lava rat upon his back.

LAVA SPEAR:

Tool carried by TOA NORIK. The lava spear could shoot a stream of molten lava at an enemy. In addition, the touch of the spear could either heat up an object and melt it instantly, or remove all heat from it in a split second. This was especially useful for turning a lava wave into an almost impenetrable wall of volcanic rock.

LE [LAY]:
A Matoran prefix meaning "air."

LE-KINI [LAY-kih-nEE]:
A temple dedicated to LEWA located in LE-WAHI on MATA NUI (2).

LE-KORO [LAY-KOAR-oh]:
Village on MATA NUI (2) and home to the LE-MATORAN. Le-Koro was led by TURAGA MATAU and protected by TOA LEWA. The village was built in the treetops above the FAU SWAMP. Visitors to the area could often hear the Le-Matoran up in the trees, chattering to each other in TREESPEAK. The village was badly damaged by the LEHVAK and many of its residents captured and enslaved by the BOHROK swarm. Le-Koro was later rebuilt. It was protected by the GUKKO BIRD FORCE led by KONGU.

LE-MATORAN [LAY-mat-OAR-an]:
A resident of LE-KORO or LE-METRU. Le-Matoran commonly had green armor and wore green masks. On METRU NUI, most Le-Matoran worked in the transport industry, either building or servicing vehicles and CHUTES, and used a slang known as CHUTESPEAK. This language was modified when they came to MATA NUI (2) to TREESPEAK.

LE-METRU

LE-METRU [LAY-mET-troo]:
Transport center of METRU NUI and site of the MOTO-HUB and TEST TRACK. Le-Metru was known for its feeling of barely controlled chaos as workers scrambled to and fro beneath a canopy of wires and cables. All chutes, ground, and air vehicles were manufactured here, and the entire chute system was supervised from here as well. Le-Metru was protected by TOA MATAU and the VAHKI VORZAKH. It suffered severe damage in the earthquake and became home to many of the species of RAHI who escaped the ARCHIVES.

LE-SUVA [LAY-SOO-vah]:
A shrine to LEWA NUVA in LE-KORO. KANOHI masks and Lewa Nuva's symbol were kept here. BOHROK-KAL stole the NUVA SYMBOL from the Le-Suva, robbing Lewa Nuva of his elemental power of air.

LE-WAHI [LAY-WAH-hee]:
A marshy, overgrown region located on the southern end of MATA NUI (2), known for its thick jungle. Le-Wahi was the site of the village of LE-KORO and home to numerous RAHI such as BRAKAS and GUKKO. LE-MATORAN live in the treetops above the FAU SWAMP. This area suffered badly at the claws of the LEHVAK during the BOHROK invasion.

LEHVAK [LAY-vahk]:
One of the six breeds of BOHROK, insectlike mechanoids controlled by KRANA who menaced the island of MATA NUI (2). The Lehvak were tied to the swampy terrain of LE-KORO and

LEHVAK

their ACID SHIELDS were powerful enough to dissolve any substance. The Lehvak normally operated in small groups and rarely worked with other Bohrok. They were responsible for the destruction of LE-KORO and the capture of most of the LE-MATORAN. They were most often active in LE-WAHI. The Lehvak returned to their nests after the coming of the BOHROK-KAL and remain there still.

LEHVAK-KAL [LAY-vahk-KAHL]:

One of the six mutant BOHROK who made up the BOHROK-KAL. Lehvak-Kal's tool was a VACUUM SHIELD which could draw in all the air from a given area, causing a destructive implosion. It could then release that air in a single blast with the power to smash through solid rock. Lehvak-Kal lost control of its power after being fed Toa power through the TOA NUVA's symbols (see BOHROK-KAL) and blasted itself into orbit.

LEHVAK-KAL

LEHVAK VA [LAY-vahk VAH]:

One of the six BOHROK VA, Lehvak Va were connected to swamp terrain. Unlike other Bohrok Va, who prided themselves on stealth, Lehvak Va were loud and aggressive creatures. They were more than willing to use their katana to defend themselves. Of all Bohrok Va, Lehvak Va stuck closest to their swarm.

LERAHK [LAY-rahk]:

One of the six RAHKSHI sent by MAKUTA to stop the HERALD and recover the KANOHI AVOHKII. Lerahk's staff was capable of poisoning anything it touched, from the ground to other beings. Along with GUURAHK and PANRAHK, Lerahk was responsible for the destruction of the village of TA-KORO. During an ensuing battle with TAHU NUVA, Lerahk scratched the TOA's mask, poisoning its foe. It took the combined power of the other five TOA NUVA to heal Tahu. Lerahk was trapped in a prison of glass due to the efforts of Tahu Nuva and LEWA NUVA.

LEWA/LEWA NUVA [LAY-wah/LAY-wah NOO-vah]:

TOA of Air and protector of LE-KORO.

LEHVAK VA

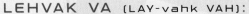
HISTORY

As is the case with the rest of his Toa team, nothing is known about Lewa's history prior to his first appearance on the island of MATA NUI (2). He was one of six Toa who had been floating in the ocean around that land for 1000 years. They were inside unique canisters and each was partially disassembled. A signal unwittingly sent by TAKUA called the canisters to shore. Lewa emerged on the shores of LE-WAHI and had to endure RAHI attacks before making it to the village of Le-Koro.

Lewa rapidly made contact with the other five Toa — ONUA, POHATU, GALI, LEWA, and KOPAKA. Together and separately, they searched for KANOHI masks and battled the Rahi servants of MAKUTA. He began a friendly rivalry with Gali, which grew out of Lewa's intense

LEWA

dislike of water. He briefly merged with Gali and Kopaka to form TOA KAITA WAIRUHA and fight the MANAS.

From the start, Lewa's impetuous nature got him into trouble. Onua had to save him twice, once when he was in thrall to an INFECTED MASK and once when his mind was stolen by a KRANA. The latter experience made Lewa a bit more serious, as well as straining his relationship with Tahu, who feared Lewa might still be influenced by the Bohrok.

Following the defeat of the twin Bohrok queens, the BAHRAG, the six Toa were transformed by ENERGIZED PROTODERMIS into TOA NUVA. When Kopaka and Tahu decided to break up the team, Lewa went along with them. Later, after the BOHROK-KAL had stolen the Toa Nuva's powers, Lewa teamed with Tahu to search for KANOHI NUVA masks.

Lewa encountered TAKUA and JALLER during their search for TAKANUVA, saving them both from an ASH BEAR. He led them both to KO-WAHI, where village drums informed him that TA-KORO had fallen to the RAHKSHI. He left the two MATORAN there while he went to join the other Toa Nuva.

Later, Lewa teamed with Tahu Nuva to imprison LERAHK, PANRAHK, and GUURAHK in a prison of glass.

Lewa Nuva and the other Toa Nuva are now journeying back to Metru Nui with the TURAGA and Matoran.

POWERS

Lewa was the master of air. He could create everything from a light breeze to a cyclone in a matter of seconds. He was extremely agile and nimble, moving through the treetops like a Rahi. He was also a highly skilled flyer.

PERSONALITY

LEWA NUVA

Lewa rarely took life seriously. To him, being a Toa was an adventure.

Although all six Toa were the same age, to an outsider Lewa might have seemed like the youngest of the group due to his boundless energy and sense of fun. Some of that enthusiasm was dampened after he was taken over by a krana, as if he suddenly realized that being a hero was not a game.

EQUIPMENT

Lewa carried an axe as a Toa, and twin AIR KATANA as a Toa Nuva. He is the only Toa to have worn both an infected mask and a krana at different points in the past. Lewa most often wore the Kanohi MIRU or MIRU NUVA, the Great Mask of Levitation.

LHII (LEE-hee):

A mythical MATORAN created by TURAGA VAKAMA to keep the memory of TOA LHIKAN alive without revealing the secrets of METRU NUI to the Matoran. Following the Matoran loss of memory on MATA NUI (2), the Turaga realized that they could not share the truth about the past without jeopardizing the safety of the villagers (see MATORAN). However, that also meant that all the old legends, particularly those of Toa Lhikan, would be lost forever. Turaga Vakama hit upon the plan of sharing some of Lhikan's exploits without revealing he was a Toa. He and Turaga NUJU crafted stories of Lhii, said to be the greatest Matoran lava surfer of all. His absence was blamed on his death in a surfing accident. Vakama even went so far as to tell JALLER he was part of the "clan of Lhii," a reference to the fact that Jaller unknowingly wore Turaga Lhikan's Noble Mask of Shielding. With the revelations about Metru Nui, the Matoran now know that Lhii never existed on Mata Nui.

LHIKAN [LEE-kan]:
TOA of Fire, protector of METRU NUI, and later a TURAGA.

LHIKAN

HISTORY

Lhikan first came to Metru Nui centuries ago along with ten other Toa in response to a call for help from Turaga DUME. The Toa encountered and defeated a KANOHI DRAGON. Afterward, Lhikan, Toa NIDHIKI, and a handful of the other heroes elected to remain in the city as its protectors.

Lhikan led the Toa to victory in the conflict with the DARK HUNTERS over the latter group's plan to establish a base in the city. During this struggle, Lhikan discovered that Nidhiki planned to betray the city. Nidhiki left with the defeated Dark Hunters and did not return for hundreds of years.

Over time, some of the Toa left the city for other islands and more adventure. More recently, Turaga Dume ordered a number of the Toa to close off all the seaways that led from Metru Nui to other lands. No explanation was given for this strange order. Lhikan remained behind in the city while his companions left to carry out their missions. None of them ever returned. Lhikan began to grow suspicious but did not know that Dume was truly MAKUTA in disguise. Still, he felt it wise to make plans in case the worst should happen. He stole the TOA STONES from the GREAT TEMPLE and infused each of them with a portion of his power. Then he gave the stones, along with maps to the Great Temple, to six Matoran: MATAU, NOKAMA, NUJU, ONEWA, VAKAMA, and WHENUA. Lhikan could not know that Makuta had expected him to attempt to create other Toa. Believing it better for his plans if the new TOA METRU were a contentious and quarrelsome lot, Makuta planted the names of six Matoran into Lhikan's mind. He believed that Vakama and the others would never be able to get along well enough to work as a team, and therefore would be no threat to him.

When Lhikan brought the Toa stone to Vakama, he was followed by the Dark Hunters Nidhiki and KREKKA. They captured Lhikan, but not before he was able to help Vakama escape. Lhikan was carried way and placed in the PRISON OF THE DARK HUNTERS.

When the six Matoran used the Toa stones to turn themselves into Toa Metru, Lhikan had met the conditions to become a Turaga: he had fulfilled his destiny (creating new heroes) and he had willingly sacrificed his Toa power. He thus turned into Turaga Lhikan.

TURAGA LHIKAN

Lhikan remained in his cell as a Turaga and so was present when Whenua, Onewa, and Nuju were thrown inside. He used the time to teach the three of them new ways of thinking and approaching problems. This helped all three to discover how to use their KANOHI mask powers.

Later, when Vakama discovered a MATORAN SPHERE containing the sleeping form of the real Dume, Lhikan's suspicions were confirmed. The Dume who had ordered the Toa out of the city and branded the Toa Metru as criminals was an impostor. At the COLISEUM, the false Dume revealed himself to be Makuta. Lhikan was furious, reminding Makuta that he had sworn at one time to protect the Matoran.

During Vakama's confrontation with Makuta at the GREAT BARRIER, Lhikan saw that Vakama was unable to properly control the VAHI, the Mask of Time. He was in mortal danger. At the last possible moment, Lhikan leapt in the path of Makuta's attack, his body wracked by dark energies powerful enough to harm a Toa. They were too much for his weakened Turaga form, and Lhikan died. Vakama took his Mask of Power as a reminder of his heroic sacrifice, and later gave the mask to JALLER. Years later, realizing the Matoran had lost all memories of Metru Nui, Vakama began telling them stories of LHII, a mythical Matoran whose exploits were based on those of Lhikan. This was Vakama's way of ensuring that his hero would never be completely forgotten.

POWERS

As Toa of Fire, Lhikan controlled heat and flame. He could hurl fireballs, melt virtually any substance, create thermal updrafts to slow falling objects, and had all the abilities of later Toa of Fire such as Vakama and TAHU.

PERSONALITY

Lhikan saw himself as very much a "big brother" figure to the Matoran. Although he was not native to Metru Nui, he was deeply loyal to his adopted city and its population. When his services were not needed to deal with an emergency, he could often be found spending time with Matoran from various METRU, listening to their probems and offering advice. After Dume became a recluse (due to the fact that it was not truly Dume but Makuta in disguise), Lhikan began resolving disputes and helping to make day-to-day decisions in the city.

EQUIPMENT

Lhikan carried two FIRE GREATSWORDS, which could be fitted together to form a shield as well as a flying board. He wore the Kanohi HAU, the Great Mask of Shielding. As a Turaga, he wore the Noble Hau.

LHIKAN [LEE-kan]:
Name given to the VAHKI TRANSPORT used by the TOA METRU to sail from METRU NUI to MATA NUI (2). It consisted of a transport body with six MATORAN SPHERES strapped to the bottom to provide buoyancy.

LHIKAN II [LEE-kan]:

Name given to the VAHKI TRANSPORT used by the TOA METRU to sail back to METRU NUI on their mission to rescue the MATORAN. It consisted of a transport body with pieces of the KARZAHNI (2) used to provide buoyancy.

LIGHTFISH:

Small, glowing fish found in the deepest underwater caves around GA-METRU and GA-KORO. GA-MATORAN on MATA NUI (2) used lightfish to provide illumination in their dwellings.

LIGHTSTONE:

A glowing crystal mined by ONU-MATORAN both in METRU NUI and on MATA NUI (2). These crystals were used to provide illumination. In their raw, unrefined state, lightstones can be so bright as to be almost blinding to unshielded eyes. It was at one time believed that lightstones had a self-contained power source, but this was largely disproved by the fact that so many of them were doused when the Metru Nui power plant was wrecked. The fact that some of the stones continued to work, particularly on Mata Nui, would seem to indicate that there was a second source of energy for them other than the Metru Nui plant. What that source might be has not yet been discovered.

LOHRAK

LOHRAK [LOH-rahk]:

A winged serpent found throughout METRU NUI and some portions of MATA NUI (2). The Lohrak was known for its sharp teeth and scaly hide covered in slime. Commonly found underground, Lohrak attacked in a swarm and were considered a dangerous menace, particularly by ONU-MATORAN miners. For a time, the creatures were even pronounced a protected species by TURAGA DUME, in hopes of stopping digging projects that might unearth more monsters. The TOA METRU fought and defeated a swarm of Lohrak after escaping the PRISON OF THE DARK HUNTERS, and later encountered a specimen mutated to monstrous size by the VISORAK.

M & D:

Visorak shorthand for "mutation and disposal."

MACKU [MAH-koo]:

A GA-MATORAN known for her canoe racing and navigational skills. On METRU NUI, she received special permission to run her own business offering canoe tours of the coastline (see MACKU'S CANOES). On MATA NUI (2), she excelled in the NGALAWA canoe racing tournaments.

Macku helped to save her village from a RAHI attack by sending TAKUA to aid the other Ga-Matoran while she sought out TOA GALI. Later, she served as part of the CHRONICLER's Company and helped defend KINI-NUI against Rahi attack. Macku joined with HAHLI to form Ga-Koro's winning KOLHII team.

MACKU

MACKU'S CANOES (MAH-koo):
Small business run by MACKU in GA-METRU. She offered guided tours of the METRU NUI coastline. Her most frequent customers were ONU-MATORAN searching for aquatic RAHI to add to the ARCHIVES.

MADU (MAH-doo):
A coconut-like fruit found on MATA NUI (2). The fruit's juices were extremely volatile and so the fruit was known to explode. Madu grew on trees.

MADU CABOLO (MAH-doo cah-BOH-loh):
An unripe MADU fruit. Also very volatile, Madu Cabolo would explode if exposed to elemental energy. When they did so, they emitted a foul-smelling gas that could be used to repel KANE-RA bulls.

MAGMA SWORDS:
Twin blades carried by TAHU NUVA. He could both channel his fire power through them and cross them in front of him to block attacks.

MAGNETIC SHIELD:
Tool carried by GAHLOK-KAL. This shield was capable of creating a magnetic force field, which proved itself capable of resisting TAHU NUVA's full power.

MAHIKI (mah-HEE-kee):
KANOHI Mask of Illusion. The Great Mask version of this, worn by TOA MATAU, actually allowed the user to shapeshift. The Noble Mask version, worn by Matau as a TURAGA, simply created illusions to confound enemies. Matau used the Great Mask to impersonate a VAHKI, NIDHIKI, and KREKKA.

MAKIKA (mah-KEE-kah):
A large and dangerous cave toad found in GA-METRU. It has few natural predators since it is poisonous to most other RAHI. MATORAN on MATA NUI (2) discovered that the Makika's acidic venom was useful for tunneling through earth and rock.

MAKOKI STONES (mah-KO-kee):
Six stone fragments used by the RAHAGA as a key to unlock the hiding place of the AVOHKII in the ARCHIVES. Later, they were collected by TAHU's TOA team shortly after their arrival on MATA NUI (2). Fitted together, the stones formed a key that opened a passage from KINI-NUI to MAKUTA's lair.

MAKUTA (mah-KOO-tah):
Master of shadows, spirit of destruction, and sworn enemy of the TOA.

HISTORY

Information on Makuta's past is sketchy at best, much of it having come from either legend or his own statements (the truth of which is open to debate). According to Matoran lore, Makuta was the GREAT SPIRIT MATA NUI's "brother" — however, since it was not a biological relationship, it is unclear just what their bond might have been. What has been verified is that at some point in the distant past, Makuta took an oath to protect the MATORAN. He was so highly regarded that he had an elite team of Toa dedicated to serving and guarding him (see TOA HAGAH).

For reasons that are unclear, Makuta's attitude changed. Both he and the larger BROTHERHOOD OF MAKUTA began oppressing and enslaving Matoran. Legend states that Makuta coveted the devotion the Matoran showed for Mata Nui (1) and wanted it for himself. He set in motion events that would eventually lead to Mata Nui falling into an unending sleep,

MAKUTA

and worked with the ENERGIZED PROTODERMIS ENTITY to create dangerous RAHI mutations. Discovering his treachery, the Toa Hagah turned on him. They succeeded in temporarily defeating Makuta, but only at the cost of being turned into RAHAGA by Makuta's lieutenant, ROODAKA.

Centuries later, Makuta reappeared, this time posing as TURAGA DUME and ruling METRU NUI. Weakened due to his earlier defeat, he was forced to rely on DARK HUNTERS to achieve his ends. He ordered many of the city's Toa to go on dangerous missions, from which they did not return. He also sent NIDHIKI and KREKKA to capture Toa LHIKAN.

His plan was simple and frightening. He would have all the city's Matoran placed into spheres that would render them comatose and erase their memories. Using the KANOHI VAHI, the Mask of Time, he would cause this to happen rapidly — years for the Matoran, but only days for Makuta. Then he would awaken them and be hailed as their rescuer.

At first, all went well. The Matoran were put to sleep. Makuta drained the energy of the city's power plant and absorbed Nidhiki, Krekka, and NIVAWK, regaining his full power. Mata Nui lapsed into unconsciousness. But the TOA METRU intervened, with VAKAMA keeping the Vahi from Makuta. In the ensuing fight, Lhikan, now a Turaga, was killed by Makuta. The six Toa then combined their powers and imprisoned Makuta behind solid protodermis branded with a TOA SEAL.

His body was trapped, but not his mind. He reached out and summoned Roodaka, SIDORAK, and the VISORAK hordes to Metru Nui. While the hordes attacked and captured the city's Rahi, Roodaka worked on a way to free Makuta.

Just how she did so has not yet been revealed, but she obviously succeeded. After the Toa Metru transported the Matoran to the island of MATA NUI (2), Makuta became a constant menace to them. Operating out of one of his numerous lairs, this one called MANGAIA, he used infected Kanohi to take over Rahi and harass the Matoran. In fact, he was not trying to destroy them. He was simply trying to keep them from ever returning to Metru Nui, for he knew if they ever did Mata Nui might reawaken.

The tide began to turn with the arrival of six Toa: GALI, KOPAKA, LEWA, ONUA, POHATU, and TAHU. They opposed Makuta, defeated his Rahi, his MANAS guardians, and the SHADOW TOA he sent against them. Then they triumphed over the master of shadows himself, apparently saving the Matoran.

But Makuta was not defeated, merely weakened. He bought time by unleashing the BOHROK on Mata Nui (2) while he regained his strength. But whatever plans he might have been making were changed by TAKUA's discovery of the Kanohi AVOHKII, the Mask of Light. Knowing the coming of a Toa of Light might mean his doom, Makuta sent his RAHKSHI to try and retrieve the mask. They were defeated by the TOA NUVA. Makuta challenged TAKANUVA, the Toa of Light, and in the resulting combat the two were merged into a combined entity called TAKUTANUVA. With Takanuva's mind dominating the entity, Takutanuva opened the gateway that led to Metru Nui.

In an act of great self-sacrifice, Takutanuva surrendered part of his life force to revive JALLER, who had been killed by a Rahkshi. Thus weakened, he could no longer support the gateway, which came crashing down even as the entity split back into its two halves. Takanuva was revived by the power of light, but of Makuta there was no sign. He is currently missing and presumed dead by the Toa Nuva.

POWERS

One of the most powerful entities in the BIONICLE universe, Makuta wielded the energies of darkness. He was an incredibly skilled shapeshifter and mimic, had strong telepathic powers, could summon a mighty vortex, and possessed all of the powers of the various Rahkshi. He also had the ability to create KRAATA from his own substance.

In his large, armored forms, he had physical strength exceeding that of a Toa. When weakened, he tended to rely more on surrogates to fight his battles. His knowledge of the universe exceeded that of both the Toa and Turaga, allowing him to use things like the Bohrok against them.

In the past, Makuta had used his powers to create Shadow Toa from the darkness inside the Toa; trigger sandstorms, tidal waves, and volcanic eruptions; transform his body into a vortex; and appear as everything from a Matoran to an armored, winged giant. He was defeated at least three times, but never for long.

PERSONALITY

Makuta was ruthless, deceitful, and capable of almost any act in the furtherance of his cause. At the same time, if asked, he would insist that everything he was doing was for the good of Mata Nui (2) and the Matoran. He saw Toa as annoyances who were commiting a crime against the universe by defying his will. His strengths were his cunning, his imagination, his ability to rebound from defeat, his vast knowledge, and his sheer willpower. His weaknesses were overconfidence, pride, and a tendency to underestimate his opponents.

EQUIPMENT

Makuta wore the Kanohi KRAAHKAN, the Great Mask of Shadows, and carried the STAFF OF DARKNESS, which channeled his power.

MAKUTA FISH (mah-KOO-tah):

An incredibly ugly breed of fish capable of leaping from the water to attack larger creatures. It got its name during a battle with TOA METRU MATAU in an underground cavern. Matau noted that the faces of the grotesque fish reminded him of Makuta, and the name stuck. TOA NOKAMA would later fashion a trident out of Makuta fish bones which she would carry with her as a TURAGA.

MANAS (MAH-nuhz):

Huge, powerful crablike creatures who served as the guardians of MAKUTA's lair during the time the MATORAN were on MATA NUI (2). The word "manas" is Matoran for "monster," and it was said that no single TOA could ever hope to defeat one of these creatures. They were first spotted by the TOA METRU while sailing from METRU NUI to Mata Nui, but did not play a large role in the battle that followed. Later, the team of TAHU, KOPAKA, LEWA, GALI, ONUA, and POHATU would be forced to form two much more powerful entities — the TOA KAITA, AKAMAI, and WAIRUHA — to defeat the Manas. Onua and Turaga WHENUA later defeated the Manas again in a subterranean cavern by unleashing a swarm of KOFO-JAGA upon them.

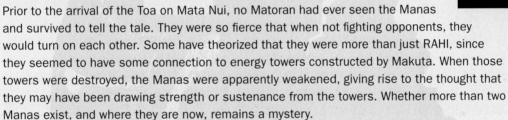

MANAS

Prior to the arrival of the Toa on Mata Nui, no Matoran had ever seen the Manas and survived to tell the tale. They were so fierce that when not fighting opponents, they would turn on each other. Some have theorized that they were more than just RAHI, since they seemed to have some connection to energy towers constructed by Makuta. When those towers were destroyed, the Manas were apparently weakened, giving rise to the thought that they may have been drawing strength or sustenance from the towers. Whether more than two Manas exist, and where they are now, remains a mystery.

MANGAI (MAHN-gigh):

The great volcano of MATA NUI (2). Molten lava still streams from this site, feeding the lava farms of TA-WAHI. A potentially destructive eruption of the Mangai triggered by MAKUTA was countered by ONUA and LEWA, who used a combination of speed and strength to dig a trench for the lava to flow into.

MANGAIA (MAHN-gigh-uh):

One of a number of lairs of MAKUTA. Mangaia was located beneath KINI-NUI. It was here that the TOA fought the MANAS, the SHADOW TOA, and Makuta himself. Later, Makuta created the RAHKSHI here and sent them forth to battle the Toa Nuva. TAKANUVA used the USSANUI to travel to Mangaia and confront Makuta.

One of the major features of Mangaia was a huge stone gateway so heavy no Toa or group of Toa could lift it. Only TAKUTANUVA, the merged being formed from Makuta and Takanuva, could open this door. The gateway later crashed down upon Takutanuva, with only Takanuva known to have survived. The door led to the shores of a protodermis sea, beyond which was the city of METRU NUI.

A pool of ENERGIZED PROTODERMIS existed in Mangaia, used by Makuta to create Rahkshi from KRAATA. This same pool was responsible for the creation of TAKUTANUVA.

MATA NUI (MAH-tah NOO-ee):

[1] The GREAT SPIRIT revered by the MATORAN. Both the GREAT TEMPLE in METRU NUI and KINI-NUI on the island of MATA NUI (2) were dedicated to him, and of course the island of Mata

Nui was named in his honor. According to Matoran legend, Mata Nui was sent from paradise by the GREAT BEINGS to care for all living things. After many thousands of years of his benevolent guidance, Mata Nui was struck down by his spirit brother MAKUTA. This resulted in Mata Nui sinking into an endless sleep and heralded a time of darkness for the Matoran.

Upon Mata Nui's fall, a team of six TOA including TAHU, GALI, LEWA, ONUA, POHATU, and KOPAKA was dispatched to awaken him. While they have made progress, they have not yet been successful in reversing the effects of Makuta's actions.

[2] Island in an unnamed sea, and home to the Matoran. The island was named after the Great Spirit Mata Nui (1) by Turaga VAKAMA. It consists of six regions: GA-WAHI, LE-WAHI, KO-WAHI, PO-WAHI, ONU-WAHI, and TA-WAHI. Each region has distinct geographic features and the climates are vastly different from one place to the other.

The TOA METRU brought the Matoran here when Metru Nui became unsafe for them. The Matoran constructed six KORO here, as well as Kini-Nui and other landmarks. RAHI also traveled from Metru Nui to this island. Initially, the Matoran were able to travel freely from place to place on the island. But Makuta used infected masks to take over Rahi and set them against the Matoran, making overland travel highly dangerous. TAHU and his team of Toa washed up on the shores of Mata Nui after spending 1000 years floating in the ocean in canisters. They defended the island from attacks by Rahi, BOHROK, BOHROK-KAL, and RAHKSHI. The Bohrok, in particular, did severe damage to the villages and the natural terrain of Mata Nui.

MATA NUI

After the rediscovery of Metru Nui, the Matoran began building boats to transport them back to that city, which had been their original home. Whether the Matoran will ever have reason to return to Mata Nui again remains to be seen.

MATA NUI FISHING BIRD (MAH-tah NOO-ee):
Clever and noisy birds often spotted splashing along the LE-METRU coastline, and later in LE-WAHI. Too fast for most aquatic predators, these birds seem to delight in teasing their enemies by flying close, then soaring away at the last moment.

MATATU (MAH-tah-too):
KANOHI Mask of Telekinesis. TOA NUJU wore the Great Mask version of this, using its power to free himself, ONEWA, WHENUA, and LHIKAN from the PRISON OF THE DARK HUNTERS. As a TURAGA, he wore the Noble Matatu, once using it to save a powerless KOPAKA NUVA from plunging into a crevasse.

MATAU (mah-TOW):
TOA METRU of Air, guardian of LE-METRU, and later TURAGA of LE-KORO.

HISTORY

Matau was in the middle of doing one of his favorite things — testing a new vehicle on the Le-Metru TEST TRACK — when TOA LHIKAN gave him a TOA STONE and a map to the GREAT

MATAU

TEMPLE. Intrigued, Matau traveled there and encountered five other MATORAN — NUJU, ONEWA, WHENUA, NOKAMA, and VAKAMA. They placed their Toa stones into the TOA SUVA and were transformed into mighty Toa heroes. Matau was thrilled, believing that being a "Toa hero" was the key to lasting fame. He teamed with Nokama to find two GREAT DISKS in GA-METRU and Le-Metru, and was part of the successful effort to use the disks to destroy the MORBUZAKH plant. When the Toa went to the COLISEUM to present the disks to Turaga DUME, Matau was convinced they would be hailed as heroes. Instead, they were branded impostors by Dume, who ordered them arrested. (The Toa

Metru did not realize at this point that Dume was MAKUTA in disguise.)

Whenua, Onewa, and Nuju were captured, with Vakama, Nokama, and Matau escaping. They survived a battle with Vahki and the DARK HUNTERS on an AIRSHIP, then stowed away on a VAHKI TRANSPORT into PO-METRU. There they fought the Dark Hunters again, formed an alliance with the KIKANALO, and helped to free their three friends and Lhikan, now a Turaga. During the battle, Matau discovered his mask power of shapeshifting and used it to confuse NIDHIKI and KREKKA.

Matau participated in the defeat of Makuta, the rescue of six Matoran spheres, and the trip to MATA NUI (2). He acted as pilot for both the *LHIKAN* and the *LHIKAN II*. His initial experience on LE-WAHI was not a positive one, as he promptly got lost in the FAU SWAMP.

On the return journey to Metru Nui, Matau grew increasingly annoyed with Vakama's harsh attitude. His mood was not improved any when the *Lhikan II* was shipwrecked and Nuju blamed "pilot error." Matau blamed Vakama for leading the Toa Metru into the trap that resulted in their being mutated into TOA HORDIKA. Of all the Toa, he had the hardest time adjusting to his new appearance and was torn between rescuing the Matoran and searching for KEETONGU, who might hold the key to a cure.

TURAGA MATAU

How the Toa Hordika transformed back into Toa Metru and escaped to Mata Nui (2) with the rest of the Matoran has not yet been revealed. But they did make it to that island with close to 1,000 sleeping villagers. The Toa Metru willingly sacrificed their power to awaken the Matoran, transforming into Turaga in the process.

As a Turaga, Matau supervised the construction of LE-KORO, as well as its reconstruction after the BOHROK invasion. Along with the Toa LEWA and the LE-MATORAN, he was fitted with a KRANA and controlled the Bohrok swarm for a short time.

He is now journeying with the TOA NUVA, the other Turaga, and the Matoran back to Metru Nui.

TURAGA MATAU

Matau was the master of air. He could summon a windstorm or cyclone, raise the air pressure in a chamber until the walls burst, or absorb all the air in a room into his body before releasing it in a massive blast. He was also a skilled flyer with the aid of his Toa tools.

PERSONALITY

Matau loved being a Toa Metru. To him, it was all excitement and fun and the chance to be remembered forever for heroic deeds. Even in the darkest moments, he never fully lost his sense of humor or his taste for adventure. Only when he was transformed into a Toa Hordika did Matau succumb to bitterness. But even then, he remained fiercely loyal to Nokama and the other Toa. Only his relationship with Vakama suffered during this period.

As a Turaga, Matau could be calm and wise one moment, and pull a practical joke the next. His motto was "talk ever-quick, and move ever-quicker." Although he could be a prankster, he was also seen as a brave leader who would never ask a Matoran to do something he would not do himself. As a result, the Le-Matoran were fiercely loyal to him.

EQUIPMENT

As a Toa Metru, Matau carried twin aero slicers that doubled as wings. He wore the Kanohi MAHIKI, the Great Mask of Illusion. As a Turaga, he carried a KAU KAU STAFF and wore the Noble Mahiki.

MATORAN (mat-OAR-an):

[1] Villagers on both METRU NUI and MATA NUI. There are six known types of Matoran: GA-MATORAN, KO-MATORAN, LE-MATORAN, ONU-MATORAN, PO-MATORAN, and TA-MATORAN, identified by the color of their armor and KANOHI. Whether other Matoran exist elsewhere remains to be seen. Matoran are the only beings so far shown to be able to evolve into TOA. Groups of six Matoran, one from each village, are capable of merging into the MATORAN NUI. The Matoran so far seen lived on Metru Nui until they were captured by MAKUTA and forced into MATORAN SPHERES. There they were thrown into a form of suspended animation. This lasted until they were brought to MATA NUI (2) and awakened by the TOA METRU. Over time, the Matoran's bodies shrank in stature and they lost all memory of their lives on Metru Nui, aftereffects of their time in the spheres.

They built six villages, or KORO, on Mata Nui and lived there for 1000 years, much of it spent fighting off RAHI sent by Makuta. The Matoran universally welcomed the coming of TAHU and his team of Toa, believing they would reawaken MATA NUI (1) and defeat Makuta.

Following the defeat of the BOHROK-KAL, the TURAGA taught the Matoran how to rebuild themselves so that they could be stronger and more agile. It is believed the Turaga may have learned this secret from the RAHAGA at some point in the past.

The Matoran are now traveling with the Toa and the Turaga back to Metru Nui to bring that city back to life.

Known Matoran have included AHKMOU, EHRYE, HAFU, HAHLI, HEWKII, JALLER, KAPURA, KONGU, KOPEKE, MACKU, MATORO, MAVRAH, NUHRII, NUPARU, ONEPU, ORKAHM, TAIPU, TAKUA, TAMARU, TEHUTTI, and VHISOLA. See individual entries.

THE MATORAN ALPHABET

◯ = A	◯ = N
◯ = B	◯ = O
◯ = C	◯ = P
◯ = D	◯ = Q
◯ = E	◯ = R
◯ = F	◯ = S
◯ = G	◯ = T
◯ = H	◯ = U
◯ = I	◯ = V
◯ = J	◯ = W
◯ = K	◯ = X
◯ = L	◯ = Y
◯ = M	◯ = Z

[2] The official language of the residents of Metru Nui and Mata Nui (2). Matoran was spoken by all villagers, Toa, and Turaga, as well as by Makuta, the DARK HUNTERS, and the KRANA-KAL. KRAHKA learned to speak Matoran through her mimicry of the Toa Metru. OOHNORAK were able to speak some Matoran, thanks to their telepathic abilities and skill at imitation, a trick they used to lure TOA HORDIKA into traps.

MATORAN NUI (mat-OAR-an NOO-ee):

A being formed by the merging of six MATORAN. The Matoran Nui has been created at least twice, once on METRU NUI by AHKMOU, EHRYE, NUHRII, ORKAHM, TEHUTTI, and VHISOLA, and once on MATA NUI by HEWKII, JALLER, KONGU, MACKU, MATORO, and ONEPU.

MATORAN SPHERE (mat-OAR-an):

Rounded silver containers in which MAKUTA imprisoned the MATORAN of METRU NUI. These spheres caused the Matoran to go into suspended animation. They were later rescued and reawakened by the TOA METRU.

MATORO (mat-OR-oh):

KO-MATORAN translator for TURAGA NUJU. During his time on METRU NUI, he spent many days and nights in the ARCHIVES studying the language and behavior of RAHI. He later opened a small trading post offering small Rahi to other MATORAN for use as pets.
Once on MATA NUI (2), Matoro swiftly built a reputation as an efficient tracker and hunter of Rahi. He gave that up when he was tapped to lead KO-KORO's KOLHII team. But easily his most important role on the island has been aide to Turaga Nuju. Only Matoro fully understands Nuju's strange language of clicks and whistles. It is his job to translate for the Turaga, even at the councils of the village leaders. This has put him in the uncomfortable position of having knowledge he cannot share with the other Matoran, or having to translate some of Nuju's ruder comments to Turaga and TOA alike.
Matoro was the first to encounter Toa KOPAKA after that hero arrived on Mata Nui. Kopaka later saved Matoro from a NUI-RAMA attack. Later, Matoro rescued TAKUA when the CHRONICLER was lost in the snowdrifts of KO-WAHI.

MATORO

MATORO'S RAHI (mat-OR-oh rah-HEE):

Small business run by MATORO in METRU NUI, selling little RAHI for use as pets.

MAVRAH (MAHV-rah):

An ONU-MATORAN archivist in METRU NUI. Along with WHENUA, Mavrah was part of a secret project to study ancient aquatic RAHI who had appeared in the ocean around the city. When it became obvious that keeping the beasts confined was a threat to the ARCHIVES and the rest of Metru Nui, TURAGA DUME ordered that the project be shut down and the Rahi driven back out to sea by the VAHKI. Unwilling to give up his work, Mavrah led the creatures out of the Archives himself and through a tunnel in the GREAT BARRIER. There he took up residence in a cavern while his Rahi lived in an underground river. He also allied with a small number of KRALHI, mechanical order enforcers who had been driven from the city long ago.

Many years later, the TOA METRU traveled that same river as they attempted to find a new land in which the MATORAN could live. Believing them to be agents of Dume sent to take him back, Mavrah unleashed his Rahi on them and attempted to kill the TOA. In the middle of a three-way battle between Toa, Rahi, and Vahki, Toa ONEWA forced Mavrah to see the destruction his methods were causing. Guilt-ridden and dismayed, Mavrah rushed to the water's edge, calling for the fighting to cease. But the battle had turned the river waters violent, and Mavrah was washed away by a sudden wave. He is presumed to be dead.

METRU (mET-troo):

Districts in the city of METRU NUI. There are six metru: GA-METRU, KO-METRU, LE-METRU, ONU-METRU, PO-METRU, and TA-METRU. See individual entries.

METRU MANTIS (mET-troo):

Nocturnal, meat-eating insectlike creatures found on both METRU NUI and MATA NUI (2). Their favorite prey was NUI-RAMA, NUI-JAGA, and other insectoids. They averaged six to eight feet in height and tended to be tame unless provoked. After the arrival of the VISORAK, Metru Mantis began feasting on them as well, and the RAHAGA considered them a potent strike force against the invaders. Metru Mantis hunted by grabbing their prey with their forelegs and then injecting a sedating venom through their bite.

METRU NUI (mET-troo NOO-ee):

Island city that floated on a PROTODERMIS sea far beneath the surface of MATA NUI (2). Metru Nui was the original home of the MATORAN who later settled on Mata Nui. It was divided into six districts, or metru: GA-METRU, KO-METRU, LE-METRU, ONU-METRU, PO-METRU, and TA-METRU. It was also known as the CITY OF LEGENDS.

During much of its existence, Metru Nui was ruled by TURAGA DUME, protected by TOA LHIKAN and other Toa, and guarded by the VAHKI. Metru Nui was once the site of a major conflict between the Toa and the DARK HUNTERS.

When MAKUTA impersonated Dume, he sent all the Toa but Lhikan out of the city and invited the Dark Hunters in to capture the remaining hero. He also unleashed the MORBUZAKH plant, which wrecked many outlying areas. Before he was through, the city power plant had been destroyed, most of the Vahki blown to pieces by a power surge, Lhikan killed, and the Matoran placed in MATORAN SPHERES that kept them comatose. The city was wracked by a major earthquake that damaged buildings throughout the metru. Only the actions of the six TOA METRU stopped Makuta before things got worse.

After the Toa Metru departed the city to search for a new home for the Matoran, the VISORAK horde moved in and shrouded the city in webs. The Toa Metru, transformed into TOA HORDIKA, had to challenge the Visorak for control of the city.

After the Matoran reached Mata Nui (2), they eventually lost all memory of Metru Nui due to the aftereffects of being in the spheres. The city was not rediscovered until TAKANUVA, the Toa of Light, defeated Makuta. The Matoran are now journeying back to the

METRU NUI

city, for legend states that only by bringing Metru Nui back to life can the GREAT SPIRIT be reawakened and peace returned to the universe.

MIO (MY-oh):

A unit of MATORAN measurement. A mio is equal to 1,000 kio, or 850 miles/1,370 kilometers.

MIRU (MEAR-roo):

The Mask of Levitation. Although often mistaken for a mask of flight, what this KANOHI actually did was to prevent a flying wearer from falling to earth. While wearing a Miru, a user could ride on air currents and rely on the mask's power to repel the ground and keep him aloft. By controlling the mask, the being could then descend slowly. The Miru did not allow flight from a standing start. This mask was worn by TOA LEWA when he first appeared on MATA NUI (2).

MIRU NUVA (MEAR-roo NOO-vah):

The more powerful version of the Mask of Levitation, this mask actually did allow a semblance of flight. With a proper head start, a user could rise into the air and remain aloft without having to rely on updrafts.

MORBUZAKH (MORE-boo-ZACK):

MORBUZAKH

An intelligent plant creature created by MAKUTA as part of his plan to capture the MATORAN of METRU NUI. The Morbuzakh was actually Makuta's second attempt at such a creation, the first being the KARZAHNI (2). When the Karzahni proved to be too ambitious and willful, Makuta banished it and made the Morbuzakh.

The purpose of this creature was to drive the Matoran away from the outskirts of the city and toward the COLISEUM, making it easier for them to be rounded up by the VAHKI. The Morbuzakh also captured a number of Matoran for Makuta. Its primary tools were its vines, which were so long they could reach anywhere in the city. The massive king root of the Morbuzakh was hidden inside the GREAT FURNACE in TA-METRU. The Morbuzakh thrived on heat and flame. It was able to spread via seeds, which clung to the ceilings of furnaces and foundries throughout the METRU. When these seeds struck a solid object, they sprouted and the vines immediately wrapped themselves around whatever was nearest. The TOA METRU were almost smothered by these baby vines.

Using the power of the GREAT DISKS, the Toa Metru were able to defeat the Morbuzakh even as it brought the Great Furnace down around itself. The king root and all its vines crumbled to dust. No further sign of it has ever been seen.

While it lived, the Morbuzakh was able to communicate by telepathy with other species and to gather information about the world outside through its vines. Shortly before its death, it claimed that its ultimate purpose was to conquer the city and enslave the Matoran. It is doubtful Makuta would have reacted well to this change of plan.

MOTO-HUB:

Site of the vehicle manufacturing factories and CHUTE system controls in METRU NUI. The Moto-Hub was the

MOTO-HUB

center of LE-METRU and the place of employment for roughly half of the LE-MATORAN. Chutes, air vehicles, and ground vehicles were all produced there, with the latter often being tried out on the TEST TRACK. KONGU worked here as a chute controller and MATAU spent much of his spare time here when he was a MATORAN.

The Moto-Hub was badly damaged in an earthquake prior to the VISORAK invasion. The TOA METRU hid here to avoid a VAHKI squad and later defeated a mutant LOHRAK who was on the loose in the structure.

MOUNT IHU [EEE-hoo]:

A high, snow- and ice-capped mountain in the center of MATA NUI (2). It was named by NUJU for IHU, his late Matoran mentor. KOPAKA found his first KANOHI mask, the HAU, on Mount Ihu, and later spied the other TOA gathering from there using his AKAKU. It would eventually become a place where Kopaka would go to be alone and think.

MUAKA [moo-AH-kah]:

A powerful tigerlike beast that plagued both METRU NUI and MATA NUI (2). Solitary hunters, Muaka were extremely quick for their size and more than strong enough to bring down most other RAHI. Muaka were particularly fond of RAHKSHI and were the only natural enemy of those creatures on Metru Nui. Perhaps because of that, MAKUTA made extensive use of Muaka when he set out to use Rahi against the MATORAN on Mata Nui. TOA KOPAKA and Toa LEWA challenged a number of Muaka shortly after arriving on the island, eventually defeating them and removing the INFECTED MASKS Makuta used to control them. KOPAKA NUVA and POHATU NUVA were menaced by a Muaka on MOUNT IHU after losing their elemental powers. TOA METRU WHENUA set a Muaka against a Rahkshi in an effort to save TEHUTTI. The Muaka relied primarily on its claws in a hunt. Sinking them into its prey, it forced the unfortunate victim to the ground and then finished the job with its teeth.

MUAKA

NAHO BAY:

A large body of water in GA-WAHI on MATA NUI (2), and site of the village of GA-KORO. Unknown to the MATORAN, Naho Bay covers one of the two openings in the surface of the island that once served as "suns" for METRU NUI. Also known as Lake Naho and Gali's Bay.

NAMING DAY:

Matoran holiday in which those villagers who have performed some great service for their KORO are rewarded with name changes. Past recipients of this honor include JALLER, HEWKII, and MACKU, among others. The exchange of gifts was also a part of Naming Day ceremonies, although that practice was more prevalent on METRU NUI than MATA NUI (2).

NGALAWA [NIH-gah-LAH-wah]:

A boat-racing competition popular in GA-KORO. Winners of Ngalawa tournaments received a COPPER MASK OF VICTORY.

NIDHIKI

NIDHIKI (nih-DEE-kee):

Former TOA of Air, betrayer of METRU NUI, and vicious DARK HUNTER. Nidhiki was one of ten Toa summoned by LHIKAN to help defend Metru Nui against the KANOHI DRAGON. He remained in the city for many years afterward, helping to defend it against RAHI and occasionally venturing to other islands. But over time, he began to feel dissatisfied with his role. TURAGA DUME and the MATORAN were not, after all, as powerful as he and the other Toa — so why should the Toa serve their interests? Powerful beings should serve only themselves, and lesser beings should obey them, he decided.

When the Dark Hunters attempted to create a base in the city, Dume opposed them and the Toa mobilized to defend Metru Nui. Nidhiki secretly made contact with the enemy and offered to betray the city into their hands. Before he could so, Lhikan discovered his treachery. The Dark Hunters were defeated and Nidhiki went with them when they departed.

How Nidhiki changed from a Toa into a monstrous being capable of functioning without a Kanohi mask is unknown. Some believe he was the subject of an experiment by the BROTHERHOOD OF MAKUTA, others that he said the wrong thing at some point to ROODAKA and she punished him with a mutation spinner. Regardless, Nidhiki found that he was not fully trusted by the Dark Hunters (since no one trusts a traitor). As a result, he was teamed with KREKKA, a strong, dumb brute who was nevertheless scrupulously honest and devoted to carrying out orders. Krekka would make sure Nidhiki did not turn their missions into occasions for personal profit. Nidhiki was also told that he would be held responsible if any harm came to Krekka. He went along with this because he felt certain he could get around Krekka at some point if he had to, and because he hoped to use his place in the Dark Hunters to someday take over the entire organization.

After many adventures together, Nidhiki and Krekka were sent to Metru Nui to aid MAKUTA in his plans to capture the Matoran. They began by capturing Toa Lhikan, an act Nidhiki found particularly satisfying. Then they intimidated AHKMOU into helping them get the six GREAT DISKS. When that plan was frustrated by the TOA METRU, they attempted to hunt down the new heroes. They battled the Toa in an AIRSHIP, in PO-METRU, and outside of the COLISEUM, without success.

Finally, Makuta used his powers to absorb Nidhiki, Krekka, and NIVAWK into his own body, enhancing his power. Nidhiki is presumed dead.

In addition to his natural cunning, Nidhiki was capable of flight and of spitting force bolts at opponents.

NIGHT CREEPER:

A nocturnal creature found in ONU-METRU. Roughly seven feet long, squat, with powerful legs, night creepers forage for small insects and rodents. RAHAGA BOMONGA once saved a night creeper from a VISORAK in Onu-Metru.

NIVAWK (NEE-vawk):

Given name of a RAHI hawk that served as a pet and spy for MAKUTA during the time he was posing as TURAGA DUME in METRU NUI. Though strong enough to transport its owner, it was used primarily to keep watch on the activities of TOA LHIKAN and later the TOA METRU. It would then report back to Makuta/Dume, who was capable of understanding its language. Makuta used a shadow claw to absorb Nivawk into his substance, later reappearing with Nivawk's wings as part of his new body. Nivawk is presumed dead.

NIVAWK

NOBLE MASKS:
See KANOHI.

NOKAMA [noh-KAH-mah]:
TOA METRU of Water, guardian of GA-METRU, and later TURAGA of GA-KORO.

HISTORY

Nokama was in the middle of a lecture on the translation of ancient texts when TOA LHIKAN gave her a TOA STONE and a map leading to the GREAT TEMPLE. She traveled there and encountered five other MATORAN — MATAU, NUJU, ONEWA, VAKAMA, and WHENUA. They placed their Toa stones into the TOA SUVA and were transformed into mighty Toa heroes. Vakama had a vision that the city was in peril and that only finding the six GREAT DISKS would save it, but not all of the Toa Metru took him seriously. It was Nokama who insisted that as long as the chance existed that his visions might be a message from the GREAT SPIRIT, the Toa were obligated to act upon them.

Nokama teamed with Matau to retrieve the Ga-Metru and LE-METRU Great Disks. The Toa Metru used these disks to destroy the MORBUZAKH plant that threatened the city. But when they went to present the disks to Turaga Dume, he denounced them as impostors and ordered their arrest.

Whenua, Onewa, and Nuju were captured, with Vakama, Nokama, and Matau escaping. They survived a battle with VAHKI and the DARK HUNTERS on an AIRSHIP, then stowed away on a VAHKI TRANSPORT into PO-METRU. There they fought the Dark Hunters again. Shortly after this battle, Nokama discovered how to trigger her mask power of translation and was able to communicate with the KIKANALO. With her help, the Toa were able to form an alliance with those RAHI and rescue the other three Toa and Lhikan (who was now a Turaga).

Nokama helped to rescue six of the Matoran, still trapped in their MATORAN SPHERES, and aided in the defeat of Makuta. During the initial voyage to MATA NUI (2), she carved a trident from the bones of a MAKUTA FISH (which would later be her symbol of office as a Turaga). She also carved an image of the six Toa Metru into the side of a tunnel.

NOKAMA

On the journey back to Metru Nui, Nokama was seriously wounded in a fight with the RAHI NUI. The Toa were forced to make a deal with KARZAHNI (2) in order to get the herbs necessary to save her life.

Along with the other Toa Metru, Nokama was transformed into a TOA HORDIKA by the VISORAK upon returning to Metru Nui. But unlike her friends, Nokama seemed to revel in the new connection she felt with nature and sea creatures as a Hordika. This, combined with her frequent rages, worried RAHAGA GAAKI, who feared that Nokama might come to like being a Hordika too much and never want to turn back.

TURAGA NOKAMA

How the Toa Hordika transformed back into Toa Metru and escaped to Mata Nui (2) with the rest of the Matoran has not yet been revealed. But they did make it to that island with close to 1,000 sleeping villagers. The Toa Metru willingly sacrificed their power to awaken the Matoran, transforming into Turaga in the process.

As a Turaga, Nokama supervised the construction of Ga-Koro. When GALI arrived, Nokama stuck to the agreement made by the Turaga not to share any information about Metru Nui and the events there. But of all the Turaga, she was the least comfortable with the arrangement. She went so far as to lead Gali to the tunnel where her carving of the Toa Metru could be seen, though she denied having any connection with the figures in the picture.

She is now journeying with the TOA NUVA, the other Turaga, and the Matoran back to Metru Nui.

TURAGA NOKAMA

POWERS

Nokama controlled the power of water. She could hurl jets of water at a foe, summon everything from a trickle of moisture to a tidal wave, calm raging waters, and survive for prolonged periods at great depths. Combined with a knack for strategy, this made her a formidable opponent. Perhaps her greatest victory was when she singlehandedly defeated three RAHKSHI.

PERSONALITY

Although she represented an element usually associated with peace and tranquility, Nokama was capable of flashes of temper and could be too sure of her own wisdom at times. Of all the Toa, she had the hardest time adjusting to the fact that her old Matoran friends did not know how to treat her after she transformed. After taking some time to get comfortable with her new self, she was able to forge friendships with the other Toa Metru that continued when they became Turaga. She was a strong supporter of Vakama, even after his actions led to the Toa Metru being transformed into Toa Hordika.

As a Turaga, Nokama was known for her logical approach to things. She had seen how often deciding things based purely on emotion had led to trouble. The GA-MATORAN respected her for the fact that she would always listen to every side carefully before making a decision on what action to take. She was strongly in favor of telling the Toa Nuva the truth about Metru Nui.

EQUIPMENT

As a Toa Metru, Nokama carried twin HYDROBLADES that could pull her through the water at high speed. She wore the KANOHI RAU, the Great Mask of Translation. As a Turaga, she carried a trident carved from Makuta fish bones and wore the Noble Rau.

NORIK (NOAR-ick):

Former TOA HAGAH of Fire, later mutated by ROODAKA into a RAHAGA. Norik had been the leader of an elite Toa team assigned to MAKUTA's personal guard. When they discovered Makuta was oppressing and enslaving MATORAN, they turned on him and attacked a fortress of the BROTHERHOOD OF MAKUTA. Norik and IRUINI were separated from the other Toa but managed to defeat the EXO-TOA and the DARK HUNTERS and drive Makuta off. They then went to rescue their friends, only to discover they had been turned by Roodaka into shrunken, twisted creatures with the faces of RAHKSHI. Although they saved their fellow heroes, they, too, were turned into Rahaga.

Norik later suggested that the Rahaga begin a search for KEETONGU, a legendary RAHI said to be able to reverse any affliction. Although Norik firmly believed that this beast existed, many of the other Rahaga did not share his faith. Still, they agreed to join him and eventually made their way to METRU NUI. There Norik saved Toa VAKAMA after he had been turned into a TOA HORDIKA, but he was unable to keep Vakama from turning away from his friends and succumbing to his bestial side.

As a Toa, Norik carried a LAVA SPEAR and a RHOTUKA SPINNER with the ability to slow an opponent. He wore the KANOHI PEHKUI, the Great Mask of Diminishment.

As a Rahaga, Iruini specialized in capturing RAHI reptiles and other crawling creatures, such as FURNACE SALAMANDERS. He carried a Rhotuka spinner with the *snare* power, which tangled the limbs of a target. His staff could be used to distract his intended target until he was ready to strike.

NORTH MARCH:
An icy pass near where KO-WAHI meets TA-WAHI. Shortly after the construction of KO-KORO, a guard post was established here by KO-MATORAN.

NOTCH:
An old portion of the CHUTE system in METRU NUI. A number of chutes met and wound around each other here. TOA MATAU retrieved a GREAT DISK from inside a FORCE SPHERE here.

NUHRII (noo-ree):

NUHRII

A TA-MATORAN mask maker in TA-METRU. Resentful of VAKAMA's success, Nuhrii decided to use the Ta-Metru GREAT DISK to create a mask that would make him famous. Unfortunately, the DARK HUNTERS also wanted the disk and arranged for Nuhrii to be trapped in a house under attack by the MORBUZAKH. Vakama rescued Nuhrii and learned the location of the disk. The TOA and MATORAN worked together to retrieve the Great Disk from the FIRE PITS. Later, Nuhrii joined with AHKMOU, EHRYE, ORKAHM, TEHUTTI, and VHISOLA to form a MATORAN NUI to aid the TOA METRU against the Morbuzakh. Shortly after this, Nuhrii was captured by VAHKI and placed into a sphere that rendered him comatose. Evidence was later discovered that Nuhrii may have been destined to become a Toa of Fire. On MATA NUI (2), Nuhrii served in the TA-KORO GUARD with honor.

NUHVOK (noo-vahk):
One of the six breeds of BOHROK, insectlike mechanoids controlled by KRANA who menaced the island of MATA NUI (2). The Nuhvok were tied to the element of earth, and their EARTH SHIELDS could weaken structures from below, causing them to collapse. Nuhvok were accomplished tunnelers and could see in the dark but had weak eyesight in daylight. The Nuhvok returned to their nests after the coming of the BOHROK-KAL and remain there still.

NUHVOK

NUHVOK-KAL (noo-vahk-KAHL):

One of the six mutant BOHROK who made up the BOHROK-KAL. Its tool was a gravity shield, capable of negating or increasing gravity around a target. After being fed Toa power via the TOA NUVA symbols (see BOHROK-KAL), Nuhvok-Kal's power turned back upon itself and transformed the Bohrok-Kal into a black hole.

NUHVOK-KAL

NUHVOK VA (noo-vahk VAH):

One of the six BOHROK VA, Nuhvok Va were connected to the element of earth. They were gifted with the ability to see in the dark and were adequate tunnelers. When threatened, they used their claws to defend themselves.

NUHVOK VA

NUI-JAGA (noo-ee-JAH-guh):

Slow-moving, scorpionlike creatures found in both PO-METRU and PO-WAHI. Pack hunters, they relied on numbers and their powerful stingers to bring down prey. MAKUTA used INFECTED MASKS to control Nui-Jaga on MATA NUI (2) and send them against the MATORAN. One Nui-Jaga was defeated by a merged entity called a MATORAN NUI, made up of HEWKII, JALLER, KONGU, MACKU, MATORO, and ONEPU. On METRU NUI, Nui-Jaga stingers were prized by collectors and were often the subject of highly dangerous hunts.

NUI-JAGA

NUI-KOPEN (noo-ee-KOH-pen):

A giant, wasplike insect and a bitter enemy of the NUI-RAMA and the KIRIKORI NUI. ROODAKA rode a Nui-Kopen to visit MAKUTA's PROTODERMIS prison on the GREAT BARRIER.

NUI-RAMA (noo-ee-RAH-mah):

Winged, insectlike creatures who menaced both LE-METRU and LE-WAHI. Their primary tool was their stinger, which could be used both for offense and for feeding (Nui-Rama fed on liquid PROTODERMIS in METRU NUI and on plant sap and other natural fluids on MATA NUI (2)). Its wings were strong enough to allow it to carry a TOA into the air, and gave it sufficient speed to outdistance its natural enemy, the GUKKO bird. Nui-Rama were among the earliest recorded RAHI menaces in Metru Nui and followed the MATORAN when they migrated to Mata Nui (2). Large numbers of them were fitted with INFECTED MASKS by MAKUTA and used against the KORO. The first Rahi encountered on Mata Nui by Toa KOPAKA was a Nui-Rama who attempted to knock him and MATORO off a cliff. Nui-Rama were also responsible for the death of IHU on Metru Nui.

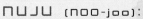

NUI-RAMA

NUJU (noo-joo):

TOA METRU of Ice, guardian of KO-METRU, and later TURAGA of KO-KORO.

> **HISTORY**

Nuju was a scholar and seer working in a KNOWLEDGE TOWER when TOA LHIKAN gave him a TOA STONE and a map to the GREAT TEMPLE. His reaction was annoyance that his work had been interrupted for such a strange gift. Still, he traveled to the temple and there encountered five other MATORAN — MATAU, NOKAMA, ONEWA, VAKAMA, and WHENUA. They placed their Toa stones into the TOA Suva and were transformed into mighty Toa heroes. From the start, Nuju regarded being a Toa and saving the city as something of an inconvenience. He once mused that the reason Toa had to be chosen by destiny for the job was that no one would ever volunteer for it. Despite this, he teamed with Whenua to find the ONU-METRU and Ko-Metru GREAT DISKS and used them to help destroy the MORBUZAKH plant that threatened the city. Nuju's stated reason for doing this was that the sooner the city was out of danger, the sooner he could go back to worrying only about Ko-Metru.

When the Toa Metru presented the Great Disks to Turaga DUME, he denounced them as impostors and ordered their arrest. (The Toa did not discover until later that this Dume was MAKUTA in disguise.) Whenua, Onewa, and Nuju were captured and locked up in the PRISON OF THE DARK HUNTERS. There they encountered a mysterious Turaga who counseled them on what it meant to be a Toa and helped Onewa and Nuju discover their KANOHI mask powers. (Later, they discovered this Turaga was in fact Lhikan.) Nuju used his mask's telekinesis power to tear stones out of the prison wall, allowing the Toa and Lhikan to escape. Shortly after, they were reunited with Vakama, Matau, and Nokama.

NUJU

Nuju aided in the subsequent battle with Makuta by using his mask powers to lift Vakama up to a plateau on the GREAT BARRIER for a showdown with their enemy. He later joined with the other Toa in using their powers to trap Makuta behind a wall of PROTODERMIS.

After the Toa's initial journey to MATA NUI (2), Nuju proved himself a hero on the return trip to Metru Nui. He teamed with Vakama to defeat the RAHI NUI that had severely wounded Nokama. It was also Nuju who deduced that KARZAHNI (2) was dying and therefore could not afford to back out of the deal it had made to save Nokama in exchange for a sample of ENERGIZED PROTODERMIS. Over time, Nuju became the most skilled of all the Toa at solving mysteries, applying careful logic and keen powers of observation.

Nuju found his intellect under siege when he was transformed along with the other Toa Metru into TOA HORDIKA. His rational side warred with the beast inside of himself, and he found his already short temper becoming even hotter and nastier. Worse, he was teamed with RAHAGA KUALUS, who persisted in wasting time talking to RAHI in their own language. Ironically, Kualus would later teach that language to Nuju and it would become the only one he ever spoke.

TURAGA NUJU

How the Toa Hordika transformed back into Toa Metru and escaped to Mata Nui with the rest of the Matoran has not yet been revealed. But they did make it to that island with close to 1,000 sleeping villagers. The Toa Metru willingly sacrificed their power to awaken the Matoran, transforming into Turaga in the process.

As a Turaga, Nuju supervised the construction of Ko-Koro. When KOPAKA arrived on Mata Nui, Nuju warned him about the threat of Makuta and his Rahi, but said nothing about Metru Nui or past events there.

The biggest change in Nuju was his language. Shortly before becoming a Turaga, he stopped speaking Matoran and spoke only the Rahi language taught to him by Kualus. MATORO served as his translator. His stated reason for the change was that if someone were not willing to make

TURAGA NUJU

the effort to understand him, that being was not worth Nuju's time to talk to. He has only been heard to speak the Matoran language twice in the last 1000 years. During the BOHROK-KAL invasion, Nuju used his mask power to save KOPAKA NUVA, who had fallen into a crevasse after beng stripped of his elemental ice power.

Nuju is one of the Turaga who strenuously objects to Vakama telling the tale of the Toa Hordika. He tried his best to talk his old friend out of it, and when that failed, he signaled his displeasure by sitting apart from the other Turaga as Vakama began the story.

Nuju is now journeying with the TOA NUVA, the other Turaga, and the Matoran back to Metru Nui.

POWERS

Nuju was the master of ice. He could cause ice storms and blizzards, travel via ice slide, and create virtually anything out of ice. Perhaps his most impressive feat was freezing attacking VAHKI in mid-leap to create an ice bridge between two Knowledge Towers for himself and Whenua.

PERSONALITY

Nuju's personality changed little between his time as a Matoran, Toa Metru, and Turaga. He was impatient with fools, had no use for those who did not plan for the future, and was more than willing to use his cutting wit to voice his dislike of anyone or anything. Despite all this, his razor-sharp mind and incredible analytical skills made him a valuable ally. Like all residents of Ko-Metru, his orientation was toward the future, so he was always thinking ahead. More than once, this helped the Toa Metru escape extremely dangerous situations.

EQUIPMENT

As a Toa Metru, Nuju carried twin CRYSTAL CLIMBERS. He wore the Kanohi MATATU, the Great Mask of Telekinesis. As a Turaga, he carried an ICE PICK and wore the Noble Matatu.

NUPARU

NUPARU (noo-PAH-roo):
An ONU-MATORAN inventor. Nuparu was employed as a RAHI Receiving Official in the ONU-METRU ARCHIVES in METRU NUI, but he could not suppress a natural talent for invention and engineering. He designed the KRALHI, the VAHKI, the KRAAHU, and the KRANUA, all of which were constructed in PO-METRU.

Nuparu's curiosity sometimes led him into dangerous situations. While searching the Archives sublevels for RAHKSHI pieces, he stumbled upon a large crack in one of the sea walls through which liquid PROTODERMIS was leaking. Returning to the surface, he warned TOA WHENUA. The TOA METRU went belowground in response to his report and encountered KRAHKA for the first time.

On MATA NUI (2), Nuparu was best known for inventing the BOXOR. This one-Matoran vehicle was used by villagers to combat the BOHROK and BOHROK VA. Nuparu's greatest regret is that he never got to see an EXO-TOA in person, because he would have loved to have studied its design and possibly reproduced it in some form. Unknown to the TURAGA, Nuparu salvaged some of the wreckage of those armored suits and is bringing it with him on the return journey to Metru Nui.

NUURAKH (NER-rahk):
VAHKI model assigned to TA-METRU on METRU NUI. These mechanoids were extremely swift and enormously patient, preferring to lurk in ambush than initiate direct confrontation. Their STAFFS OF COMMAND allowed them to fill a MATORAN's mind with a single overriding directive. The TOA METRU battled Nuurakh on their initial journey from Metru Nui to MATA NUI (2).

O

ONEPU

ONEPU (oh-NEE-poo):
An ONU-MATORAN. Onepu served as an archivist in METRU NUI, but did not have the patience for the work. He preferred to be out capturing RAHI rather than just waiting for them to be brought in by VAHKI. He was best known for leading an expedition that discovered an intact BOHROK nest beneath LE-METRU.
On MATA NUI (2), Onepu was appointed captain of the USSALRY, the Onu-Matoran defense force. He established himself as a great rider of USSAL crabs and was a five-time winner of the GREAT USSAL RACE.

ONEWA (AH-new-wah):
TOA METRU of Stone, guardian of PO-METRU, and later TURAGA of PO-KORO.

HISTORY

Onewa was employed as a carver in Po-Metru when TOA LHIKAN gave him a TOA STONE and a map to the GREAT TEMPLE. He traveled there and encountered five other MATORAN — MATAU, NOKAMA, NUJU, VAKAMA, and WHENUA. They placed their Toa stones into the TOA Suva and were transformed into mighty Toa heroes.

After Vakama had a vision warning of the destruction of the city, Onewa reluctantly agreed to join the others to find the six GREAT DISKS. From the start, he clashed with Toa Vakama, whom he derisively referred to as "fire-spitter." Still, he teamed with the new Toa of Fire to recover both the TA-METRU and Po-Metru disks. Vakama even saved Onewa's life twice, once from a MORBUZAKH vine and once when the two of them were about to be incinerated in the PROTODERMIS RECLAMATION FURNACE. Later, Onewa identified AHKMOU as the Matoran who had betrayed the city to the DARK HUNTERS. The Toa used the Great Disks to defeat the Morbuzakh plant that threatened the city.

TOA ONEWA

When the Toa Metru presented the Great Disks to Turaga DUME, he denounced them as impostors and ordered their arrest. (The Toa did not discover until later that this Dume was MAKUTA in disguise.) Whenua, Onewa, and Nuju were captured and locked up in the PRISON OF THE DARK HUNTERS. There they encountered a mysterious Turaga who counseled them on what it meant to be a Toa and helped Onewa and Nuju discover their KANOHI mask powers. (Later, they discovered this Turaga was in fact Lhikan.) Onewa used his mind control mask power to make Whenua sit down on the cell floor. Shortly after, they escaped the cell and were reunited with Vakama, Matau, and Nokama.

Onewa aided in the ensuing battle with the Dark Hunters by making KREKKA attack NIDHIKI. Later, he joined his power with that of the other Toa Metru to trap Makuta behind a wall of solid PROTODERMIS.

The Toa Metru then departed Metru Nui with the six Matoran spheres. Along the way, they encountered monstrous sea RAHI and powerful KRALHI under the command of an ONU-MATORAN named MAVRAH. During a huge battle between the Toa, the Kralhi, the VAHKI, and the RAHI, Mavrah was swept into the underground river by a great wave. Onewa prevented Whenua from sacrificing his life to save Mavrah.

After reaching MATA NUI (2) and then returning to Metru Nui, Onewa and the other Toa Metru encountered VISORAK. All six Toa were captured and mutated by Visorak venom into TOA HORDIKA. As half Toa, half beast, Onewa found it difficult to control his rage. Later, he stumbled upon a secret lair of Makuta's that contained evidence that Ahkmou may have been destined to become Toa of Stone.

TURAGA ONEWA

How the Toa Hordika transformed back into Toa Metru and escaped to Mata Nui (2) with the rest of the Matoran has not yet been revealed. But they did make it to that island with close to 1,000 sleeping villagers. The Toa Metru willingly sacrificed their power to awaken the Matoran, transforming themselves into Turaga in the process. As a Turaga, Onewa supervised the construction of PO-KORO. Of all the villages, it looked the most like its Metru Nui counterpart. Onewa became known for his firm and fair resolutions of disputes, earning the nickname "Referee." He also invented the sport KOLHII. When POHATU arrived, Onewa informed him of the threat Makuta posed to the island but did not share any information regarding Metru Nui or his life as a Toa.

During the BOHROK invasion, Onewa led the Po-Matoran across the coast to GA-KORO to avoid the TAHNOK. Still, it was only the Toa's defeat of the BAHRAG that saved the Po-Matoran from the PAHRAK.

Onewa is now journeying with the TOA NUVA, the other Turaga, and the Matoran back to Metru Nui.

TURAGA ONEWA

POWERS

Onewa was the master of stone. He could cause jagged pillars of stone to erupt from the ground, stone hands to grab enemies, or stone walls to form around a target. He also had the ability to shatter stone at will, a power he used effectively during the battle with the ENERGIZED PROTODERMIS ENTITY.

PERSONALITY

Onewa was courageous and daring as a Toa, but not always the easiest to get along with. He was always quick with a wisecrack, and frequently made Vakama and Whenua the butt of his jokes. Like Matau, he could see the thrilling side of being a Toa, but he also knew that it was serious business.

Perhaps because he had provoked so many arguments as a Toa, he became skilled at resolving them as a Turaga. Where once he had lived only for the present, he came to see the virtues of an awareness of both past and future.

EQUIPMENT

As a Toa Metru, Onewa carried twin proto pitons. He wore the Kanohi KOMAU, the Great Mask of Mind Control. As a Turaga, he carried a STONE HAMMER and wore the Noble Komau.

ONU (oh-NOO):
A Matoran prefix meaning "earth."

ONU-KINI (oh-NOO-KIH-nee):
A temple dedicated to ONUA located in ONU-WAHI on MATA NUI (2).

ONU-KORO (oh-NOO-KOAR-oh):
A village of tunnels, caves, and mines located beneath the surface of ONU-WAHI. It was home to TURAGA WHENUA and the ONU-MATORAN and was protected by TOA ONUA. Onu-Koro was the site of PROTODERMIS mines as well as USSAL crab races. The village was flooded by the GAHLOK during the BOHROK invasion, and later destroyed by the RAHKSHI. The ONU-SUVA was located here.

ONU-MATORAN (oh-NOO mat-OAR-an):
A resident of ONU-KORO or ONU-METRU. Onu-Matoran commonly had black armor and wore purple or orange masks. On both METRU NUI and MATA NUI (2), Onu-Matoran were skilled miners. They also served as archivists in the Onu-Metru ARCHIVES. Onu-Matoran generally have good night vision but weak eyes in the daylight. Their favorite sport is USSAL crab racing, and they make up the membership of the USSALRY.

ONU-METRU (oh-NOO-MET-troo):
Home of the archivists and miners in METRU NUI. Onu-Metru was best known for the presence of the ARCHIVES, place of employment for most Onu-Matoran in the city. It was also the site of solid PROTODERMIS mines, with blocks of the substance shipped by boat and airship to PO-METRU for carving. Onu-Metru was also the site of the PRISON OF THE DARK HUNTERS.

ONU-SUVA (oh-NOO-SOO-vah):
A shrine to ONUA NUVA in ONU-KORO. KANOHI masks and Onua Nuva's symbol were kept here. BOHROK-KAL stole the NUVA SYMBOL from the Onu-Suva, robbing Onua Nuva of his elemental power of earth.

ONU-WAHI (oh-ᑎOO-WAH-hee):

A largely barren region located in northwestern MATA NUI (2). On the surface, it appeared nothing lived there but the occasional RAHI. In fact, there was a thriving village in the tunnels beneath the surface. ONU-KORO was home to the ONU-MATORAN. TOA ONUA's canister washed up on the shore of ONU-WAHI. Onu-Wahi suffered serious damage during the BOHROK invasion, and the village was destroyed when the RAHKSHI attacked. Subterranean tunnels linked Onu-Wahi to other regions.

ONUA/ONUA NUVA (oh-ᑎOO-ah/oh-ᑎOO-ah ᑎOO-vah):

TOA of Earth and protector of ONU-KORO.

ONUA NUVA

HISTORY

Onua's early history is a mystery. He was one of six Toa who had been floating in the ocean around MATA NUI (2) for 1000 years. They were inside unique canisters and each was partially disassembled. A signal unwittingly sent by TAKUA called the canisters to shore. Onua emerged from his canister on the coast of ONU-WAHI and instinctively headed underground. There he met ONEPU and TURAGA WHENUA.

Later, he made contact with the other five Toa — GALI, KOPAKA, LEWA, POHATU, and TAHU. Together and separately, they searched for KANOHI masks and battled the RAHI servants of MAKUTA. It was during this period that Onua saved Lewa, who'd had an INFECTED MASK affixed to his face and been transported to a NUI-RAMA nest.

He briefly merged with Pohatu and Tahu to form the TOA KAITA called AKAMAI and battle the MANAS. During the invasion of the BOHROK, he risked his life to help Lewa when the latter's mind was taken over by a KRANA.

Following the defeat of the twin Bohrok queens, the BAHRAG, the six Toa were transformed by ENERGIZED PROTODERMIS into TOA NUVA. Onua said nothing as his teammates grew arrogant and quarrelsome, nor did he step in to prevent Tahu and Kopaka from splitting up the team. This made Gali angry with Onua for his failure to act.

During the BOHROK-KAL invasion, Onua teamed with Whenua to find KANOHI NUVA, encountering and driving off Manas in the process. When the RAHKSHI attacked Onu-Koro, he battled them alongside Pohatu. He was later part of the Rahkshi's final defeat.

He and other Toa Nuva are now journeying back to that city with the Turaga and MATORAN.

POWERS

Onua is the master of earth. He can erect walls of earth in an instant, cause the soil to strike a foe like a battering ram, or make the dirt shift under an enemy's feet so that he sinks into the ground. He is a skilled tunneler, often helping ONU-MATORAN to dig new mine shafts. He has excellent night vision, but his eyesight is weak in daylight.

PERSONALITY

Onua was arguably one of the wisest of the Toa as well as being the least talkative. This caused problems, for he was too quick to let the others go their own way without speaking up, even when he knew they were making a mistake. He has tried to be the conscience of the Toa, helping them to keep a sense of perspective about their place in the universe.

EQUIPMENT

Onua relied on his claws as a Toa and on a pair of QUAKE BREAKERS as a Toa Nuva. He most often wore a Kanohi PAKARI or PAKARI NUVA, the Great Mask of Strength.

OOHNORAK (ooh-NOAR-ack):

One of the six breeds of VISORAK that invaded METRU NUI. Oohnorak have limited telepathic abilities and are skilled mimics, allowing them to trap a foe by speaking in the voice of a trusted friend. The Oohnorak used this trick to get TOA MATAU to open a hangar door and let them in. Oohnorak RHOTUKA SPINNERS are capable of numbing a target, making an escape extremely difficult.

ORKAHM (OR-kam):

An USSAL crab rider in LE-METRU. Orkahm was one of six MATORAN to discover the locations of the legendary GREAT DISKS. Orkahm was slow and meticulous and known for having little imagination. His favorite Ussal crab was PEWKU.

ORKAHM

He originally intended to find some way to profit from his knowledge of the Le-Metru Great Disk's location, but shortly after finding it, he began being followed by NIDHIKI and KREKKA. Lured to an out-of-the-way spot, he was trapped in a snare set by AHKMOU. The TOA METRU of Air, MATAU, came to his rescue. Orkahm led Matau to the Great Disk, which was stuck inside a FORCE SPHERE in one of the CHUTES.

Later, Orkahm joined with Ahkmou, VHISOLA, TEHUTTI, EHRYE, and NUHRII to form a MATORAN NUI to aid the Toa in their battle against the MORBUZAKH. Shortly afterward, he was captured by VAHKI and put into a SPHERE. He remained there, comatose, until awakened on MATA NUI (2) by the Toa Metru. Evidence was later discovered that Orkahm may have been destined to become a Toa of Air. Orkahm later became a GUKKO rider in LE-KORO.

P

PAHRAK (PAH-rahk):

One of the six breeds of BOHROK, insectlike mechanoids controlled by KRANA who menaced the island of MATA NUI (2). The Pahrak were tied to the element of ice and their STONE SHIELDS could cause violent seismic disruptions. The Pahrak came dangerously close to destroying GA-KORO, stopped once by HAHLI and MACKU's efforts and once by the TOA's defeat of the BAHRAG. The Pahrak returned to their nests after the coming of the BOHROK-KAL and remain there still.

PAHRAK

PAHRAK-KAL

PAHRAK-KAL [PAH-rahk KAHL]:
One of the six mutant BOHROK who made up the BOHROK-KAL. Its tool was a PLASMA SHIELD, capable of superheating any substance until it becomes plasmoid. It could also be used defensively to melt incoming projectiles. After being fed Toa power via the TOA NUVA symbols (see BOHROK-KAL), Pahrak-Kal superheated, melted through the floor, and vanished, possibly falling all the way through to the core of the planet.

PAHRAK VA [PAH-rahk VAH]:
One of the six BOHROK VA, Pahrak Va was connected to the element of stone. Slow-moving, this Bohrok Va proved the easiest for the MATORAN to capture. It used stone hammers to defend itself.

PAHRAK VA

PAKARI [PAH-kar-EE]:
The KANOHI Mask of Strength, capable of increasing the physical power of the wearer. ONUA wore the Great Mask of Strength when he first washed ashore on MATA NUI (2).

PAKARI NUVA [PAH-kar-EE NOO-vah]:
The powerful Great Mask of Strength worn by ONUA NUVA. It was capable of increasing his strength and that of those around him to their ultimate. See KANOHI NUVA.

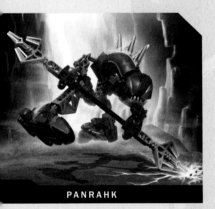
PANRAHK

PANRAHK [PAHN-rahk]:
One of the six RAHKSHI sent by MAKUTA to stop the HERALD and recover the KANOHI AVOHKII. Panrahk was able to use its staff to make any object fly into tiny fragments. This Rahkshi's energies were so potent that small explosions would go off wherever it walked. Along with GUURAHK and LERAHK, Panrahk was responsible for the destruction of the village of TA-KORO. Panrahk was trapped in a prison of glass through the efforts of TAHU NUVA and LEWA NUVA.

PAPA NIHU REEF [PAH-pah nee-HOO]:
Name given to the ONU-WAHI coastline on MATA NUI (2).

PARAKREKKS [PAH-rah-KRECKS]:
These vicious amphibians follow in the wake of the PROTOCAIRNS, feeding off of the rubble the larger creatures leave behind. Long after the protocairns have died, these nasty beings linger, tearing down structures with their claws and feasting on the fragments. Extremely good at finding concealment, they can be very difficult to root out once they have gotten a foothold in a place. Left unchecked, they can eventually destroy an entire city due to their rapacious appetite.

PEHKUI [peh-KOO-ee]:
Mask of Diminishment, worn by TOA NORIK. This mask allows a user to shrink to a minimum height of six inches while still retaining normal strength and power.

PEWKU (POO-koo):

A retired USSAL racing crab who was friends with TAKUA. Pewku originally served in METRU NUI pulling an USSAL CART, driven by ORKHAM. After migrating to MATA NUI (2), Pewku was a racing crab and later a means of transport for MATORAN traveling between ONU-KORO and PO-KORO. She was TAKUA's companion during the search for TAKANUVA. She has since been adopted by JALLER.

PHASE DRAGON:

Flying reptilian RAHI of METRU NUI, known for its great speed and ability to alter its density so as to pass unharmed through solid objects. Although frightening in appearance, phase dragons were largely harmless as long as there were vehicles for it to chase. Once Metru Nui became a dead city, phase dragons became a menace to anything that moved. None of these creatures were ever seen on MATA NUI (2).

PHASE DRAGON

PLACE OF SHADOW:

Name given by the MATORAN to a pass along the border of KO-WAHI and TA-WAHI on MATA NUI (2). This area was avoided at all costs, even by the BOHROK. TAHU NUVA, KOPAKA NUVA, and GALI NUVA came here in search of KANOHI NUVA masks.

PLASMA SHIELD:

Tool carried by PAHRAK-KAL. The plasma shield was able to emit a stream of superheated plasma at a temperature of roughly 2,000 degrees.

PO (POH):

A Matoran prefix meaning "stone."

PO-KINI (POH-kih-NEE):

A temple dedicated to POHATU located in PO-WAHI on MATA NUI (2).

PO-KORO (POH-koar-OH):

Village on MATA NUI (2) and home to the PO-MATORAN. Po-Koro was located in the desert to the far north of the island. Structures here were carved from rock and intended to blend in with the surrounding area. The climate was harsh, with unrelenting heat and sandstorms. During the BOHROK invasion, the Po-Matoran temporarily fled their village and took up residence in caves.

PO-MATORAN (POH-mat-OAR-an):

A resident of PO-KORO or PO-METRU. Po-Matoran commonly had tan armor and wore black or dark orange masks. On both METRU NUI and MATA NUI (2), Po-Matoran were known as extremely skilled carvers. Po-Matoran, as a rule, hate water and cannot swim. The sport of KOLHII originated among the Po-Matoran and they were some of its best players.

PO-METRU (POH-MET-troo):

Home of the carvers in METRU NUI. Unlike the other districts of the city, Po-Metru is largely a wild and barren place, dotted with mountains and canyons. Po-Matoran labor out of doors, assembling goods and carving great statues. Po-Metru is protected by TOA ONEWA and is home to the SCULPTURE FIELDS, the FIELDS OF CONSTRUCTION, the ASSEMBLER'S VILLAGE, the PRISON OF THE DARK HUNTERS, and the PROTODERMIS WAREHOUSE. One of the six GREAT DISKS was found here. Three of the TOA METRU were held captive here, and the other three came to Po-Metru to save them and LHIKAN. A major skirmish between VAKAMA, NOKAMA, and MATAU and the DARK HUNTERS took place in Po-Metru.

PO-SUVA [POH-soo-VAH]:
A shrine to POHATU NUVA in PO-KORO. KANOHI masks and Pohatu Nuva's symbol were kept here. BOHROK-KAL stole the NUVA SYMBOL from the Po-Suva, robbing Pohatu Nuva of his elemental power of stone.

PO-WAHI [POH-wah-HEE]:
A barren, rocky wasteland located in the far northern region of MATA NUI (2). It was home to PO-KORO and the PO-MATORAN. TOA POHATU's canister washed up on the shore of Po-Wahi. Numerous RAHI live here, including NUI-JAGA, SAND TARAKAVA, TUNNELERS, HUSI, and many more. Po-Wahi suffered some damage during the BOHROK invasion, but was largely spared by the BOHROK-KAL and RAHKSHI.

POHATU/POHATU NUVA [poe-HAH-too/poe-HAH-too NOO-vah]:
TOA of Stone and protector of PO-KORO,

HISTORY

Nothing has been revealed about Pohatu's history prior to his first appearance on the island of MATA NUI (2). He was one of six Toa who had been floating in the ocean around that land for 1000 years. They were inside unique canisters and each was partially disassembled. A signal unwittingly sent by TAKUA called the canisters to shore. Pohatu's canister washed up on the shores of PO-WAHI. He first encountered another Toa in spectacular fashion, when he accidentally buried KOPAKA in a rockslide.

Later, the two of them made contact with the other heroes of Mata Nui — GALI, LEWA, ONUA, and TAHU. Together and separately, they searched for KANOHI masks and battled the RAHI servants of MAKUTA.

POHATU

Pohatu briefly merged with Tahu and Onua to form the TOA KAITA called AKAMAI and fight the MANAS. Following the defeat of Makuta, he joined the other Toa in battling the BOHROK invasion. Pohatu teamed with Gali, Kopaka, and Onua to trap a swarm of TAHNOK in TIRO CANYON in PO-WAHI.

Following the defeat of the twin Bohrok queens, the BAHRAG, the six Toa were transformed by ENERGIZED PROTODERMIS into TOA NUVA. Despite the increase in power, Pohatu remained modest and friendly. After the BOHROK-KAL stole the Toa's elemental powers, Pohatu teamed with Kopaka to track down KANOHI NUVA.

Pohatu was in attendance at the KOLHII match when it was revealed that TAKUA had discovered the Kanohi AVOHKII, the Mask of Light. Pohatu later joined with Onua in a futile effort to defend ONU-KORO against the RAHKSHI. During this period, he was infuriated to discover that the Turaga had been keeping captured KRAATA in a Po-Wahi cave without informing him.

The two Toa Nuva were part of the final defeat of the Rahkshi, aided by TAKANUVA, the Toa of Light. Pohatu Nuva and other Toa Nuva are now journeying back to METRU NUI with the TURAGA and MATORAN.

POWERS

Pohatu is the master of stone. He can create rockslides, make stone spring from the ground, bring rock walls into being by his will, and more. His strength is prodigious, particularly in his legs. He is capable of kicking a massive boulder a distance of several miles.

PERSONALITY

Pohatu has always been the most easygoing of the Toa. His philosophy from the start was that everyone would be better served by getting along, and he maintained that attitude even in the face of such extreme personalities as Tahu and Kopaka. He is widely regarded as a loyal and reliable comrade and a good being to have beside you in a fight. He rarely took himself or others too seriously. Like most residents of Po-Wahi, he disliked water and could not swim.

EQUIPMENT

Pohatu initially carried no special Toa tool, relying on his own strength, As Pohatu Nuva, he wielded CLIMBING CLAWS, which could be thrown or put together to form a KODAN BALL. He most often wore a Kanohi KAKAMA or KAKAMA NUVA, the Great Mask of Speed.

POKAWI (POH-kah-WEE):
Flightless fowl that live high among the peaks of PO-METRU, feeding on whatever vegetation that might be there. Their high vantage point is all that saves them, since they can usually spot predators long before they get too close. On MATA NUI (2), they were known for scattering in all directions when enemies approached, confusing them with their sudden movement.

POUKS (POOKS):
Former TOA HAGAH of Stone later mutated by ROODAKA into a RAHAGA. Pouks had been part of an elite Toa team charged with being MAKUTA's personal guard. When they discovered Makuta was oppressing and enslaving MATORAN, they turned on him and attacked a fortress of the BROTHERHOOD OF MAKUTA. Pouks was struck by one of Roodaka's RHOTUKA SPINNERS and mutated into a shrunken creature with the head of a RAHKSHI. He was later rescued by TOA IRUINI and Toa NORIK, who also ended up being mutated.
What masks and tools Pouks carried as a Toa has not yet been revealed.
As a Rahaga, Pouks specialized in capturing large land RAHI, such as KIKANALO and MUAKA. He carried a Rhotuka spinner with the *lasso* power, which skimmed just above the ground and then wrapped around the legs of a target, bringing it down and immobilizing it. He also carried a staff that could be used to make an invisible mark on Rahi so that they could be tracked.

Pouks was familiar enough with the natural movements of Rahi that he could spot impersonations by KRAHKA. He persuaded Krahka to side with the TOA METRU against the VISORAK, and later rode with her and Toa ONEWA on the back of a TAHTORAK.

PRISON OF THE DARK HUNTERS:

A series of cells inside a cave network in ONU-METRU, used by the DARK HUNTERS to keep important prisoners. LHIKAN, WHENUA, NUJU, and ONEWA were held here after their capture. Lhikan, then a TURAGA, taught the three TOA METRU skills that would help them focus and learn to use their KANOHI mask powers. Both Onewa and Nuju discovered their powers while in captivity, and Nuju's Kanohi MATATU, the Mask of Telekinesis, made it possible for him to tear stones from the wall and free them. The prison of the Dark Hunters was guarded by squads of VAHKI.

PROTOCAIRNS (PROE-toe-CARE-nz):

Surely one of the most bizarre creatures ever seen on METRU NUI, perhaps only their rumored origin is stranger than their behavior. According to legend, the Protocairns were once a small group of villagers from another land who willingly exposed themselves to ENERGIZED PROTODERMIS. They were transformed into monstrous amphibious beasts. Every hundred years or so since then, Protocairns appear on the shore of various islands and wreak enormous destruction, actually disintegrating large portions of the coastline. After a short time of this, the Protocairns die and their bodies fuse together, forming new land in place of the old they destroyed. While they live, they are extremely difficult to stop, although VAHKI squads have had success driving them away over the past few centuries.

PROTODERMIS:

The most important substance in the BIONICLE universe. Protodermis can exist in solid, liquid, and gaseous form, and virtually everything known to the MATORAN is made of it. This includes Toa armor and organic tissue, buildings, tools, KANOKA DISKS, KANOHI masks, and even the silver sea that surrounds METRU NUI.

Solid protodermis was mined in both ONU-METRU on Metru Nui and ONU-KORO on MATA NUI (2). All buildings, statues, and other structures on both islands were made from solid protodermis.

Liquid protodermis, such as makes up the Metru Nui ocean, must be purified before being used to create items. (See PROTODERMIS PURIFICATION.) No significant sources of liquid protodermis existed on Mata Nui. Due to the fact that liquid protodermis took the place of water for the Metru Nui Matoran, it was dubbed the "stuff of life."

The third, and rarest, form of protodermis is ENERGIZED PROTODERMIS.

PROTODERMIS PURIFICATION:

A process performed in GA-METRU on METRU NUI to remove impurities from liquid protodermis so that it could be used in the making of KANOKA DISKS. Liquid protodermis was drawn from the sea into the GREAT TEMPLE. Here a special group of GA-MATORAN waited to begin purification work. While some read ancient passages calling on the GREAT SPIRIT MATA NUI for aid and protection, others supervised the rapid heating and cooling needed to cleanse the liquid. Once this was done, the liquid protodermis lost its silver coloring and become a clear fluid with a blueish tinge.

PROTODERMIS RECLAMATION FURNACE:

An enclosure containing an extremely hot flame, used to melt down flawed creations in TA-METRU. Items stored in the PROTODERMIS RECLAMATION YARD were sent here to be reduced to liquid protodermis. NIDHIKI attempted to kill VAKAMA and ONEWA here.

PROTODERMIS RECLAMATION YARD:

Area of TA-METRU in which damaged masks and tools were kept prior to their being melted down. TOA VAKAMA journeyed here while searching for the missing NUHRII. The Matoran caretaker of the facility is reported to talk to the KANOHI masks in his care as if they were living beings.

PROTODERMIS WAREHOUSE:

Structures in PO-METRU that held an assortment of parts awaiting assembly. Components of VAHKI, furniture, and other items were shipped to Po-Metru from TA-METRU and put together in ASSEMBLER'S VILLAGES. TOA ONEWA came to a protodermis warehouse during his search for AHKMOU.

PROTO DRAKE

PROTODITES (PROE-toe-DIGHTS):

Microscopic creatures accidentally freed in the ARCHIVES and still infesting some sections. These creatures were being studied by archivists when efforts to escape by a KRAAWA rocked their container and shattered it. The protodites spread rapidly, kept in check only by their one predator, the ARCHIVES MOLES. Whether any protodites made it to MATA NUI (2) is unknown.

PROTO DRAKE:

Amphibious creatures found in the waters off GA-METRU. These creatures got their name from their habit of bathing in molten PROTODERMIS, which was believed to be their way of burning off parasites that clung to their skin. They were regarded with respect by the GA-MATORAN, particularly because they helped to keep coastal areas safe by feeding on sharks. Proto drake were later spotted off the coast of TA-WAHI on MATA NUI (2).

QUAKE BREAKERS:

ONUA NUVA's twin Toa tools which could dig through earth and rock, as well as serve as all-terrain treads when attached to his feet.

R

RAHAGA (rah-HAH-gah):

Name given to six former TOA HAGAH who were transformed by ROODAKA into shrunken, bent creatures with the heads of RAHKSHI. The name was coined by Roodaka as a play on the words "Hagah" and "Rahkshi." Rahaga were partially RAHI and had enhanced sense and agility as a result. Each carried a staff and had a RHOTUKA LAUNCHER as part of their anatomy. The Rahaga continued to oppose Roodaka and the VISORAK, making every effort to rescue Rahi before the Visorak could capture them. The Rahaga acted to save the TOA HORDIKA from certain death and to educate them about their new forms, new powers, and hopes for a cure for their condition. The six Rahaga were BOMONGA, GAAKI, IRUINI, KUALUS, NORIK, and POUKS (see individual entries).

RAHI (rah-HEE):

Overall name applied to all animals, fish, birds, insects, and reptiles by the MATORAN. A rough translation of the term is "not us," since it is used by Matoran to describe living things other than themselves. The majority of Rahi are sentient, multi-celled biomechanical beings, ranging from dangerous and hostile beasts to easily domesticated creatures. The precise origin of the different species is unknown to the Matoran, since the Rahi they have encountered have all migrated from other lands.

RAHI NUI (rah-HEE NOO-ee):

A bizarre creature that appeared to be a combination a MUAKA, a TARAKAVA, a NUI-JAGA, a NUI-RAMA, and a KANE-RA bull. It was created by MAKUTA to serve as a tracking beast for the DARK HUNTERS NIDHIKI and KREKKA. In addition to its natural tools — horns, wings, teeth, power forelegs, and hindlegs — the Rahi Nui originally possessed all the base KANOKA DISK powers, including *teleportation*. Using that particular ability, it could home in on TOA wherever they might be. The Rahi Nui actually fed on Toa power, making it immune to elemental blasts. The first recorded encounter was with the TOA METRU, during which the Rahi Nui severely wounded NOKAMA. It was defeated by NUJU and VAKAMA and its atoms dispersed. Over 1000 years later, the Rahi Nui reappeared on MATA NUI (2), minus its special powers. It was defeated by the TOA NUVA with the aid of TURAGA Vakama. Its current whereabouts are unknown.

RAHKSHI (RAHK-shee):

Powerful and destructive armored beings created by MAKUTA to do his bidding. A Rahkshi consists of a suit of armor that houses a KRAATA, a wormlike creature that controls the being's movements and actions. Without a kraata, Rahkshi armor is unable to move or act. Rahkshi are created by exposing kraata to ENERGIZED PROTODERMIS. Over time, the protodermis evolves the kraata into a suit of Rahkshi armor. A second kraata then crawls into the head of the armor and activates it. Since kraata are created by Makuta, Rahkshi have been nicknamed the "sons of Makuta." There are 42 known types of Rahkshi, differentiated by their powers and the color of their armor.

Most Rahkshi on METRU NUI were "wild Rahkshi," beings operating without orders from Makuta and acting like pure beasts. They lived in tunnels underneath the city, occasionally venturing out and battling VAHKI. Some of these Rahkshi ended up on display in the ARCHIVES.

When the search began for the TOA of Light on MATA NUI (2), Makuta unleashed six Rahkshi against the TOA NUVA and Matoran: GUURAHK, KURAHK, LERAHK, PANRAHK, TURAHK, and VORAHK (see individual entries). So powerful were they that even Makuta expressed reluctance about setting them free. All six were defeated by the Toa Nuva and TAKANUVA, and their parts were used to build the USSANUI.

Rahkshi Power Chart

A Rahkshi's power can be identified by the color of its armor. This chart contains all known Rahkshi, although it is possible that others may exist which have not yet been encountered.

Rahkshi Armor Color	Power
Gold	Weather Control
Tan	Elasticity
Yellow	Heat Vision
Tan-Blue	Illusion
Blue-Green	Teleport
Black-Brown	Quick Healing
Red-Orange	Laser Vision
Blue-Silver	Gravity
Blue-White	Electricity
Yellow-Green	Sonics
Orange-Black	Vacuum
Tan-Red	Plasma
Black-Gold	Magnetism
Aqua-Marine	Fire Resistance
Red-Yellow	Ice Resistance
Light Purple	Mind Reading
Blue-Gold	Shapeshifting
Black-Red	Darkness
Green-Brown	Plant Control
Light Blue	Molecular Disruption (inorganic)
Silver	Chain Lightning
Black-White	Cyclone
Black-Green	Density Control
Red-Gold	Chameleon
Blue-Purple	Accuracy
Magenta	Rahi Control
Orange	Insect Control
Blue-Black	Stasis Field
Gray	Limited Invulnerability
Purple	Power Scream
Red-Silver	Dodge
Gray-Black	Silence
Black-Purple	Adaptation
Blue-Yellow	Slow

Gray-Green	Confusion
Maroon	Sleep
Red	Fear
Black	Weakness
White	Anger
Blue	Disintegration
Green	Poison
Brown	Shattering

RANAMA (rah-NAH-mah):

Long considered a pest by MATORAN in TA-METRU, the Ranama are giant fire frogs who thrive in molten PROTODERMIS. Their presence in that fluid forced TA-MATORAN to filter it carefully before using it to mold tools and masks. Ranama fed on small insects, leaping out of molten protodermis vats to snare them with its tongue. They later made their way to MATA NUI (2), where they lived in molten lava in TA-WAHI.

RAU (ROW):

RAU

KANOHI Mask of Translation. The Great Mask version of this allowed TOA NOKAMA to understand both written and spoken languages. She used its power to communicate with the KIKANALO as well as to translate ancient writings related to the GREAT DISKS. The Noble Rau, worn by Nokama as a TURAGA, enabled translation of written languages only.

RAZORFISH:

Although called a fish, this creature is actually an aquatic mammal. Its primary defense was the razor-sharp scales that lined its body. Brushing against a razorfish could result in a serious wound. They were found both in the ocean around METRU NUI and the waters surrounding MATA NUI (2).

RAZOR WHALE:

Massive aquatic mammals who rely on the sharp spines on their backs to protect them from predators. At a certain point in their lives, the spines naturally fall off, making it possible for MATORAN to ride the great beasts. TOA HORDIKA NOKAMA made a point of defending the razor whales against the VISORAK BOGGARAK. Since few specimens were ever sighted off MATA NUI (2), it is unclear how many of the species still survive.

RAZOR WHALE

RED STAR:

A blazing star in the heavens above MATA NUI (2). Of all the celestial bodies, it is this one that most governs the interpretation of prophecies about the island and its inhabitants.

RHOTUKA LAUNCHER (roe-TOO-kah):

A tool, either natural or artificially created, capable of hurling an energy spinner a long distance at a target. These were used for both offense and defense. The RAHAGA, TOA

HORDIKA, KEETONGU, VISORAK, and some RAHI had natural launchers as parts of their bodies. Toa IRUINI, Toa NORIK, ROODAKA, and SIDORAK carried mechanical launchers.

RHOTUKA SPINNER (roe-TOO-kah):

A wheel of energy generated by the willpower of the user and able to be hurled great distances using a RHOTUKA LAUNCHER. These spinners were the primary offensive and defensive tools of the TOA HORDIKA, RAHAGA, KEETONGU, and VISORAK, and were also used by ROODAKA, SIDORAK, TOA IRUINI, Toa NORIK, and some RAHI. The power of the spinner was determined by the individual being who launched it — for example, due to his identification with his element, Toa Hordika VAKAMA launched fire spinners, something no one else could do. Sidorak, who favored blind obedience from his horde above all else, could generate a spinner that produced such obedience in anyone it struck. Generating a Rhotuka spinner cost the user energy, so only a certain number could be created in a given time.

ROCK LION:

Little is known about this creature, which was said to occupy the lowest levels of the ARCHIVES. Those few MATORAN who claimed to have seen one said that it had sharp teeth and claws and a mane which became white-hot when the beast was angered. No rock lion was ever seen on MATA NUI (2).

ROCK RAPTOR

ROCK RAPTOR:

A successful predator in PO-METRU, rock raptors suffered badly at the claws of VISORAK ROPORAK until only a few specimens remained. Prior to the arrival of the VISORAK, rock raptors were known for capturing much larger prey by using their natural tools to trigger rockslides. Their aggressive, independent nature made it impossible for the RAHAGA to help them against the hordes and most raptors were captured or killed.

ROODAKA (roo-DAHK-ah):

Viceroy of the VISORAK and lieutenant to MAKUTA.

HISTORY

Little is known of Roodaka's past. She has stated that she came from a land where ruthlessness and the ability to deceive were required to survive, two traits she had in abundance. She committed her first betrayal while participating in a rite of passage with a companion, which involved successfully scaling a living mountain. When her partner's foot became caught, Roodaka abandoned him to die while she completed the climb.

How she met Makuta and SIDORAK are stories that have yet to be told. But later years found her partnered with Sidorak as lieutenants to Makuta, a job she enjoyed. Both of these powerful beings attempted to gain favor in the eyes of their employer, with neither succeeding at truly outdoing the other. After the TOA HAGAH attacked the BROTHERHOOD OF MAKUTA, Roodaka ambushed them and used her KANOKA DISK to transform them into bestial RAHAGA.

ROODAKA

Sidorak claimed credit for this idea and was rewarded with command of the VISORAK horde, with Roodaka as his viceroy. Together, they led the horde to many victories in many lands. Sidorak hoped to cement an alliance with Roodaka and so gain influence in her native land. Roodaka, on the other hand, schemed to eliminate Sidorak and rule by the side of Makuta. Both got their opportunity when Makuta was defeated and imprisoned by the TOA METRU. Responding to his mental summons, they led the horde to METRU NUI. The final conflict between the two would be played out in the ruined city.

POWERS

Roodaka was immensely strong and capable of harnessing her body's natural shadow energy and unleashing it in a devastating blast. Her catcher claw could snatch Kanoka disks out of the air so she could fling them back at her foe.

PERSONALITY

Roodaka was cunning, cruel, and thoroughly evil. A grand strategic thinker, she saw all other beings as pawns in her game. The only entity she admired was Makuta, and her time on Metru Nui was spent devising a means of rescuing him from his prison. Roodaka could be subtle, scheming, and capable of brilliantly complex plans one moment, and irrational and violent the next. Her favored approach to problems was to work on the weak spot of an opponent and twist them until they were willing to do her dirty work for her. Roodaka enjoyed the loyalty of the BOGGARAK who made up her personal guard, but many of the other Visorak feared and hated her.

EQUIPMENT

Roodaka carried a Kanoka disk launcher. Her disk was capable of causing instantaneous, permanent mutation of whomever it struck. She also carried a shard of the solid PROTODERMIS that imprisoned Makuta.

ROPORAK [ROE-poe-RACK]:
One of the six breeds of VISORAK who invaded METRU NUI. Roporak have the power to blend in with their surroundings, becoming virtually invisible. This makes them excellent spies for the horde. Their RHOTUKA SPINNERS can disrupt the function of living creatures, causing an abrupt "power outage" effect. Of all Visorak, Roporak are capable of launching their spinners the farthest distance.

ROPORAK

RORZAKH [ROAR-zahk]:
VAHKI model assigned to ONU-METRU on METRU NUI. These mechanoids were relentless, willing to continue a pursuit even to their own destruction. Their Staffs of Presence allowed them to see and hear whatever their target saw or heard. The Rorzakh used this power on TOA WHENUA to lead him, NUJU, and ONEWA into a trap in the PRISON

RORZAKH

OF THE DARK HUNTERS. The TOA METRU also battled Rorzakh in the COLISEUM after being branded traitors by MAKUTA in his disguise as DUME.

RUKI [ROO-kee]:

Small fish found in the waters around both METRU NUI and MATA NUI (2). Although no threat individually, schools of Ruki had been seen to drive off TARAKAVA and other much larger creatures. Their powerful jaws made them a consistent problem for GA-MATORAN, since they would chew through nets, dams, and any other object they might find in the water.

RURU [ROO-ROO]:

KANOHI Mask of Night Vision. The Great Mask version, worn by TOA WHENUA, allowed him not only to see in the dark but to have X-ray vision as well. The Noble Ruru, worn by Whenua as a TURAGA, allowed night vision only.

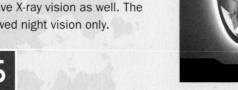

RURU

S

SAND SNIPE:

A small, biting insect found in PO-METRU. Sand snipes could be annoying creatures, often burrowing beneath MATORAN armor and biting the organic PROTODERMIS underneath. Fortunately, they were easy to trap. Living in a barren METRU, they were enthralled by the sight of liquid protodermis and would march headlong into any puddle and promptly drown. This odd quirk led to the Matoran saying "foolish as a sand snipe."

SAND TARAKAVA [TAH-rah-KAH-vah]:

This smaller cousin of the aquatic TARAKAVA made its home in the sandy wastes of PO-METRU and PO-WAHI. Its usual hunting method was to lurk beneath the sand and then strike when prey passed near. It was a natural enemy of the KIKANALO, usually preying on the weak or injured in a herd.

SCHOOLS:

GA-METRU was the educational center of METRU NUI and boasted many schools. Among the subjects taught here were PROTODERMIS PURIFICATION, translation, and MATORAN history. Ga-Metru employed Matoran from other districts to do menial tasks so that GA-MATORAN could focus on their studies. Prior to becoming a TOA, NOKAMA was a teacher in a Ga-Metru school and VHISOLA was one of her students.

SCULPTURE FIELDS:

Great, barren plains in PO-METRU used for the creation and display of massive statues. Anything too big to be carved in an enclosed space is worked on here. Portions of the Sculpture Fields became unstable due to RAHI activity, and MATORAN were barred from entire sections. TOA ONEWA pursued AHKMOU through the Sculpture Fields. The Po-Metru GREAT DISK was found embedded in a rock pillar here.

SCULPTURE FIELDS

SEA SPIDER:

An amphibious RAHI that first appeared off GA-METRU after the VISORAK invasion. The RAHAGA rapidly discovered that the sea spiders were a natural predator of the Visorak, one of the only ones known. Sea spider venom shrinks its prey to a more manageable size. The creature then throws its target into stasis using its spinner. Sea spiders have never been spotted anywhere on or around MATA NUI (2).

SEA SPIDER

SECTOR THREE:

An area of LE-METRU just across the PROTODERMIS canals from TA-METRU. It had long been the site of numerous CHUTE breakdowns, which were eventually tied to the MORBUZAKH. LE-MATORAN repair squads who traveled there vanished, never to return, even when protected by VAHKI. Despite its reputation, ORKAHM allowed himself to be lured there by AHKMOU, part of the latter's efforts to get his hands on the six GREAT DISKS. Orkahm walked into a trap there and had to be rescued by TOA MATAU.

SEEKING:

The name given to the study of prophecies in KO-KORO.

SENTRAKH (sen-TRAHK):

The unliving guardian of the SHADOWED ONE's keep. Sentrakh possesses four different powers — *illusion, darkness, molecular rearrangement, mind wipe,* and the RHOTUKA SPINNER power of *dematerialization* (which can cause targets to become insubstantial ghostlike figures, unable to touch or be touched by anything physical). Sentrakh is singlemindedly devoted to the Shadowed One and has in the past been used to discipline DARK HUNTERS who have failed in their tasks. It is said that the Shadowed One's isle is haunted by the living ghosts of those Dark Hunters.

SHADOW TOA (TOE-ah):

Dark essences of GALI, KOPAKA, LEWA, ONUA, POHATU, and TAHU, given independent life by MAKUTA. The Shadow Toa were unleashed against their counterparts shortly after the TOA arrived on MATA NUI (2) as a test of their power. Faced with essentially fighting themselves, the Toa still managed to triumph by acknowledging that the darkness was a part of them, just as it was a part of all beings. This realization enabled the Toa to reabsorb the Shadow Toa back into their bodies, ending their threat.

SHADOWED ONE:

Legendary leader of the DARK HUNTERS, the Shadowed One is said to reside in another land, from which he directs the actions of his mercenaries. His power is rumored to be second only to that of the BROTHERHOOD OF MAKUTA. It was he who dispatched NIDHIKI and KREKKA to METRU NUI in answer to MAKUTA's summons, but he remains unaware that Makuta was responsible for the disappearance of both his operatives. He believes the TOA defeated Nidhiki and Krekka, and he has vowed vengeance upon all Toa, everywhere. The Shadowed One's staff can create solid, crystalline PROTODERMIS, and his RHOTUKA SPINNER induces temporary madness.

SIDORAK (sih-DOAR-ack):
King of the VISORAK horde.

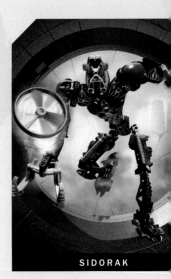
SIDORAK

HISTORY

In his early life, Sidorak was a minor power in a land filled with conflict. He rapidly discovered that by claiming credit for victories won by those beneath him, he could advance in the eyes of his leaders. If a commander objected to the credit being stolen, Sidorak would simply dispatch him on a dangerous mission from which he would not return.

This talent for treachery attracted the attention of MAKUTA. Sidorak was made one of that powerful being's lieutenants, along with ROODAKA. He immediately saw the advantage that might be gained if he and Roodaka formed an alliance, but she refused to agree. Instead, the two ended up competing for Makuta's favor, with Roodaka doing her best to hamper Sidorak.

When the TOA HAGAH turned on Makuta, and Roodaka transformed them into RAHAGA, Sidorak claimed credit for the idea. Makuta rewarded his cleverness by making him king of the Visorak, while Roodaka became viceroy. Sidorak grew into the job, becoming a respected leader of the horde and carrying them to many victories. He continued to hope that he and Roodaka could join forces at a some point, a wish that may have blinded him to her true intentions.

POWERS

Sidorak's primary power was his strength. Although not at the level of KEETONGU, he was far stronger than a TOA. He was also an excellent strategist and tactician, having masterminded a number of Visorak campaigns. He was skilled at manipulation, so much so, in fact, that it never occurred to him that he might be manipulated in turn.

PERSONALITY

Sidorak was not a king who hid in a fortress — he preferred to be out leading his Visorak into battle. Deep down, though, he knew that he had not really earned the position he held, and it made him try that much harder to be a successful and ruthless conqueror. He came across most of the time as confident, strong, and in control. He had done a good job at hiding from the Visorak any doubts he may have had about his leadership. Unfortunately, he had not managed to hide them from Roodaka.

EQUIPMENT

Sidorak carried a herding blade which could be used to communicate orders to the Visorak in the field. He also carried a RHOTUKA LAUNCHER with an *obedience* spinner which would force whoever it struck to obey his commands.

SILVER CHUTE SPIDER:
A voracious predatory arachnid whose favorite hunting ground was near METRU NUI CHUTES. Its favorite prey was the GUKKO bird, which it would trap using fast-acting paralyzing venom

in its webs. GA-MATORAN made a study of this creature's incredibly light and strong webbing, with the hope of duplicating it, but their efforts were unsuccessful. Interestingly, silver chute spiders were the only RAHI not hunted by the VISORAK hordes. As a result, many survived to make their way to LE-WAHI on MATA NUI (2).

SILVER CHUTE SPIDER

SONIC SHIELD:
Tool carried by KOHRAK-KAL. This shield could create a sonic barrier that responded to blows with a sound so loud it could stun a TOA NUVA.

SPINY STONE APE:
A tremendously strong RAHI that lived in caves in PO-METRU and PO-WAHI. Aggressive only when threatened, the stone ape relied on its claws, blade-tipped tail, and spiny armor when fighting. Its normal reaction to an intruder was to roll up into a defensive ball and growl, warning away anyone foolish enough to enter its lair. Stone apes favored the caves carved out of the canyon walls by ROCK RAPTORS.

SPIRIT STARS:
Points of light said to appear in the sky to represent TOA. Following the path of a spirit star in the night sky above METRU NUI enabled Toa VAKAMA, Toa NOKAMA, and Toa MATAU to find the prison in which LHIKAN was being held. After the TOA METRU defeated MAKUTA, Lhikan's spirit star split into six new ones, representing the new Toa.
Six stars above MATA NUI (2) were believed to represent TAHU and his team of Toa. The appearance of a seventh star above the island heralded the coming of TAKANUVA, the Toa of Light.

STAFF OF DARKNESS:
Tool carried by MAKUTA through which he could channel his dark energies. Makuta used this as a sort of KOLHII STAFF in his battle with TAKANUVA.

STAFF OF LIGHT:
Tool carried by TAKANUVA. In the final combat with MAKUTA, Takanuva used this as a KOLHII STAFF, catching and hurling balls of energy with it.

STARS, METRU NUI (MET-troo NOO-ee):
A sky full of stars seemed to light the METRU NUI night, despite the fact that the city was inside a hollow cavern. It is clear that these stars were not the same as those in the skies above MATA NUI (2), but exactly what their true nature might have been has never been discovered. Still, beings as diverse as KO-MATORAN scholars and MAKUTA himself studied the stars to divine prophecies of the future and the will of the GREAT SPIRIT MATA NUI (1).

STONE HAMMER:
TURAGA ONEWA's tool and badge of office.

STONE RAT:
Voracious rodents who lived beneath the ground in METRU NUI. A stone rat plague once struck TA-METRU when the creatures were driven from their nests by NUI-RAMA. Later, the TOA METRU encountered stone rats while searching for KRAHKA.

SUBTERRANEAN WORM:
Great, blind, pale, white-tentacled creatures that lived in the deepest tunnels beneath ONU-WAHI on MATA NUI (2). They were believed to eat raw PROTODERMIS and the appearance of one was enough to shut down an Onu-Matoran mine for good. ONUA NUVA and WHENUA encountered one of these creatures while searching for KANOHI NUVA masks. Onua defeated it by slamming two rocks together and deafening the beast.

SUUKORAK

SUUKORAK [SUE-coe-rack]:
One of the six breeds of VISORAK that invaded METRU NUI. Suukorak have a natural resistance to cold and the ability to slow their life processes down to almost zero, making it extremely difficult for others to detect their presence. Suukorak RHOTUKA SPINNERS create an electrical field around a target. The field surrounds and moves with the target, gradually shrinking as time goes on. It is impossible to escape the field without sustaining a shock, so a prisoner's only hope is that the field dissipates before it contracts completely.

TA [TAH]:
A Matoran prefix which means "fire."

TA-KINI [TAH-kih-NEE]:
A temple dedicated to TAHU located in TA-WAHI on MATA NUI (2).

TA-KORO [TAH-koar-OH]:
Village on MATA NUI (2) and home to the TA-MATORAN. Ta-Koro was located in the Lake of Fire and its citizens lived in homes made of cooled lava. A small lava stream flowed through the village, providing it with heat. Ta-Koro was governed by TURAGA VAKAMA and protected by TOA TAHU and the TA-KORO GUARD. The village was destroyed by the RAHKSHI, vanishing beneath the lava without a trace. It has not been rebuilt.

TA-KORO GUARD [tah-KOAR-oh]:
Defense force that protected the village of TA-KORO against all threats. The Guard was led by JALLER.

TA-MATORAN [TAH-mat-OAR-an]:
A resident of TA-KORO or TA-METRU. Ta-Matoran commonly had red armor and wore red or yellow masks. On METRU NUI, most Ta-Matoran worked in foundries and forges, creating KANOHI masks and other items for use throughout the city. On MATA NUI (2), many Ta-Matoran were lava farmers or members of the TA-KORO GUARD.

TA-METRU [TAH-MET-troo]:

Home of the "makers" on METRU NUI, where molten PROTODERMIS was fashioned by skilled workers into tools, KANOHI masks, and other items used throughout the city. Ta-Metru was filled with factories and foundries, and the temperature in the METRU was too hot for most other MATORAN to handle. The skies above Ta-Metru were traditionally filled with steam and smoke, making it a place residents of other metru preferred to avoid. Ta-Metru was the site of the GREAT FURNACE, where the final battle with the MORBUZAKH plant took place. The FIRE PITS, PROTODERMIS RECLAMATION YARD, PROTODERMIS RECLAMATION FURNACE, and VAKAMA'S FOUNDRY could all be found here. One of the six GREAT DISKS was hidden in a fire pit in this metru.

TA-SUVA [TAH-soo-VAH]:

A shrine to TAHU NUVA in TA-KORO. KANOHI masks and Tahu Nuva's symbol were kept here. BOHROK-KAL stole the NUVA SYMBOL from the Ta-Suva, robbing Tahu Nuva of his elemental power of fire. The suva was destroyed, along with the village itself, by the RAHKSHI.

TA-WAHI [TAH-wah-HEE]:

The hot, volcanic region surrounding TA-KORO on MATA NUI (2). Lava falls, rivers of molten magma, and other fiery features can be found here, flowing from the mouth of the MANGAI volcano. It is home to TA-MATORAN and scores of RAHI that thrive on heat and flame. TOA TAHU's canister washed up on the shore of Ta-Wahi. This region was the site of one of the first BOHROK attacks, as well as a devastating onslaught by the RAHKSHI that resulted in the destruction of Ta-Koro. The largest Matoran KOLHII stadium is also located here.

TAHNOK [TAH-nahk]:

One of the six breeds of BOHROK, insectlike mechanoids controlled by KRANA that menaced the island of MATA NUI (2). The Tahnok were tied to the element of fire and their FIRE SHIELDS could melt any substance. Dangerous and unpredictable, the Tahnok were the most aggressive of all the Bohrok swarms. They were part of the initial attack on TA-KORO and a subsequent one on PO-KORO. Later, a swarm of Tahnok (minus their krana) was led by TAHU NUVA against the BOHROK-KAL. They were sent into space due to NUHVOK-KAL's negation of gravity and remain in orbit. The rest of the Tahnok returned to their nests after the coming of the Bohrok-Kal and remain there still.

TAHNOK

TAHNOK-KAL [TAH-nahk-KAHL]:

One of the six mutant BOHROK who made up the BOHROK-KAL. Its tool was an electricity shield, able to be used both for defense and to hurl lightning bolts. After being fed Toa power via the TOA NUVA symbols (see BOHROK-KAL), Tahnok-Kal was overloaded with electricity and its moving parts fused together.

TAHNOK-KAL

TAHNOK VA [TAH-nahk VAH]:

One of the six BOHROK VA, Tahnok Va were connected to the fire element. They used their FIRESTAFFS to defend themselves in combat and to light their way through the dark BOHROK tunnels. Upon realizing the Tahnok Va were not living creatures, the TA-MATORAN diverted a lava stream into the path of some of the couriers and melted them.

TAHNOK VA

TAHTORAK [tah-TOAR-ack]:

The largest land RAHI ever seen in METRU NUI, the intelligent, reptilian Tahtorak stood over 40 feet tall. It was more than powerful enough to destroy a city, with a single sweep of its tail able to bring down entire buildings. It is believed that the Tahtorak was once a herd animal in another land and was mysteriously transported or teleported to Metru Nui.

It made a home far beneath the ARCHIVES maintenance tunnels, where it slumbered. It was awakened by the TOA METRU's battle with the KRAHKA and later tore its way through the surface, demanding to know "the answer." (RAHAGA POUKS later theorized that the answer it seeks is just how it ended up in Metru Nui, so far from its home.) The TOA defeated it by weakening the ground beneath its feet, sending it plunging back down below.

The Tahtorak reappeared after the VISORAK invaded the city. Summoned by Krahka, the great beast allied itself with her, the Toa, and the Rahaga. The Tahtorak fought a great battle against the monstrous ZIVON, which ended when both creatures and Krahka were transported into the zone of darkness by a KAHGARAK spinner. None of the three have been seen since.

TAHTORAK

TAHU/TAHU NUVA [TAH-hoo/TAH-hoo NOO-vah]:

TOA of Fire on MATA NUI (2), leader of the TOA NUVA, and protector of TA-KORO.

HISTORY

Nothing is known about Tahu's history prior to his first appearance on the island of Mata Nui. He was one of six Toa who had been floating in the ocean around that land for 1000 years. They were inside unique canisters and each was partially disassembled. A signal unwittingly sent by TAKUA called the canisters to shore. Tahu emerged on the coast of TA-WAHI, assembled himself, and headed into the CHARRED FOREST. There he walked into a RAHI trap set by JALLER. The MATORAN set him free upon realizing that this was indeed the Toa whose arrival they had awaited for so long.

Tahu rapidly made contact with the other five Toa — GALI, KOPAKA, LEWA, ONUA, and POHATU. Together and separately, they searched for KANOHI masks and battled the Rahi servants of MAKUTA. Over time, Tahu came to be acknowledged as the group's leader, though that role did not always sit well with the others.

The Toa of Fire led his friends into battle against the SHADOW TOA and later against Makuta himself. He also briefly merged with Pohatu and Onua to form the TOA KAITA called AKAMAI. During the invasion of the BOHROK, Tahu began to display a recklessness and lack of patience that grated on the nerves of Kopaka. At one point, Tahu's impetuous nature led to his being trapped in a TAHNOK nest. Only by using his powers to superheat the air in the nest and cause an explosion was he able to escape. (It was during this period that Tahu was briefly stripped of his mask and forced to wear a parasitic KRANA, but this is an encounter he has refused to speak about.)

Following the defeat of the twin Bohrok queens, the BAHRAG, the six Toa were transformed by ENERGIZED PROTODERMIS into TOA NUVA. Tahu Nuva grew, if anything, more overconfident

TAHU

and arrogant. This led to arguments with Kopaka and eventually a decision to split up the team. None of the Toa Nuva could know that this would leave them vulnerable to a later attack by the BOHROK-KAL. It was Tahu's potentially dangerous use of the Kanohi VAHI, the Great Mask of Time, that helped to end that threat.

Despite how close the Toa came to being defeated in that instance, Tahu Nuva had not yet learned a badly needed lesson about unity. His stubbornness alienated him from Gali. When the Rahkshi attacked Ta-Koro, Tahu Nuva attempted to challenge them on his own. The result was defeat, the destruction of the village, and a scratch from the poisonous LEHRAK. The poison ravaged Tahu Nuva's system, causing him to easily become enraged and turn on his friends. It took Kopaka's ice power to stop his rampage, and the power of all five Toa Nuva to remove the poison.

Their unity now restored, the Toa Nuva challenged the Rahkshi and won with the aid of TAKANUVA, the Toa of Light.

Tahu Nuva and other Toa Nuva are now journeying back to Metru Nui with the TURAGA and Matoran.

POWERS

Tahu was the master of heat and flame. In his time on Mata Nui (2), he created everything from small brush fires to raging infernos; used his flame to fuse a wall of sand into glass; superheated the air in an enclosed space until it caused an explosion; and created cages and other structures made of flame. Tahu also had in theory the ability to absorb all heat and flame in an area into himself, but never demonstrated this skill. He was an accomplished lava surfer and has a natural resistance to extreme heat.

PERSONALITY

Tahu took being a leader extremely seriously. This often caused him to be impatient with the other Toa, too quick to take on dangerous tasks, and not inclined to include his comrades in strategy sessions. While very protective of the other Toa, especially Gali, he had a habit of plunging into risky situations without waiting for a plan. He could be fierce, short-tempered, and stubborn, but was also an extremely brave and loyal Toa.

EQUIPMENT

Tahu carried a fire sword and (as Tahu Nuva) twin magma swords. He most often wore a HAU or HAU NUVA, the Great Mask of Shielding. He was also the only one of the six Toa to ever wear the Kanohi Vahi, the Great Mask of Time.

TAIPU (TAY-poo):

Taipu was a junior ONU-MATORAN archivist of no particular renown on METRU NUI. On MATA NUI (2), he served as a miner in ONU-KORO. He first met TAKUA while participating in a digging project to construct a tunnel to LE-WAHI. He informed the newcomer about Onu-Matoran mining and what was known about TOA ONUA. Later, Taipu was captured by a swarm of NUI-RAMA and an infected Toa LEWA. Only Onua's intervention saved him. Taipu would later join with Takua, KAPURA, KOPEKE, TAMARU, MACKU, and HAFU in the CHRONICLER's Company and defend KINI-NUI against RAHI attack. He participated in a great battle with various forms of Rahi which ended successfully, thanks to the intervention of the TA-KORO GUARD, the ONU-KORO USSALRY, and the LE-KORO GUKKO BIRD FORCE.

TAKANUVA [TAH-kah-ΠOO-vah]:
The TOA of Light, also known as the "Seventh Toa."

TAKANUVA

HISTORY

Matoran legend stated that in a time of great darkness, a defender would emerge who would wield the power of Light. His coming would be heralded by the discovery of the KANOHI AVOHKII, the Mask of Light. The mask was discovered by a MATORAN named TAKUA. He and his best friend, JALLER, were sent by the TURAGA on a mission to bring the mask to the waiting Toa. The mission proved to be extremely dangerous, as MAKUTA sent his RAHKSHI to find the HERALD of the Seventh Toa and the mask. Takua eventually realized that he was the one destined to become the Toa of Light, and putting on the mask, he was transformed.

As Takanuva, he helped to defeat the Rahkshi. With the assistance of the Toa, he built a vehicle called the USSANUI from Rahkshi parts and used it to travel to Makuta's lair. There light and darkness clashed, until the two powerful beings fell into a pool of ENERGIZED PROTODERMIS and were merged into one entity, TAKUTANUVA.

After being returned to his individual form, Takanuva used his light powers to help illuminate the newly rediscovered METRU NUI. He returned to Mata Nui with the TOA NUVA to oversee the building of transport craft and is currently preparing for the return to Metru Nui. He believes that he has fulfilled his destiny — defeating Makuta — but only time will tell if Takanuva has achieved all that he was meant to achieve.

POWERS

Just as Tahu controls fire and Gali water, Takanuva controls light. He can illuminate the darkness, create blinding flares, focus his power into a laser beam, and create holographic images of himself. He has also been experimenting with other potential powers, such as increased speed and the creation of solid light projections.

PERSONALITY

Although now a Toa, Takanuva has not changed a great deal from when he was Takua. He still has an insatiable curiosity about new things and new places and prefers exploring to doing more mundane work. He is awed by the power and responsibility he has as a Toa and by being in the company of Tahu and his other heroes. He has proven to be a good student of their training, driving himself hard to master his powers. What he has not shared with them is that he secretly worries Makuta will return someday and seek vengeance for the defeat at Takanuva's hands. The Toa of Light is determined to be ready should that happen. Although he has been welcomed into the company of the other Toa, Takanuva still feels most comfortable with his Matoran friends, especially Jaller and HAHLI.

EQUIPMENT

Takanuva carries the STAFF OF LIGHT, which he can use to channel and direct his powers. He wears the Kanohi Avohkii, the Mask of Light.

TAKEA [TAH-kay-AH]:

An ocean predator, the Takea's name means "king of sharks" in MATORAN (2). Takea consider virtually everything in the water an enemy, from TARAKAVA to Matoran fishing boats. The TOA METRU witnessed Takea sharks attacking prehistoric beasts along the underground river that linked METRU NUI to MATA NUI (2).

TAKU [TAH-koo]:

A small, ducklike bird distantly related to the GUKKO. It is best known for its ability to dive deep beneath the water in search of fish.

TAKUA [tah-KOO-ah]:

A TA-MATORAN, former CHRONICLER, and currently TAKANUVA, the TOA of Light.
Little is known about Takua's life on METRU NUI. He worked in TA-METRU as a toolmaker and operated a small business offering souvenirs from other METRU he had picked up in his wanderings. Unfortunately, since he often made these trips during his working hours, he attracted a lot of attention from VAHKI patrols. A running joke in Ta-Metru was that an entire squad was assigned just to keep watch on Takua.

TAKUA

On MATA NUI (2), Takua continued to be more interested in exploring than working. But his life changed when the TURAGA asked him to travel the island and collect the TOA STONES. These had been hidden long before by the TOA METRU, but the Turaga believed that MAKUTA might attempt to steal them. Takua carried out his task and brought all six stones to the KINI-NUI. When he placed them there, beams of light shot up into the sky. Takua was carried high in the air by one of the beams, then slammed onto the ground, the blow resulting in amnesia. Without realizing it, Takua had succeeded in summoning TAHU and the rest of the Toa from the sea, where they had been floating in canisters for 1000 years.

Stripped of his memory, Takua stumbled into more adventures as he wandered the island. He helped to save GA-MATORAN trapped underwater, aided ONU-MATORAN miners, aided PO-MATORAN dealing with infected COMET balls, and helped save the LE-MATORAN and Toa LEWA from NUI-RAMA. As a reward for his service, he was named CHRONICLER of the Toa.
One of his first acts was to form the CHRONICLER's Company to aid in the defense of the island. When the Toa went to battle Makuta underground, the Chronicler's Company was assigned to defend Kini-Nui from RAHI attack. Before going below, Toa GALI established a mind link with Takua so he would be aware of all that went on and could keep an accurate record.
After the defeat of the Rahi, Takua journeyed down to MANGAIA to witness the Toa's fight with Makuta. He saw both this and the awakening of the BOHROK, and barely escaped with his life. During the Bohrok invasion, Takua aided the Le-Matoran and the Ga-Matoran. He and his best friend, JALLER, journeyed with Tahu for a brief time after the appearance of the BOHROK-KAL.
Takua's greatest adventure began when he wandered off before a KOLHII match and found a lava cave. Fascinated by a strange stone marker, he was investigating it when Jaller found him.

Stumbling, he dropped the marker, which dissolved in the lava to reveal the KANOHI AVOHKII, the legendary Mask of Light.

Although the mask's illumination clearly fell on Takua, marking him as the HERALD of the Seventh Toa, he did not want the responsibility. He convinced the Turaga that it was Jaller who was meant to be the herald. Together, the two were sent by Turaga VAKAMA to find the Toa of Light and bring him his mask. Accompanied by PEWKU, Takua's pet USSAL crab, they set out. Their journey took them through LE-WAHI and KO-WAHI and ONU-WAHI, dodging RAHKSHI attacks along the way. It became clear that the Rahkshi were seeking the herald and the mask. Takua continued to refuse to accept responsibility for the quest, even going so far as to quit the journey entirely at one point after Makuta warned him that continuing would cost Jaller his life. It was, in fact, Jaller's sacrifice that saved Takua from the TURAHK and made the MATORAN realize what he must do. As Jaller lay dying, Takua donned the Mask of Light and transformed into Toa TAKANUVA. Vakama later told him that after being a Chronicler for so long, "you have finally found your own story."

TAKUTANUVA [tah-KOO-tah-ΠOO-vah]:

A merged entity formed when TAKANUVA and MAKUTA fell into a pool of ENERGIZED PROTODERMIS together during their battle. The creature that emerged had a mask formed of half the KANOHI AVOHKII and half the Kanohi KRAAHKAN. Due to the fact that Makuta's mask had been torn off him just prior to immersion, Takutanuva was apparently dominated by Takanuva's more benevolent personality. Takutanuva used his great strength to open the gateway leading from Makuta's lair to METRU NUI. He then used a portion of Makuta's life force to revive the dead JALLER. The gateway immediately collapsed on the weakened Takutanuva. The Toa of Light survived, his body reconstituted by the power of light, but of Makuta there was no sign.

TAMARU [tah-MAH-roo]:

A friendly, fast-talking LE-MATORAN, Tamaru once dreamed of being an AIRSHIP pilot in METRU NUI. Unfortunately, he washed out of training due to a fear of heights. He later opened his own shop, Tamaru's Transports, renting and selling used vehicles and failed test-track prototypes.

On MATA NUI (2), Tamaru similarly failed to become a GUKKO rider and ended up working as the keeper of the LE-KORO throwing disk range. He served as part of the Chronicler's Company, a small force assembled by TAKUA to protect KINI-NUI from RAHI attacks. Later, he was one of only two Le-Matoran who were not captured by the BOHROK and fitted with a mind-controlling KRANA. He joined with the other Le-Matoran, KONGU, along with Takua and NUPARU to lure TOA LEWA, TURAGA MATAU, and the rest of the Le-Matoran into a trap and remove their krana.

TARAKAVA [tah-RAH-kah-VAH]:

TARAKAVA

Lizardlike amphibians who live in shallow waters, around both GA-METRU and GA-KORO. Their common hunting method is to lurk beneath the water until a target comes by and then strike with their powerful forearms. Tarakava tend to avoid deep water, as it is home to TAKEA sharks and other natural enemies of this RAHI. These beasts were among the creatures used by MAKUTA against the TOA and MATORAN on MATA NUI (2). Although the Rahi caused a great deal of destruction, GA-MATORAN on Mata Nui showed a willingness to care for those Tarakava who had been freed from Makuta's dark influence.

TARAKAVA NUI (tah-RAH-kah-VAH NOO-ee):
A mutant version of the TARAKAVA and one of the last creatures created by MAKUTA and the ENERGIZED PROTODERMIS ENTITY. The Tarakava Nui was responsible for wrecking early efforts to build the village of GA-KORO on MATA NUI (2), before it was temporarily driven off by TURAGA NOKAMA and the GA-MATORAN.

TEHUTTI (tuh-HOO-tee):
ONU-MATORAN archivist who discovered the location of the ONU-METRU GREAT DISK. Initially, Tehutti planned to give the disk as a gift to the ARCHIVES, thus securing his reputation as a master archivist. But when NIDHIKI threatened him, the MATORAN thought better of his plan. Rescued from a wild RAHKSHI by TOA WHENUA, Tehutti led him and Toa NUJU to the proper section of the Archives where the disk could be found.
Later, Tehutti joined with AHKMOU, EHRYE, NUHRII, ORKAHM, and VHISOLA to form the MATORAN NUI and assist the TOA METRU against the MORBUZAKH. After they had split back into their separate forms, Tehutti departed for Onu-Metru. He was captured on the way by VAHKI and placed in a MATORAN SPHERE. Evidence was later discovered that Tehutti may have been destined to become a Toa of Earth.
He would later be rescued by the Toa Metru and transported to MATA NUI (2), where he worked as a miner.

TEHUTTI

TEST TRACK:

TEST TRACK

A portion of the MOTO-HUB in LE-METRU devoted to testing new land vehicles. MATAU was a frequent visitor here when he was a MATORAN, often volunteering to test the latest creations. Like the Moto-Hub in general, the test track was badly damaged by the earthquake that struck METRU NUI. Matau was using the test track when LHIKAN gave him a TOA STONE.

TIRO CANYON (tee-ROE):
A gorge in the desert of PO-WAHI on MATA NUI (2). POHATU, GALI, ONUA, and KOPAKA combined forces to trap a swarm of TAHNOK here and rob them of their KRANA.

TOA (TOE-ah):
Heroes who serve the GREAT SPIRIT MATA NUI (1), defend the MATORAN and other innocent beings, and honor the three virtues: Unity, Duty, and Destiny. All Toa seem to have certain things in common, including the ability to use Great KANOHI Masks of Power, control of a single elemental power, and possession of a tool to focus that power. Toa commonly operate in groups of six, although smaller and larger groups have been known to exist when circumstances dictate. Certain Toa are known to have begun their lives as Matoran, while others may have been Toa for the entirety of their existence. Known means of transforming from Matoran to Toa include via the power of TOA STONES (the TOA METRU) and by donning the Mask of Light (TAKANUVA). Whether these are the only ways a Matoran can become a Toa is unknown.

Toa are said to have a destiny to fulfill. Once they have done so, they will at some point be presented with a great choice. If they choose to sacrifice their Toa power for the greater good, then they will be transformed into TURAGA, respected leaders of the Matoran. If they choose to retain their power, they can remain as Toa indefinitely. Toa have been active on METRU NUI, MATA NUI (2), and in numerous other lands. Toa have faced numerous foes including MAKUTA, the RAHKSHI, the BOHROK, the BOHROK-KAL, the MORBUZAKH, KARZAHNI (2), the RAHI, the DARK HUNTERS, ROODAKA, SIDORAK, and KRAHKA, among others. Their greatest and most persistent enemies to date have been Makuta and the Dark Hunters.

Known Toa include BOMONGA, DUME, GAAKI, GALI, IRUINI, KOPAKA, KUALUS, LEWA, LHIKAN, MATAU, NIDHIKI, NOKAMA, NORIK, NUJU, ONEWA, ONUA, POHATU, POUKS, TAHU, VAKAMA, and WHENUA (see individual entries).

TOA HAGAH [TOE-ah HAH-gah]:

Name given to the six elite TOA whose job was to safeguard MAKUTA. Each Toa Hagah wore unique armor that identified him or her as a member of this special group. The Toa Hagah later discovered that Makuta was oppressing and enslaving MATORAN and turned against both him and the BROTHERHOOD OF MAKUTA. They were later turned into RAHAGA by ROODAKA. The six Toa Hagah were BOMONGA, GAAKI, IRUINI, KUALUS, NORIK, and POUKS.

TOA HORDIKA [TOE-ah hoar-DEE-kah]:

Name given to the six TOA METRU who were transformed into half hero, half beast forms by the venom of the VISORAK. The Toa Hordika were equipped with new tools and KANOKA LAUNCHERS, but had to constantly fight their own bestial sides. They challenged the Visorak and aided the RAHAGA in their search for KEETONGU.

TOA KAITA [TOE-ah KIGH-ee-TAH]:

Two distinct beings formed by the merging of the six TOA. WAIRUHA was created when GALI, KOPAKA, and LEWA combined, and AKAMAI by the joining of TAHU, ONUA, and POHATU. The Toa Kaita were first seen by Gali in a vision. Later, the Toa chose to bring them into being to defeat the MANAS guardians of MAKUTA. They have not been seen to form Kaita since that time.

Although the TOA METRU also had the potential to form Toa Kaita, they never did so simply because they did not know how to accomplish the feat.

TOA KAITA NUVA [TOE-ah KIGH-ee-TAH NOO-vah]:

Two distinct beings who could have been formed by the merging of the six TOA NUVA. Although the potential for such a union existed, the Toa Nuva are not known to have ever joined in this way.

TOA METRU [TOE-ah MET-troo]:

Name given to the six TOA heroes who defended METRU NUI against MAKUTA, the MORBUZAKH, and the DARK HUNTERS. The six Toa Metru were MATAU, NOKAMA, NUJU, ONEWA, VAKAMA, and WHENUA. It is believed that these six were the first Toa to have this designation, as the previous Toa serving in Metru Nui were not native to that city (see LHIKAN and NIDHIKI).

TOA METRU

TOA NUVA (TOE-ah NOO-vah):

Heroes gifted with greater strength, stronger armor, and greater control of their elemental powers than ordinary TOA possess. Toa Nuva also have the ability to use KANOHI NUVA, masks that allow the wearer to share their power with those in close proximity. The only known means of transforming a Toa into a Toa Nuva is via exposure to ENERGIZED PROTODERMIS. Only six Toa Nuva have ever been known to exist: GALI NUVA, KOPAKA NUVA, LEWA NUVA, ONUA NUVA, POHATU NUVA, and TAHU NUVA.

Originally Toa on MATA NUI (2), these six heroes were immersed in energized protodermis shortly after their defeat of the BAHRAG. The experience transformed them and made them more powerful than before. Although that enhanced power for a time threatened to shatter their unity, they were able to combine forces to defeat the BOHROK-KAL and the RAHKSHI. They are currently preparing to lead the TURAGA and MATORAN back to METRU NUI.

TOA STONES (TOE-ah):

Powerful relics that have loomed large in the history of the Matoran civilization. From all evidence, it appears that Toa stones are ordinary rocks until they are invested with some portion of a TOA's power. Once so invested, they seem always to be linked to the creation of or the coming of Toa heroes. Two sets of Toa stones are currently on record as existing. Toa LHIKAN shared his power with six stones in METRU NUI, which were later used to transform six MATORAN into the TOA METRU. Those same Toa Metru later put a portion of their power into six more stones and hid them on the island of MATA NUI (2), in places they believed only a true Toa could reach. One thousand years later, a Matoran named TAKUA found the stones and placed them on the KINI-NUI, unwittingly triggering a signal that brought TAHU and five other Toa to shore. Whether more Toa stones exist elsewhere is unknown.

TOWERS OF THOUGHT:

Special structures in the METRU NUI district of KO-METRU intended for scholarly projects requiring absolute silence. A squad of VAHKI KEERAKH was always in the area to insure that the work of the MATORAN in the Towers of Thought was not disturbed.

TRANSPORT CARTS:

Wheeled vehicles used for transporting exhibits through the subterranean tunnels of the ARCHIVES.

TREN KROM BREAK:

An area marked by lava streams outside of TA-KORO, site of a number of lava farms and IGNALU lava surfing competitions.

TRIDENT OF NOKAMA (noh-KAH-mah):

TURAGA NOKAMA's tool and badge of office. It was crafted to resemble the tridents that GA-MATORAN used to catch fish in GA-METRU. Nokama carved it while still a TOA from the bones of a MAKUTA FISH.

TUNNEL STALKER:

A gigantic desert RAHI from PO-METRU known for its unusual hunting technique. The stalker lurks in tunnels just below the sand, with its bladed tail poised to strike. When it picks up movement from above, it lunges up through the ground and traps whatever luckless creature was going by. Only two specimens of tunnel stalker were ever seen in METRU NUI, one of which was captured by the VAHKI and put in the ARCHIVES. Tunnel stalkers did make scattered appearances in PO-WAHI on MATA NUI (2). In addition to its tail, the tunnel stalker could rely on sharp pincers and mandibles to defend itself.

TUNNELER:
A reptilian creature of PO-METRU capable of taking on the properties of any physical object used against it (a fireball, for example, turns it into a creature of fire). TOA VAKAMA and Toa ONEWA defeated one by tricking it into turning itself to glass. They have appeared periodically in PO-WAHI on MATA NUI (2).

TURAGA (too-RAH-gah):
Leaders of the MATORAN and protectors of the legends of the TOA. Turaga come into being when Toa have fulfilled their destiny and have chosen to sacrifice their Toa power for the greater good. That act leads to the transformation of Toa to Turaga. The city of METRU NUI was led by Turaga DUME, a benevolent leader who was captured and impersonated by MAKUTA for many months. He remains somewhere in the city, comatose inside a silver sphere. The six TOA METRU fulfilled their destiny by saving the Matoran from Makuta and sacrificed their power to awaken those same Matoran from their comas. In that instant, they transformed into Turaga MATAU, Turaga NOKAMA, Turaga NUJU, Turaga ONEWA, Turaga VAKAMA, and Turaga WHENUA. In these forms, they oversaw the construction of the six villages of MATA NUI (2) and helped to defend the Matoran from the attacks of RAHI.

When TAHU and his team of Toa arrived on the island, the Turaga chose to tell them only part of the truth about the past. It was not until the defeat of Makuta and the rediscovery of Metru Nui that the Turaga shared with Tahu and the others the fact that they had once been Toa and that the Matoran had once lived on Metru Nui.

Once a Toa becomes a Turaga, he loses the ability ever to wield Toa power or use Great Masks of Power again. Turaga are able to master Noble Masks of Power and have limited elemental abilities. Physically, they are slightly stronger than Matoran but nowhere near as powerful as Toa. Although generally wise and able leaders, Turaga have shown themselves capable of resentment, deception, and lack of trust. How much recent revelations about their past will damage the relationship between the Turaga and the TOA NUVA remains to be seen.

Known Turaga have included Dume, LHIKAN, Matau, Nokama, Nuju, Onewa, Vakama, and Whenua.

TURAGA NUI (too-RAH-gah NOO-ee):
Legend states that if six TURAGA merge their minds and bodies, they will form a great and wise leader called a Turaga Nui. To this point, the idea remains merely legend, as no Turaga have ever been known to attempt this.

TURAHK (TER-rahk):
One of the six RAHKSHI dispatched by MAKUTA to capture the HERALD of the Seventh TOA. Turahk's job was to fill the TOA NUVA with fear so that they would forget their duty to MATA NUI (1). Using its staff, it could cause a foe to break into a terror-filled run or freeze in fear. Turahk killed JALLER by overwhelming him with fear, but the MATORAN was later brought back to life by TAKUTANUVA. Turahk was defeated by TAKANUVA, the Toa of Light.

TWO-HEADED TARAKAVA [tah-RAH-kah-VAH]:

A mutant aquatic beast (see TARAKAVA) created by the ENERGIZED PROTODERMIS ENTITY. TOA NUJU encountered this creature in the ARCHIVES.

U

USSAL [uss-SUL]:

Crablike creatures long domesticated by MATORAN and used for both racing and transport. Docile and friendly, Ussal seem to genuinely enjoy Matoran company. In METRU NUI, they were used to pull carts and carry heavy loads. On MATA NUI (2), they served much the same purposes, along with being used for sport in Ussal crab races and for defense. The most famous Ussal crab is PEWKU, who originally belonged to a LE-MATORAN named ORKAHM and later became the companion of TAKUA. After Takua became TAKANUVA, he gave Pewku to his best friend, JALLER.

USSAL

USSALRY [uss-SUL-ree]:

The ONU-MATORAN defense force on MATA NUI (2) consisting of MATORAN riding on USSAL crabs. The Ussalry was under the command of an Onu-Matoran named ONEPU. The Ussalry was instrumental in helping to defend KINI-NUI against attacking RAHI and ONU-KORO against invading BOHROK.

USSANUI [uss-ah-NOO-ee]:

Vehicle constructed by TAKANUVA and the TOA NUVA for transport to MAKUTA's lair. The Ussanui was built using RAHKSHI parts and was powered by KRAATA. The vehicle was wrecked when Takanuva used it to break into the lair. Whether or not it will be repaired remains to be seen.

V

VACUUM SHIELD:

Tool carried by LEHVAK-KAL. The vacuum shield could absorb and hold a large amount of air for a long period of time before releasing it in a powerful blast.

VAHI [VAH-hee]:

The Great Mask of Time. This mask was able to either slow down or speed up time around a target. Originally created by TOA VAKAMA using all six of the GREAT DISKS, it was lost in the ocean surrounding METRU NUI during battle with MAKUTA. Vakama later recovered the mask and brought it to MATA NUI (2).
One thousand years later, Vakama, now a TURAGA, gave the mask to TAHU NUVA. The Toa of Fire used the mask to slow down time around the BOHROK-KAL and prevent them from freeing the BAHRAG. Tahu later returned the mask to Vakama's care, where it remains.

VAHKI [VAH-kee]:

Mechanical order enforcement units who patrolled METRU NUI. There were six models of Vahki: BORDAKH, KEERAKH, NUURAKH, RORZAKH, VORZAKH, and ZADAKH. They were put into operation after the failure of the KRALHI experiment. Vahki received recharges of power in their HIVES, located throughout Metru Nui.

VAHI

The primary purpose of a Vahki was to maintain order. This involved anything from containing a RAHI rampage, to pursuing a lawbreaker, to making sure MATORAN worked when they were scheduled to do so. Vahki communicated by speaking the Matoran language at an extremely high speed. Turaga DUME's chambers contained technology that could slow the speech down enough to be understood.

Vahki were capable of three modes of transport: flight, walking on two legs, and walking on four legs using their tools as forelegs. They were equipped with stun staffs, nonlethal devices that acted on the mind rather than the body of the target. The point was to correct behavior without damaging valuable workers.

When the Metru Nui power plant was destroyed by MAKUTA, a power surge struck the hives and destroyed most of the Vahki. Those that survived were altered for the worse. Their speech centers had slowed so that other beings could understand them. Their stun staffs had become incredibly destructive. In addition, their fundamental mission had been warped. They now believed that living things created disorder, and that therefore the way to maintain order was to eliminate anything that lived.

The Vahki were used by Makuta (posing as Dume) to capture Matoran, guard the PRISON OF THE DARK HUNTERS, and battle the TOA METRU. After their transformation, small squads of Vahki continued to patrol the city, often clashing with VISORAK.

VAHKI HUNTER [VAH-kee]:

Massive RAHI who seem to have a particular hatred for machinery. They have been known to use their claws and teeth to demolish VAHKI, FIRE DRONES, and other mechanical creations. Once confined to PO-METRU and TA-METRU, they later spread out all over METRU NUI. Vahki Hunters spent most of their time underground, emerging only to strike before returning to the safety of their tunnels.

VAHKI TRANSPORT [VAH-kee]:

A vehicle propelled by mechanical insectoid legs and used to transport VAHKI squads, KRAAHU, and KRANUA to trouble spots. NOKAMA, VAKAMA, and MATAU snuck onboard a transport while fleeing from the DARK HUNTERS. The transports were being used to carry the MATORAN SPHERES to the COLISEUM. Later, the TOA METRU used a Vahki transport with spheres affixed to the bottom as a boat to escape METRU NUI, and a second transport to sail back again.

VAKAMA [vah-KAH-mah]:

TOA METRU of Fire, guardian of TA-METRU, and later TURAGA of TA-KORO.

Vakama began his life as a TA-MATORAN working in a foundry. Shortly after being promoted to mask maker, he was asked by Turaga DUME (secretly MAKUTA in disguise) to make the KANOHI VAHI, the Mask of Time. Later, he was visited by Toa LHIKAN, who gave him a TOA STONE. Lhikan warned him that dark times were coming to METRU NUI. Before he could explain, NIDHIKI and KREKKA attacked. Lhikan was captured, but not before helping Vakama escape.

Vakama traveled to the GREAT TEMPLE and encountered five other MATORAN — MATAU, NOKAMA, NUJU, ONEWA, and WHENUA. They placed their Toa stones into the Toa suva and were transformed into mighty Toa heroes. Vakama had a vision that the city was in peril and that only finding the six GREAT DISKS would save it.

Despite many dangers, the TOA METRU succeeded in finding the disks, eluding the VAHKI, and destroying the MORBUZAKH plant that threatened the city. But when they went to present the disks to Turaga Dume, he denounced them as impostors and ordered their arrest.

Whenua, Onewa, and Nuju were captured, with Vakama, Nokama, and Matau escaping.

VAKAMA

They survived a battle with Vahki and the DARK HUNTERS on an AIRSHIP, then stowed away on a VAHKI TRANSPORT into PO-METRU. There they fought the Dark Hunters again, formed an alliance with the KIKANALO, and helped to free their three friends and Lhikan, now a Turaga. Vakama believed they had achieved what they set out to do, and was crushed to find out that Lhikan had wanted them to save the Matoran, not him. Already plagued with self-doubt, discovering he had made such a serious error was a blow to his confidence. Despite this, he led the Toa against Makuta and the Dark Hunters. They succeeded in rescuing six Matoran, still in the MATORAN SPHERES in which the Vahki had placed them. Vakama confronted Makuta, using the Vahi he had made by combining the six Great Disks. During the battle, Vakama's inability to control the Vahi placed him in mortal danger. Lhikan intervened at the last moment, taking a blow meant for Vakama and dying as a result. Vakama and Makuta battled to a stalemate until the other Toa Metru arrived and their combined might trapped Makuta behind a wall of solid PROTODERMIS.

The Toa Metru then departed Metru Nui with the six Matoran spheres. After a dangerous journey, they reached the island of MATA NUI (2). There Vakama suggested they create Toa stones and hide them in places on the island only one with the heart of a true Toa could reach. This, he believed, would ensure that a new generation of Toa would follow the Toa Metru someday.

On the return journey to Metru Nui to rescue the rest of the Matoran, Vakama grew short-tempered and frustrated. He blamed himself for Lhikan's death and the fate of the Matoran. Eager to prove he deserved to be a Toa, he recklessly led the Toa Metru into the heart of the city, where they were captured by the VISORAK. The venom of these creatures mutated the Toa into TOA HORDIKA, half hero, half beast. Vakama saw this as another example of his poor leadership, and the other Toa, particularly Matau, blamed him as well.

Vakama's mood was not improved by the discovery of evidence that apparently indicated that NUHRII, a Ta-Matoran, had been destined to become the Toa of Fire. Convinced now that his becoming a Toa Metru was a mistake from the start, Vakama grew increasingly bitter and distant from his friends.

TURAGA VAKAMA

TURAGA VAKAMA

How the Toa Hordika transformed back into Toa Metru and escaped to Mata Nui with the rest of the Matoran has not yet been revealed. But they did make it to that island with close to 1,000 sleeping villagers. The Toa Metru willingly sacrificed their power to awaken the Matoran, transforming into Turaga in the process.

As a Turaga, Vakama supervised the construction of TA-KORO. When TAHU arrived, Vakama welcomed him but did not share any information regarding Metru Nui or his life as a Toa. He revealed details about the BOHROK and RAHKSHI only after those enemies had appeared on Mata Nui.

Finally, after consulting with the other Turaga, Vakama chose to share the tales of Metru Nui with the TOA NUVA. Over the objections of Onewa and Nuju, he has begun relating the history of the Toa Hordika.

Vakama lived in PO-METRU after the destruction of Ta-Koro. He is now journeying with the Toa Nuva, the other Turaga, and the Matoran back to Metru Nui.

POWERS

Vakama was the master of fire. Among the powers he demonstrated on Metru Nui were the ability to create and absorb heat and flame, to survive for a brief period in molten protodermis, and to turn stone red-hot with just a touch of his hand. He was also capable of creating a nova blast, a massive explosion of flame, but wisely refrained from ever doing so. He was skilled with a KANOKA LAUNCHER and had a natural resistance to extreme heat.

PERSONALITY

Vakama was always a reluctant hero. Most of the time, he did not feel he deserved to be a Toa or that he was equal to what was being asked of him. At first, he reacted by hanging back and letting others take the lead. Later, he tried so hard to be a leader that he irritated his fellow Toa. He was the most affected emotionally by the transformation into a Toa Hordika, because he blamed himself for leading the Toa into a trap.

As a Turaga, Vakama was wise and patient, but highly secretive. After realizing that the Matoran had lost their memories of Metru Nui, it had been his suggestion that the Turaga never tell them of the city until some chance existed that they could go back there. It was also his idea to create the fiction of LHII to preserve some fragment of the memory of Lhikan. His experiences with the false Dume made it difficult for him to fully trust powerful beings, including Toa Tahu, so a great deal of time passed before he told the Toa Nuva the truth about the past.

EQUIPMENT

As a Toa Metru, Vakama carried a Kanoka disk launcher that could also be used as a rocket pack for flight. He wore the Kanohi HUNA, the Great Mask of Concealment. As a Turaga, he carried a fire staff and wore the Noble Huna.

VAKAMA'S FOUNDRY [vah-KAH-mah]:

One of a number of forges in TA-METRU in the city of METRU NUI. Vakama used this work area to create KANOHI masks. It was here that he first began work on the VAHI, and this was also the site of TOA LHIKAN's battle with NIDHIKI and KREKKA.

VATUKA [VAH-too-kah]:

A legendary creature of stone. TURAGA WHENUA was once captured by the Vatuka in the tunnels of ONU-WAHI and later rescued by TAKUA. It is now believed the Vatuka may have been a creation of the ENERGIZED PROTODERMIS ENTITY, who once sent a similar stone creature against the TOA METRU.

VENOM FLYERS:

Flying RAHI can be extremely difficult for the largely land-bound VISORAK to capture. That is why each horde travels with a small group of venom flyers. Naturally skilled at aerial maneuvers and captures, the venom flyers make extremely effective hunters. While they lack the extra powers normal Visorak have, their spinners can negate the ability of a target to fly, regardless of whether their ability is based on natural or mechanical means.

VHISOLA [vih-SO-lah]:

A GA-MATORAN. Vhisola was a student of NOKAMA's on METRU NUI and considered the future TOA METRU to be her best friend. But from the beginning, Vhisola was possessive of Nokama and got angry if she spent time with her other friends. When Nokama became a Toa Metru, Vhisola decided to use her knowledge of a GREAT DISK's location to make herself more famous than her friend.

But the plan backfired. Vhisola's knowledge attracted the attention of NIDHIKI, who pursued her in hopes of getting the disk. TOA Nokama ended up saving the MATORAN. Vhisola shared the location of the disk and her theory that the Great Disks could be used to defeat the MORBUZAKH. Later, Vhisola joined with AHKMOU, NUHRII, TEHUTTI, EHRYE, and ORKHAM to form a MATORAN NUI and help in the fight against the Morbuzakh. Shortly after that, she was captured by VAHKI and placed in a sphere that rendered her comatose. Evidence was later discovered that Vhisola may have been destined to become a Toa of Water. Vhisola would later be revived on MATA NUI (2) by the Toa Metru.

VHISOLA

VISORAK [vih-SOAR-ack]:

Spiderlike creatures who operate as a horde under the command of SIDORAK and ROODAKA. The Visorak invaded METRU NUI following the initial departure of the TOA METRU for MATA NUI (2). Their primary focus seemed to be the capture and either containment or mutation of RAHI. Little is known about the Visorak's point of origin, but an ancient tablet in the ARCHIVES states that their name meant "poisonous scourge" in their own language. They were also known as the "stealers of life." The Visorak were well organized, cunning, efficient, and highly skilled at the job of hunting. They had been active in a number of different places before coming to Metru Nui, and had driven herds of Rahi before them. Almost all of the Rahi who were in Metru Nui had arrived there as a result of fleeing the hordes.

The Visorak had four natural tools:

1. **Webbing:** Visorak produced webbing from internal glands and spun it using their mouths. It was strong enough to support a large number of the creatures as they moved from place to place. It could also be used to form a thick cocoon strong enough to hold the most powerful Rahi.

2. **Pincers:** All Visorak had strong, sharp pincers that could inflict a painful bite.

3. **Venom:** Visorak venom was mutagenic, capable of transforming Rahi or other targets into horrifying versions of their former selves. The most common venom delivery system was barbs in the cocoons. Visorak venom turned the Toa Metru into TOA HORDIKA, as well as causing many other mutations among the Rahi. The only known cure for the effects of Visorak venom was the counteragent abilities of KEETONGU.

4. **Rhotuka spinners:** Visorak have natural RHOTUKA LAUNCHERS and can generate wheels of energy by willpower. All Visorak have a default spinner power that can stun and paralyze an opponent, in addition to their other powers.

Although intelligent creatures, Visorak were unable to understand or speak the Matoran (2) language, with one exception (see OOHNORAK). Their relationship with Sidorak was a simple and straightforward one: They gave him their loyalty in return for his providing them with constant opportunities to hunt.

There were six known Visorak breeds: BOGGARAK, KEELERAK, OOHNORAK, ROPORAK, SUUKORAK, and VOHTARAK.

VISORAK caption: VISORAK

VISORAK BATTLE RAM [vih-SOAR-ack]:

A massive siege vehicle capable of shattering the thickest wall in METRU NUI. The battle ram was so large and heavy, it required five VISORAK to pull it.

VOHTARAK

VOHTARAK [VOT-ah-rack]:

One of the six breeds of VISORAK who invaded METRU NUI. Vohtarak had a natural resistance to fire and heat. Their preferred method of attack was to charge wildly while launching multiple spinners. They were also capable of making "berserker charges," during which their outer shells became virtually invulnerable. Vohtarak RHOTUKA SPINNERS caused a burning sensation in a target, so intense that it would distract him from any other action.

VOLO LUTU [VOE-loe LOO-too]:

A launcher that could be used to grab on to objects over great distance. TAKUA used a Volo Lutu launcher in ONU-WAHI during his search for the VUATA MACA CRYSTALS.

VOPORAK [VOE-poe-RACK]:

A huge and powerful servant of the DARK HUNTERS with an intriguing history. He came from an island populated by a highly competitive and prideful species. Anytime any of them succeeded in building something, their neighbors would grow jealous and destroy it. This resulted in a land made barren and a culture that bordered on anarchy.

Voporak might have remained there forever had an emissary of the BROTHERHOOD OF MAKUTA not arrived, seeking a being of power. Seeing that Voporak dominated his region, the Brotherhood selected him for an experiment in mutation. Combining ENERGIZED PROTODERMIS, the RHOTUKA SPINNER of ROODAKA, and possibly other more dangerous ingredients, they succeeded in transforming Voporak into a being sensitive to shifts in time.

Believing it inevitable that one day the KANOHI VAHI, the Mask of Time, would be created, the Brotherhood now had a servant capable of tracking it and capturing it.

In the interim, Voporak was loaned out to the Dark Hunters to learn discipline. He discovered that he now gave off a temporal force field that aged any power used against him. For example, a rock thrown at him would age rapidly and crumble to dust before ever striking him. He also found that his touch could age anyone and anything if he willed it to do so.

After VAKAMA used the Vahi against MAKUTA, Voporak sensed its power and began heading for METRU NUI. While the legend of what happened when he arrived there has not yet been told, it is known that Voporak survived the encounter and may well be seeking out the TOA NUVA following TAHU's use of the Vahi.

VORZAKH (VOAR-zahk):

VAHKI model assigned to LE-METRU on METRU NUI. These mechanoids were known for being destructive, preferring to smash through an obstacle rather than going around or over it. Their Staffs of Erasing allowed them to temporarily eliminate higher mental functions in their targets. A group of VORZAKH destroyed a CHUTE in an effort to capture TOA MATAU.

VORZAKH

VUATA MACA (voo-AH-tah MAH-cah):

A tree that provided fruit which the ONU-MATORAN used for energy. The tree, in turn, was energized by VUATA MACA CRYSTALS. Prior to the coming of the TOA to MATA NUI (2), the Vuata Maca tree was poisoned. TAKUA was asked to locate two Vuata Maca Crystals to cleanse the tree and make the fruit safe again.

VUATA MACA CRYSTAL (voo-AH-tah MAH-cah):

Two objects that provided energy to the VUATA MACA tree. TAKUA retrieved these in ONU-WAHI in order to cleanse poison from the tree.

WAHI (wah-HEE):

Regions on the island of MATA NUI (2). There are six wahi: GA-WAHI, KO-WAHI, LE-WAHI, ONU-WAHI, PO-WAHI, and TA-WAHI.

WAIKIRU (WHY-kee-ROO):

A walruslike creature that dwelled on the shores of GA-METRU. Swift and agile in the water, they were clumsy on land. They relied on their tusks to drive away predators, primarily TAKEA sharks. On MATA NUI (2), TOA GALI placed the species under her protection after a storm she summoned accidentally injured a number of the beasts.

WAIRUHA (ware-ROO-hah):

One of the two TOA KAITA who defeated MAKUTA's MANAS guardians. Wairuha was formed by the merging of TOA GALI, Toa KOPAKA, and Toa LEWA. He wore the KANOHI RUA, the Silver Mask of Wisdom. Following the defeat of the Manas, the Toa split back into their individual forms again and have not formed Wairuha since.

WAIRUHA NUVA (ware-ROO-hah NOO-vah):

A TOA KAITA NUVA formed by the merging of KOPAKA NUVA, GALI NUVA, and LEWA NUVA. Wairuha Nuva came into being only once, when the TOA NUVA joined together in an ultimately futile effort to defeat the BOHROK-KAL.

WALL OF HISTORY:

A large stone structure in TA-KORO upon which TAKUA the CHRONICLER recorded the history of MATA NUI (2). The wall was destroyed along with the rest of Ta-Koro during the RAHKSHI attack. HAHLI, Takua's successor as Chronicler, has begun a new wall in GA-KORO.

WALL OF PROPHECY:

A large structure of ice in KO-KORO upon which was recorded the prophecies and legends regarding the GREAT SPIRIT MATA NUI. Unknown to the MATORAN, the Wall of Prophecy largely duplicated the function of METRU NUI's KNOWLEDGE TOWERS.

WATER SHIELD:

Tool carried by the GAHLOK. It was capable of drawing water from any source and then redirecting it at a target. Gahlok used their water shields to flood ONU-KORO.

WHENUA (wen-NOO-ah):

TOA METRU of Earth, guardian of ONU-METRU, and later TURAGA of ONU-KORO.

HISTORY

Whenua was working in the ONU-METRU ARCHIVES when Toa LHIKAN gave him a TOA STONE and a map to the GREAT TEMPLE. He traveled there and encountered five other MATORAN — MATAU, NOKAMA, NUJU, ONEWA, and VAKAMA. They placed their Toa stones into the Toa suva and were transformed into mighty Toa heroes.

After Vakama had a vision warning of the destruction of the city, Whenua joined with the others to find the six GREAT DISKS. He teamed with Nuju to recover both the KO-METRU disk and the ONU-METRU disk. The Toa Metru used the disks to destroy the MORBUZAKH plant that threatened the city.

WHENUA

Afterward, Whenua led the Toa into the maintenance tunnels beneath the Archives to stop a possible flood. Whenua was captured by KRAHKA, who impersonated him to try to capture the other Toa Metru. He was the subject of a failed rescue attempt by Nuju, but both were later saved by the other Toa.

When they emerged from the tunnels and went to present the Great Disks to Turaga DUME, he denounced them as impostors and ordered their arrest. (The Toa did not discover until later that this Dume was MAKUTA in disguise.) Whenua, Onewa, and Nuju were captured and locked up in the PRISON OF THE DARK HUNTERS. There they encountered a mysterious Turaga who counseled them on what it meant to be a Toa and helped Onewa and Nuju discover their KANOHI mask powers. (Later, they discovered this Turaga was in fact LHIKAN.) After Nuju's telekinesis power helped them escape, Whenua discovered that his mask lit up the darkness and so led the way. Shortly after, they were reunited with Vakama, Matau, and Nokama.

Whenua aided in the ensuing battle with the DARK HUNTERS and the rescue of six Matoran, still trapped in MATORAN SPHERES. He joined his power with that of the other Toa Metru to trap Makuta behind a wall of solid PROTODERMIS.

The Toa Metru then departed Metru Nui with the six Matoran spheres. Along the way, they encountered monstrous sea RAHI and powerful KRALHI under the command of an ONU-MATORAN named MAVRAH. Whenua had once been a friend and colleague of Mavrah and was deeply disturbed by the fact that his old companion was now either badly misguided or insane. During a huge battle between the Toa, the Kralhi, the VAHKI, and the RAHI, Mavrah was swept into the underground river by a great wave. Onewa prevented Whenua from sacrificing his life in a vain attempt to save the Matoran.

After reaching MATA NUI (2) and then returning to Metru Nui, Whenua and the other Toa Metru encountered VISORAK. Although he had once read something in the Archives about these creatures, Whenua did not immediately identify them and was harshly criticized by Vakama because of it. Shortly after, the Toa were captured and mutated by Visorak venom into TOA HORDIKA. As half Toa, half beast, Whenua found the lure of being a full Rahi was strong. It was only the presence of RAHAGA BOMONGA that kept him from running off and joining the wild packs of beasts that roamed the city.

TURAGA WHENUA

TURAGA WHENUA

How the Toa Hordika transformed back into Toa Metru and escaped to Mata Nui with the rest of the Matoran has not yet been revealed. But they did make it to that island with close to 1,000 sleeping villagers. The Toa Metru willingly sacrificed their power to awaken the Matoran, transforming into Turaga in the process.

As a Turaga, Whenua supervised the construction of ONU-KORO. When ONUA arrived, Whenua informed him of the threat Makuta posed to the island but did not share any information regarding Metru Nui or his life as a Toa. He led the rebuilding of the Onu-Koro mines after they were flooded by a BOHROK attack and aided Onua in his search for Kanohi NUVA masks.

Whenua is now journeying with the TOA NUVA, the other Turaga, and the Matoran back to Metru Nui.

POWERS

Whenua was the master of earth. He could cause earthquakes, raise earthen walls, and even make hands of earth reach out and grab an enemy. His time as an archivist left him with an encyclopedic knowledge of Rahi and Metru Nui history. He had strong night vision but his eyes were weaker in daylight.

PERSONALITY

Whenua was not the boldest of Toa, preferring to hang back and analyze a situation before plunging in. The only exception to this is when the Archives were threatened, at which point Whenua behaved like a mother ASH BEAR defending her territory. He quarreled often with Nuju and Onewa, though he and the Toa Metru of Stone later became good friends. He firmly believed history repeated itself and that a knowledge of the past was essential to success.

As a Turaga, Whenua had a reputation for fairness and honesty. Although he had a more balanced view of life, he still believed the answer to many problems lay in memories of what had gone before.

EQUIPMENT

As a Toa Metru, Whenua carried twin earthshock drills. He wore the Kanohi RURU, the Great Mask of Night Vision. As a Turaga, he carried the drill of ONUA and wore the Noble Ruru.

WIDGETS:
Currency used on MATA NUI (2), which took the place of barter and trading systems on the island. It was based on the protodermic currency used on METRU NUI.

ZADAKH (ZAY-dahk):
VAHKI model assigned to PO-METRU on METRU NUI. These mechanoids were huge, strong, fast, and fearless, and usually quick to plunge into a fight. Their Staffs of suggestion left a target susceptible to influence for the duration of the effect. The TOA METRU battled Zadakh in the CANYON OF UNENDING WHISPERS.

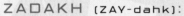

ZADAKH

ZIVON (ZEE-vahn):
A massive RAHI, well over 30 feet tall, who has been known to assist the VISORAK hordes in battle. Its head resembles that of a Visorak, but its claws are crablike and its stinger that of a NUI-JAGA. When fighting something of its own size, it will seize the enemy in its claws and then sting repeatedly. Its hard shell protects it from most damage. The Zivon is also capable of shooting webbing from its legs to entangle a foe.

The Zivon has four natural RHOTUKA LAUNCHERS as part of its anatomy. Its spinners target the senses of a foe, rendering him temporarily blind, deaf, or mute, or robbing him of his sense of touch. Although they are quite effective, the Zivon was rarely seen to use them, preferring physical combat.

The Zivon lived in a dimension of darkness which could be accessed only by the RHOTUKA SPINNERS of a KAHGARAK. Though technically an ally of the Visorak, its appearance was not welcomed by the hordes. The Zivon considered the spider creatures to be a delicacy and had been known to consume a large portion of the horde in celebration following a victory. This creature made one appearance in METRU NUI, summoned by order of SIDORAK. It fought TAHTORAK and the KRAHKA before being sent into the darkness again by a Kahgarak spinner, along with both of its opponents. Whether it still survives inside that realm of shadows is unknown.

ZIVON

BIRTH OF A DARK HUNTER

Toa Lhikan crept silently through the dark streets of Ta-Metru. The night was utterly silent, as if his adopted home had become a city of the dead. Even the shadows seemed touched by the fear that gripped Metru Nui.

He started to summon a small flame, then stopped. Turaga Dume had warned him about betraying his position through the use of his powers. The enemy would track back to the source of the flame, and if he were to be caught too far from the Coliseum . . . well, he had seen what was left of other Toa who had gotten careless.

You can afford a mistake or two against a Rahi beast, he reminded himself. *But not against these opponents. All they need is the slightest opening, and —*

A sound came from up above — metal scraping against stone, no doubt on one of the rooftops. An ambush? The Dark Hunters were more than capable of that — and worse. Lhikan activated his Mask of Shielding, throwing a force field around himself, and readied his fire great swords. Whoever — or whatever — was after him was in for a surprise.

A familiar mask appeared over the edge of the foundry roof. "Relax, brother. It's me."

Toa Nidhiki leaped down and landed beside his comrade. His emerald armor was scarred and pitted from countless battles. "Midnight walks, now?" he whispered. "What's the matter, the war not giving you enough exercise?"

"You were supposed to stay at the Coliseum, with the others," Lhikan replied.

"I got bored. Besides, six Toa to guard one Turaga should be enough."

"Not if I'm right," said Lhikan, his expression grim. "Not if he's been targeted by who I think. Half the legion could be in that building, and he still wouldn't be safe."

Beneath his Kanohi Mask of Stealth, Nidhiki flashed a smile. "You worry too much, brother. You always have. Remember the time the tops of all those Ko-Metru Knowledge Towers were being shattered? You were sure the Kanohi dragon was back. Turned out to be ice bats with attitude."

"Then humor me," said Lhikan. "I'm going west and circling around. You go north. Use your mask, stay out of sight, and for Mata Nui's sake, if you see Dark Hunters, go for help this time."

"You take all the fun out of constant violence, Lhikan," Nidhiki chuckled, already fading into the shadows.

Toa Nidhiki wandered through the broad avenues of Ga-Metru, past temples and schools and canals. Of all the metru in the city, this was his least favorite. It just seemed so clean and orderly. He got the feeling that if a little water sloshed onto the street, they would call out half a dozen Vahki patrols and declare a metru-wide emergency.

He had long ago shut down his Mask of Stealth, which allowed him to travel in a ghostlike form, barely visible and completely silent. As effective as the mask was, he found it disconcerting not to be able to hear his own footsteps. Lhikan would have called his action "taking an unnecessary risk." But Nidhiki seriously doubted that any Dark Hunter would be caught dead in this picture-perfect, sky-blue, oh-so-proper pit of a metru.

Something scuttled through the shadows to his right. He jumped a little at the sight of a chute spider heading off on its night's hunt. It was something he would never admit to his brother Toa, but Nidhiki had always had a morbid disgust of chute spiders, Nui-Jaga, Nui-Rama . . . really anything insectoid. Were it up to him, Metru Nui would have been purged of multilegged crawling things a long time ago.

Nidhiki waited until the spider was well out of sight before moving on, a little more cautiously than before. It was only that extra bit of wariness that allowed him to spot the figure that flitted from shadow to shadow. It was the first time he had ever seen anyone who seemed as at home in the shadows as he did. Intrigued, he followed.

Two things rapidly became apparent. The first was that his quarry wasn't a Toa — she wore no Kanohi mask and she was much too good at slipping unseen and unheard through the night. Toa, as a general rule, were not very good at sneaking. It went against their image of being proud and very public heroes. Nidhiki was an exception to that rule. Where he came from, Toa struck from the shadows or they did not live long.

The second was her destination. She was on a direct course southwest toward the Coliseum. Normally, it wouldn't have worried Nidhiki, not with the kind of security around that place. But what if this Dark Hunter was good enough to make it inside, and then do who knows what to Turaga Dume?

Nidhiki stopped, unlimbered his scythe, and aimed for where she would be, not where she was. Then he unleashed a narrow, focused, hurricane-strength blast of wind at his target.

She never turned. She never cried out. She simply leaped aside as if he had soft-tossed a Kodan ball at her, landed silently, and spun in his direction. Her smile was a challenge.

"I appreciate the little breeze," she said softly. "Hunting is hot work."

"Then maybe you need a little more chilling," he replied. This time he sent elemental air power from both sides of his tool, bracketing her. To his amazement, she did a somersault from a standing start, neatly evading both blasts. Before she had even reached her feet, she had hurled two daggers at him. One whistled past his mask while the other sliced his right shoulder armor as it flew by.

"I guess they don't teach dodging in Toa training," the female Dark Hunter said. "No wonder your city is falling."

Nidhiki glanced from the new gash in his emerald armor to his foe. She had missed on purpose, he was certain. With her aim, if she had wanted to kill him, he would be dead.

"Not my city," he replied. "But a place I am protecting just the same."

"Oh. A matter of honor?"

Nidhiki paused before answering. "Let's say no better offers."

He took his eyes off her for a fraction of a second to ready his scythe. When he looked back up, she was gone, vanished like a wisp of smoke in the night wind. Nidhiki stood completely still, not even breathing, his legs tense and ready to spring. A veteran of a thousand fights, he knew better than to panic. Not knowing where she was, any move he made could be the wrong one. He mentally triggered his mask and disappeared into the shadow.

"Oh, you're good."

Her voice was coming from above. She was perched among the chutes, watching. It was a perfect hiding place — a wind strong enough to dislodge her would bring the chute braces down on his head, while climbing up after her would be nothing short of suicide.

"I could kill you now, Toa," she continued. "But I've filled my quota today. So I am just going to leave you here and go finish off your precious Turaga. If you're scared of the dark . . . well, you probably should be."

Nidhiki kept silent, until another dagger buried itself in the wall behind him.

"Don't stay quiet on my account," the Dark Hunter said. "I already know where you are. I can smell your fear."

The Toa forced himself to relax. He had been in tough spots before and talked his way out of them. This was just one more. "You'll never make it. It's too well guarded."

"Watch me. Unless . . . you have a better plan?"

"We're on opposite sides, remember?"

"We don't have to be." Her voice was above and behind him now. He whirled around, but still could not see her. "How many Toa did you start out with? A hundred? Two hundred? And what do you have left, maybe a few dozen? The Dark Hunters have half the city, and we'll soon have the other half. When it's over, you'll be just one more mask in the pile."

The words struck hard. In the months since Turaga Dume had refused the Dark Hunters a base on Metru Nui, countless Toa had fallen. Most were struck down from the shadows, never knowing their enemy was there. Oh, there had been some victories — Nidhiki had routed more than his share of the enemy, and Lhikan was worth six Toa in battle — but they all knew the numbers were against them. It was only a matter of time.

"If you want to die, I will be more than happy to oblige," she added. "But if you want to live . . . something might be arranged."

A long moment went by. Then Nidhiki lowered his scythe. A second later, the Dark Hunter known as Lariska dropped to the ground in front of him. She still held her daggers at the ready.

"The Shadowed One — my employer — is always looking for new talent," she said. "Help us capture the Coliseum and you can name your price."

The full impact of what he was about to do struck Nidhiki then. If he betrayed the Toa, his name would go down in infamy . . . or would it?

Who's going to tell? he asked himself. *The Toa will all be dead. Matoran? They'll believe whatever they are told to believe. And the Dark Hunters? Right, like anyone's going to listen to them.*

"Metru Nui," he said firmly. "I give you Dume, Lhikan, and the rest, and I get the city to rule. That's my price, take it or leave it."

Lariska grinned. "Actually, I think my choices are take it or kill you where you stand. But I'll let that pass. Meet me here tomorrow night — I'll give you our answer."

The next day lasted for an eternity. Nidhiki spent his time wandering the halls of the Coliseum, imagining himself in control of it all. Now and then, he felt a little twinge of guilt over what he was about to do. But then he reminded himself that it was Dume's fault, and the other Toa's fault, for ever thinking they had a chance against the Dark Hunters.

As the twin suns set, Lhikan approached. "Nidhiki, there you are. There's a boat coming from the south, carrying supplies. I need you to meet it."

"Sure," Nidhiki replied, grateful for an excuse to slip away. "Can't have a siege to the bitter end without supplies, right?"

He left before Lhikan could answer.

"It's a deal," said Lariska. "Tomorrow you lead Lhikan and the Coliseum guard into the Canyon of Unending Whispers in Po-Metru. We'll be scattered in the caves and foothills.

Once it's over, I'm to take care of Dume personally . . . and the city will be yours, Nidhiki. What do you plan to do with it?"

Nidhiki sat down on a bench and stretched his legs. "Maybe you should stick around, Lariska, and find out."

Nidhiki's news struck the Coliseum like a lightning bolt. The Dark Hunters had established a base camp in a Po-Metru canyon. All their operations were being coordinated from there. One swift strike and the war would be over.

"But we'll need every Toa we can muster," he told Lhikan. "We can't afford to lose this opportunity because we left some behind to guard the Coliseum."

Lhikan looked at Dume. The Turaga nodded. "Nidhiki speaks the truth. We may never have such a chance again."

"All right," said Lhikan. "I'll assemble the guard. We move out at once."

Less than fifteen minutes later, they were on the march, over one hundred Toa with Lhikan and Nidhiki in the lead. Clouds of dust kicked up under their armored feet as they traveled well-worn paths through Po-Metru. Each of them had lost a brother or a sister Toa in this war, and all wanted it to end. But not before they had made the Dark Hunters pay in full for their crimes.

Side by side, they marched into the Canyon of Unending Whispers. The clang of their footsteps echoed again and again. The sun baked the barren rock for as far as the eye could see. A few Rahi flyers swooped and dove in the bright sky. Of a Dark Hunter base camp, there was no sign.

"Where is it?" demanded Lhikan, turning to Nidhiki. "You said the war could end today."

"And so it will," replied the Toa of Air. All around, Dark Hunters rose from their hiding places, weapons leveled at the assembled heroes. "Sorry it had to be this way, brother."

Lhikan shook his head. "Not half as sad as I am . . . and don't call me 'brother' again."

The Toa of Fire's arm shot up. Suddenly, Toa rose up from the tops of the canyon walls, a dozen, a hundred, then two hundred, and still more. They said nothing, merely aimed their tools at the now-surrounded Dark Hunters. The hunters were now the hunted, and they looked to Lariska for guidance. She assessed the odds, then shrugged, dropped her daggers and rose.

"Very neat," she said to Nidhiki. "You had me fooled."

Lhikan shoved Nidhiki toward the Dark Hunter lines. "He didn't deceive you. Though I wish he had."

"How did you know?" the Toa of Air asked his former friend.

"The other night. The boat carrying supplies," Lhikan replied. "You left without asking where it was docking. I went after you to give you the information, and stumbled on your meeting with your deadly new friend."

"And all these new Toa?"

"The 'supplies' we were promised from the south. With Dark Hunter eyes and ears everywhere, Dume and I thought it best not to talk of reinforcements out loud. Once I knew what you were planning, I ordered them here to spring a trap of our own."

"And now what?" asked Lariska. "Do you march us all into the sea?"

The Toa of Fire met her gaze, his eyes cold. "A messenger was sent to the Shadowed One before you even reached the canyon. You will be allowed to walk out of here the same way you walked in, provided the Dark Hunters leave Metru Nui and never come back." He turned and pointed to Nidhiki. "Starting with him."

Nidhiki's expression was one of disbelief. "Go with them? But I'm a Toa, Lhikan. I'm your brother in arms!"

Lhikan turned his back on the traitorous Toa of Air. "No. No, you're not. You lost the right to call me 'brother' when you betrayed us all. Get out, Nidhiki — of my sight and of this city. Get out before I kill you."

SIX MONTHS LATER

Nidhiki sat on a stone bench, watching a team of Dark Hunters train. Their mission was to penetrate a heavily defended island and steal a stone known as the Makoki. He didn't know all the details, but apparently the Shadowed One intended to split the rock up into six pieces and thus make six times the profit in ransoming it back.

The Dark Hunter squad was, for the most part, professional and efficient. They made it over and around every obstacle Nidhiki had set up, and effectively eliminated any target dummies that popped up. All of them, that is, except for one big blue brute who lacked any semblance of grace, style, or stealth. After watching him demolish a barrier he was supposed to slip quietly under, Nidhiki had seen enough.

"Krekka!" he snapped. "You just woke up every Toa for kios around. A Toa of Fire has spotted your team and you're about to be the guest of honor at a Dark Hunter bake. What are you going to do?"

The blue Dark Hunter pondered for a very long time. Then he smiled and said brightly, "Smash him?"

"He's up there," Nidhiki said, pointing up to a nonexistent fortress. "You're down here."

Krekka looked up to where his instructor was indicating, but saw nothing. "He's not up there. Did he run away?"

"No, but why don't you?"

"Because I like it here."

Without another word, Nidhiki stalked off. It was time he and the Shadowed One had a talk.

"They're ready," Nidhiki reported. "All of them but the blue idiot. Keep him here, send me, and we'll get your rock for you. I promise."

The Shadowed One smiled, but did not look up. "And we all know what your pledges are worth, don't we, 'Toa' Nidhiki?"

Nidhiki restrained himself from saying what came to mind. He had seen how the Shadowed One dealt with insubordination. Instead, he tried a different approach. "I know how Toa think. I know how they will try to defend the stone. I should be going on this mission."

"Your knowledge of your former allies makes you too valuable as a trainer for me to risk losing," said the Shadowed One, not even trying to sound convincing. "Krekka goes. You stay."

Nidhiki felt fury rising in him. In the six months since he had come to the Shadowed One's island, he had done nothing but help prepare other Dark Hunters for missions, wander among the rocks, and stare at the ocean. If there were such a thing as a Toa of

Boredom, he would be it. And now to be passed over for that hulking, clumsy mass of muscle — it was too much.

"He's a moron," he said through clenched teeth.

That got the Shadowed One's attention. He locked eyes on Nidhiki and rose to his full height. His voice sounded like ice breaking. "And you're a traitor. You turned your back on your ideals, your friends, your city, all to save your own worthless hide. Why would you *ever* think I would trust you, Nidhiki?"

The Toa of Air had nothing to say. After all, the Shadowed One was correct. He had turned against everyone who relied on him. The Toa didn't want him, and the Dark Hunters were just using him for his knowledge. He belonged nowhere.

"But . . . I am not without appreciation of your talents," the Shadowed One continued. "So perhaps you are right — perhaps you would serve us best in the world beyond this island. I assume you would want only the most dangerous missions?"

Nidhiki smiled, hardly able to believe the Shadowed One had come around to his way of thinking. "Those are the ones with the greatest reward."

"Indeed. Too dangerous for any Dark Hunter to do alone, however. You will need a partner. Fortunately, the very one for the job is waiting outside my chamber."

Nidhiki turned to the door, confident he knew who was about to walk through. He and Lariska had been close companions since the disaster on Metru Nui. There would be no one better to team up with him.

The door opened. Nidhiki started to say her name . . . and then the sound died in his throat.

Standing in the doorway . . . in fact, so broad he had cracked the doorway . . . was Krekka.

"Tell me the plan again."

Krekka started to reply, then stopped, as if the thought in his head had just flown away like a hungry Gukko bird. He looked lost for a moment. Then he suddenly brightened as he remembered what it was Nidhiki asked to hear.

"We get there. I keep quiet and try to look scary. When we find the spot, I smash open the gate. You go inside. I stay outside."

"Why?" asked Nidhiki.

"Because you said so."

"Then what?" This was the fourth time Nidhiki had run Krekka through the plan, start to finish, and he would do it four more times if he had to.

"You smash up the place and then come out. We leave and come back here. You turn the weapons over to the Shadowed One and I keep my mouth shut, and . . . and . . ."

Nidhiki frowned. "And no one gets hurt."

"Oh, right!" said Krekka. "I always forget that part."

It was a fairly straightforward job. Some Matoran on a nearby island had developed a new kind of launcher. Nobody knew just what it was meant to fire, but the Shadowed One wanted it anyway. Supposedly, there were only a few models in existence. Once they were stolen, and the equipment used to create them smashed to bits, it would be a while before any more could be built.

There were problems, of course. There was a Toa on the island, but Lariska had agreed to go ahead and set up a diversion. The Matoran posted guards around their village but did not cover one access point, which involved a climb up a sheer cliff. They assumed no one could get up that way.

They had never met Krekka.

The big blue Dark Hunter slammed his fist into the side of the cliff, creating an instant handhold. He began to climb, punching holes in the rock as he did so. Nidhiki came up after him. They were halfway up when Nidhiki realized something was very wrong.

"Wait a minute, Krekka," he said. "I thought Lariska said you could fly?"

Krekka responded with his usual look of puzzlement. Then he nodded vigorously. "Oh, that's right. Forgot."

If I pushed him right off this cliff, no one would ever know, Nidhiki grumbled to himself. *And I would, too, except the Shadowed One said I'm responsible for his well-being.*

Krekka walked quickly to the door of the armory and smashed it down with one swing. Then he obediently stopped, turned around, and allowed Nidhiki to go in alone.

The launchers were easy to find. There were three of them, but Nidhiki grabbed only one for transport back to the Shadowed One's island. Then he dug a hole in the rocky floor of the building and placed the other two inside. No one would ever think to look for stolen goods in the very place from which they were stolen — and now that Nidhiki knew where they were, he could come back and grab them anytime. After all, he might have a use for them someday that the Shadowed One would not approve of.

He was just beginning to fill the hole when the shadow of Krekka fell on him. "What are you doing" asked the big Dark Hunter.

"I told you to stay outside!"

"I just remembered, Shadowed One said I have to stay with you all the time on a job," Krekka answered. "What are you doing, Nidhiki?"

"What does it look like I'm doing? Listen, Krekka, we'll bring one back to the Shadowed One, and then we'll keep the other two for us. Wouldn't you like a new toy to play with?"

Krekka shook his head. "Shadowed One says everything goes back to him. Nothing gets left."

"Krekka —"

"Shadowed One says no!" Krekka said, slamming his fist into the wall. The whole building shook as it might come down on top of them. Worse, the volume of his voice was attracting Matoran attention. Nidhiki could hear guards coming this way. He had been told to make sure the Dark Hunters' involvement in this theft was kept secret, and that was now in jeopardy.

"All right," said Nidhiki, gathering up the three launchers and wishing he could use them on Krekka. "But just because you asked so nicely."

———————————————————————

Nidhiki first spotted the stranger walking through the stone courtyard of the Shadowed One's fortress. Tall, powerful, with jet-black armor, she moved like a serpent, her eyes darting from left to right. She was new, and anything new on the island was always of interest to him.

"I wouldn't," said Lariska. She had appeared beside him without him ever being aware she was near. "She's trouble."

"What kind?"

"She wants Dark Hunter training, and she's willing to pay. But she's not joining. Says she has plans of her own. So the Shadowed One is giving her a few hours to change her mind, then she's being sent back where she came from."

"And she needs our skills — so her plans involve theft, murder, and betrayal," Nidhiki muttered. "Sounds like my kind of evening."

Before Lariska could stop him, he was on his way to greet the new arrival.

"Get out of my way."

Nidhiki didn't move. He had found out the newcomer's name was Roodaka, but precious little else about her. Still, he could make a few educated guesses and the best way to confirm them was face-to-face. *If you can call what she's got a 'face,'* he noted.

"Just trying to make you feel welcome," he said lightly. "This is a very friendly island we have here — heavily defended, home to several hundred killers, and unfailingly lethal to trespassers . . . but friendly."

Roodaka started to push past him. "I have no need of friends."

Nidhiki blocked her again. "Then how about a business partner? Listen — I've been stuck on this rock for over a year now. The only time I get off is when they send me on some errand with a drooling idiot. I want out of here."

"And this concerns me how?"

"You're looking to get hired on by someone, or you're already working for them," Nidhiki replied. "Someone who needs beings with my kind of talent. Introduce me. If I get in, I'll see you're rewarded."

Roodaka nodded. When she spoke again, it was in a conspiratorial tone. "And what of the Shadowed One and the other Dark Hunters?"

Nidhiki shrugged. "They will keep doing what they do. I was meant for bigger things. I was — I *am* — a Toa. I should be running puny islands like this, not working on them."

The tall ebony figure smiled. "I think we can do business together. Meet me at the dock in full darkness. We will conclude our arrangement then."

Midnight found Nidhiki standing by the water's edge. The island was silent, much like Metru Nui had been a year before, the night he met Lariska. He hadn't told her about his meeting with Roodaka or his plans to leave the island. She wouldn't have understood. She was a Dark Hunter, by profession and by nature. The notion that in some part of his heart he still saw himself as a Toa would have been laughable to her.

She was too short-sighted, he decided. Her horizon stopped on the borders of the island. He still had the lean, powerful look of a Toa. He still had a Toa's powers. All he would have to do would be to find some island where they never heard of Lhikan or Dume or Metru Nui, and the population would line up to welcome him. Anything he wanted would be his, and maybe . . . maybe he might even be a hero again.

After all, I look the part, he reminded himself. *Of course, that won't matter if Roodaka doesn't show up soon.*

He stared out at the ocean, wondering about his past and his future. He remembered the first time he saw Metru Nui. It was the day he and a handful of other Toa arrived in answer to a summons to help fight the Kanohi dragon. They were strangers to each other, but brothers just the same — they all shared the responsibilities and the risks of being Toa. It was a special bond, nothing like what the Dark Hunters shared. And, to Nidhiki's surprise and dismay, he found he missed it. Sure, maybe they weren't really his friends . . . maybe they were too quick to turn on him, instead of trying to understand why he did what he did . . . maybe they couldn't see past their jealousy and resentment of the only Toa smart enough to look out for himself.

If it weren't for me, the war would still be going on, he reminded himself. *The Shadowed One would be sitting in the Coliseum right now. But do I get gratitude? No. I get exiled. Well, I'll find a place where they need a Toa, and aren't too particular about what kind. And if Lhikan or one of those Metru Nui heroes tries to take it away from me, I'll make them regret the day they put on a Kanohi. All I need is for Roodaka to help me get what I deserve . . .*

Rhotuka spinners, being pure energy, make very little noise when they fly. Even if the one Roodaka launched had, Nidhiki would never have heard it over the noise of his own thoughts. All he knew was the black pain when it struck, the world spinning in front of his eyes, the bizarre sensation of his muscles shifting, altering, becoming something alien.

It lasted for six seconds. To Nidhiki, it lasted for an eternity. When it was over at last, he walked . . . no, he wasn't walking, at least not like before . . . to the water's edge. All he could see were the dark waves.

"Let us help." The voice belonged to the Shadowed One. A moment later, the entire beach was bathed in torch light. And now Nidhiki could see his reflection in the water.

He screamed for a very long time.

Roodaka watched with amusement as Nidhiki tried to master his new body. He was stumbling about on the sand, trying to move like a Toa but a prisoner of the monstrous form her mutation spinner had given him. She turned to the Shadowed One.

"Can I assume I have purchased my training?" she asked.

"Most definitely," the Shadowed One replied. He thought again how amazing her powers seemed to be. Nidhiki's head and arms had changed their shape. Most grotesque of all, his lower body now resembled that of a huge, four-legged insect. The sight was too much even for some of the assembled Dark Hunters. Lariska had already fled back to the fortress.

"You really should have known," the Shadowed One said to Nidhiki. "Roodaka wanted something from me. She attempted to use the report of your conversation to buy it, but I insisted on more. If you were still deluding yourself that you could go back to being a Toa, that you could wash the stain of treachery off your spirit that easily, I was going to strip that dream from you once and for all." The Shadowed One laughed, a harsh and grating sound. "You are a monster, Nidhiki. Matoran seeing you would run screaming. You will never be cheered, never be admired, *never* be hailed as a savior by the crowds. What are you now? A Toa of Nightmares? A hero, Nidhiki, or a horror? No, I think you will find your place is now, and forevermore, with the Dark Hunters. For who else would have you?"

Nidhiki's eyes blazed with hatred. The Shadowed One paid no heed. Instead, he simply smiled and put a hand on the ex-Toa's shoulder.

"It's ironic, in a way," said the leader of the Dark Hunters. "Your friend Lhikan could have ended your misery back on Metru Nui, but he chose not to. No doubt he thought he was doing you a favor when he allowed you to leave, unharmed, with us." The Shadowed One turned and walked away, saying, "Someday, you really should thank him properly."

One by one, Roodaka and the others departed. No one spoke of a word of mourning for the Toa who had just died . . . and no one spoke a word of welcome for the Dark Hunter that had just been born.

GALI NUVA

KOPAKA NUVA

LEWA NUVA

ONUA NUVA

POHATU NUVA

TAHU NUVA

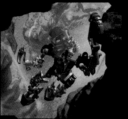

GALI

KOPAKA

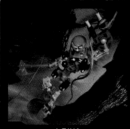

LEWA

ONUA

POHATU

TAHU

TURAGA WHENUA

TURAGA NOKAMA

TURAGA MATAU

TURAGA ONEWA

TURAGA VAKAMA

TURAGA NUJU

TOA WHENUA

TOA NOKAMA

TOA MATAU

TOA ONEWA

TOA VAKAMA

TOA NUJU

TOA HORDIKA VAKAMA

TOA HORDIKA NOKAMA

TOA HORDIKA WHENUA

TOA HORDIKA ONEWA

TOA HORDIKA MATAU

TOA HORDIKA NUJU

BIONICLE®